Jack the Ripper
in St. Louis
A Victorian Whodunit

Mayhaven Award for Fiction

Fedora Amis

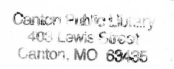

Mayhaven Publishing, Inc

P O Box 557

Mahomet, IL 61853

USA

Cover Illustration and Design by Doris Replogle Wenzel

Copyright © Fedora Amis 2013

First Edition—First Printing 2013

Library of Congress Cataloging Number: 2012953144

ISBN 13 978 193227828-6

ISBN 10: 193227828-1

Chapter One
June 1897

The reign of terror began when St. Augustine goosed Grandma McBustle. Grandma had been living with her second son Easton's family for seventeen years. One June night she unaccountably forgot the house possessed a fully plumbed bathroom on the second floor right next to her own bedroom.

While the moon was still up and the sun hours away from rising, she walked down the stairs, passed by the first floor necessary and through the back door on her way to the outhouse. Apparently she also forgot the exact location of the facility. Instead of opening the wooden slatted door to the privy, she opened the wooden slatted gate to the Bappels' back yard and turned around to do her business.

Whereupon St. Augustine, the Bappels' congenial St. Bernard, came to investigate. His cold wet nose quite discouraged Grandma from completing her errand. And, indeed, shocked her so badly she butted her head against the two-by-four latchpost of the gate—which rendered her unconscious.

St. Augustine tried to lick her out of her comatose condition. When that failed to rouse her, St. Aug did what came naturally. For a hundred and fifty doggy generations the monks of Saint Bernard's Monastery had bred the big dogs to rescue winter's victims from the Alps. St. Augustine rescued Grandma.

On the scales Grandma registered just ninety-two pounds. At one hundred eighty-two pounds St. Aug outweighed her nearly two-to-one. True to his ancestry, the kindly nurse dragged Grandma McBustle through the Bappel lettuce patch into his shed. There he tended her as best he could—sometimes by applying generous amounts of salivation to hydrate her and sometimes by sitting on her to keep her warm.

Grandma believed in the doctrine of the true woman. She prized herself on her piety, her amiability, her gentility. She considered herself a model of propriety and circumspection. Being goosed by a big dog changed all that.

Morning routine in the McBustle Boarding House kept the family from missing Grandma for quite some time. She rarely made an appearance until the breakfast gong. Unlike the rest of the McBustle women at Bricktop, she took meals with the paying guests. More accurately, she presided over the boarders and rang a tinkly bell to call for help from the kitchen if the cream jug needed refilling or the coffee had grown cold.

When she failed to appear to lead the boarders in saying grace, Mother sent eldest daughter Jemima to Grandma's room. When Jemmy returned without the grand dame, Mother dispersed the four daughters to seek her throughout the house. Still no Grandma.

Eggs and grits grew cold as Mother enlisted the boarders to fan out and search the neighborhood. Mother and Gerta the cook dragged the Chinese gong outside for convenient banging to signal the searchers as soon as Grandma had been retrieved. The four daughters launched their efforts in the back yard.

Jack the Ripper in St. Louis

Jemmy stood poised to open the door to the now-unused carriage house when she heard a whine coming from the Bappel's outbuildings. At first she thought it was the neighbors' massive dog; but then she recognized something that might be a word—though not a word she would dare repeat in polite company. She walked over to the fence and stood on tiptoe to peep between the pointed slats.

She couldn't see anything, but she heard words—louder now, and more distinct. "Get off me, you whoreson beast." Jemmy had never heard a swear word pop from between those lips before, but she recognized beyond possibility of doubt the voice of her own lady grandmother.

Jemmy hurried to the unlatched gate and pushed it open. She picked up her feet gingerly as her slippers sank into the dirt of the mashed down lettuce patch. She stopped when she heard Mr. Bappel's screen door bang shut. He said, "Miss McBustle. Why, might I ask, are you tromping down my new lettuce?"

"I'm dreadfully sorry, Mr. Bappel, but I believe my grandmother is in your doghouse."

"A peculiar place for your grandmother, Miss McBustle."

"Yes, it is, Mr. Bappel."

Mr. Bappel had been a boy drummer when he lost a leg during the "War of the Rebellion" as Yankees are wont to call the Civil War. Still, he moved across the ground lightly on one good leg and one crutch. The pair of them reached the shed door at nearly the same instant. When they peered in, they saw a sight most tragic-comical, though common courtesy forbade either to laugh out loud.

Grandma McBustle was endeavoring to push the brute off with one hand and to pull dog hairs from her mouth with the other. Meanwhile, St. Augustine, apparently convinced he had a live one in his bachelor pad, was attempting to propagate the species on Grandma's leg. Mr. Bappel sent the doggy sinner yelping with a crutch thwack to his hind haunches. St. Aug lumbered into the shadows in the far corner of the shed to whimper.

By now, the other girls had arrived. Jemmy tossed out orders. "Merry, run tell Gerta to bang the gong—and have Mother call the doctor—and make hot tea. Randy, fetch a tent tarp from the basement. Nervy, get a blanket from Grandma's bed."

Soon the Bappel yard was aswarm with Bappels and McBustles. Mr. Bappel apologized for the fact he could offer little assistance in the Grandma retrieval project. He hollered up at his notoriously lazy son Bunks, but Bunks stayed abed.

Mother and Gerta eased Grandma onto the canvas and picked up the head end. Randy and Jemmy took the legs end, and the four maneuvered Grandma into the front parlor. Little did they know how long the parlor would be thus occupied.

While they awaited the doctor, they did their best to calm the old lady with sponge baths and chamomile tea. But Grandma's feathers had been permanently ruffled.

When Jemmy urged her to take a spoonful of tea, Grandma bit the hand that fed her with the result that she spilled hot tea on her own chin. "Stop trying to scald me with tea. Bring my Pinkhams at once."

Grandma was devoted to Lydia E. Pinkhams Vegetable Compound. She said the older a person grows, the more Pinkhams herbal recipe becomes necessary to make the blood circulate.

When Mother suggested that the main ingredient smelled suspiciously like whiskey, Grandma said that liquor comes from plants. Herbs were plants so, naturally, Mrs. Pinkhams elixir would smell like whiskey. But the panacea could not, in fact, be liquoritous. Grandma would never allow alcoholic abomination admittance to her lips.

When Jemmy returned with the Pinkhams and a fresh spoon, Grandma threw the spoon on the floor in favor of a speedier alternative. She tipped the bottle up and swilled down half its contents. She licked her lips, then settled down to barking at her bevy of attendants who were trying to wash her scratches and apply salve—Gerta's special concoction of beeswax, aloe vera, goldenseal, comfrey and lard. "Don't touch that lower limb. I believe it to be broken."

"But Grandma, how can I get the lettuce out of your scratches if I—"

"You'd think I was a rag doll, tattered and torn, ready to be burned in the trash barrel instead of your own grandmother."

"But Granny, the scrapes won't heal right if you won't let—"

"That's the way youngsters treat their elders these days. Ready-made shoes and tinned milk. What's wrong with milk from a cow, I'd like to know."

"I'm as gentle as I know how to be. If you would just—"

"Where is that doctor? That young quack. I expect he'll refuse to bleed me. Has no respect for hundreds of years of medical treatment. Knows nothing at all."

"But Granny, doctors quit bleeding people long ago. They say bleeding makes folks weak—that it makes them sicker."

"Where's my Pinkham's?" When Jemmy handed her the bottle, she drained the contents then took up railing where she had left off.

"This camp cot is a misery. Why can't I go upstairs to my own bed?"

"We couldn't bear to cause you another moment's pain if we didn't have to. Now if you would—"

"Stop that. I'll have another taste of Pinkham's."

Jemmy turned the bottle upside down to demonstrate. "You drank it—even the last drop."

Just then, the doctor made his appearance. In his jolliest bedside manner he said, "Mrs. McBustle, I hear you had a set-to with a St. Bernard.

Next thing I know, you'll probably take up fisticuffs with a hundred pound catfish and ring me up to put beefsteak on the FISH'S eye."

Grandmother was in no mood for joviality. "You whoreson beast. Bleed me or get out."

The doctor's voice went from jocund to strained. "Modern medicine frowns upon the bleeding of patients, Mrs. McBustle, as I have told you every time I have seen you in the last thirteen months. Bleeding is a practice based on folklore, not on modern science."

"Then give me my Pinkham's and get out of my house, you whoreson beast."

The doctor's voice went from strained to sharp. "You'd save money by buying straight bourbon whiskey. But since I wouldn't carry whiskey around with me any more than I would carry Pinkham's poison, I will give you something better." He produced two laudanum pills and helped her wash them down with lukewarm tea.

He was a marvel of efficiency as he poked and prodded to find her sore spots. Grandma was less than appreciative. She said, "In future, you will do me the common courtesy to ask permission before you lay hands upon me. You take improper liberties, Sir. I will not abide it."

She let out a wail a banshee would have envied when he moved her right leg. He looked pleased as he said, "Now we've found the trouble. You have a broken leg."

She said, "I don't tolerate swearing or the use of obscene words by anyone in my house. You will apologize immediately and in future keep a civil tongue in your head."

The doctor looked confused and turned to Jemmy for an explanation. With hand to face, Jemmy hid her reply as she silently mouthed, "Leg." Aloud she said, "Grandmother, I am sure letting the doctor tend to your LOWER RIGHT LIMB will make you feel much better."

Jack the Ripper in St. Louis

The doctor rolled his eyes and waited for the opium to work its will. By the time Grandma began snoring, he had set and splinted her leg as well as immobilized the index finger of her right hand with wooden tongue depressors. From then on Granny aimed an accusatory finger at every person who came within pointing distance. She used it to wreak more destruction than a Colt .45.

Mother had been on the telephone to Uncle Erwin and Aunt Delilah who wanted the medical report straight from the doctor's mouth.

Mr. Bell's invention allowed him the efficiency of telling the whole family at once.

"Yes, Mr. McBustle, I will send the bill to you. No, I don't foresee anything life threatening. Of course, whether she walks after her lower right limb knits is entirely up to her willingness to exercise it back to strength." Then the doctor was off with a quick tip of his flat-crowned straw hat and the promise to return the next day.

He returned every day that week. And every day that week Grandma McBustle told him in a progressively louder voice, "Bleed me or get out, you whoreson beast." By the end of the week, the doctor's jollity had dimmed to a sullen smirk.

The primary object of Grandma's wrath and the primary receiver of all beratings and scourges was not the doctor or even Mother. The burden of caring for the sick invariably fell to the most hapless and available person of the distaff persuasion—the eldest daughter. At Bricktop, that unfortunate female happened to be young Jemima McBustle.

At seventeen Jemmy stood at the crossroads of her life with the whole world open to her, a brave new world where women might dare to challenge male supremacy in any field.

Jemmy stayed up nights wondering where life as a trailblazer for other women to follow might lead. At the same time, she felt the pull of security and the life of leisure which would be hers if she chose to wed a prominent and wealthy man.

Circumstances had placed both paths within her reach. Because her father had no sons, he reared his daughters as businesswomen. Only Minerva showed any real aptitude, but he expected all of his girls to receive diplomas from public coeducational schools.

Jemmy took pride in walking up to the third floor of the Gothic inspired Peabody School to matriculate at St. Louis Branch High School No. 3.

When a tornado blew away most of her school, her guardian, Uncle Erwin, saw to it that she finished her education at the prestigious Mary Institute, the school on Lucas Place for the daughters of the city's protestant well-to-do.

She had tasted life on both sides. Luxury beckoned, but had its price—freedom. A career beckoned, but had its price—censure. Then too, Jemmy had no clear idea of what career she wanted.

She envied Minerva—just thirteen, but already the family accountant. Nervy kept the books in clear numbers in perfect columns. Once a month Uncle Erwin sent his man to audit the ledgers. Nervy looked forward to the man's visits as if he were President McKinley. She asked endless questions about amortization and insurance and other words too abstract for Jemmy to remember. The pair talked ceaselessly about gas bills and the best time of year to buy coal.

Jemmy envied Nervy's certainty about what to do with her life. When she could find no comparable obsession in her own personality, she tried to cook one up—no luck. She liked acting. Her little theatre directors called her a good actress. But she couldn't possibly go on the professional stage and disgrace the family.

Before Grandma became cantankerous, Jemmy had planned to spend the summer of 1897 exploring and thinking. Aunt Delilah would surely help.

Jack the Ripper in St. Louis

Society maven and wife to her guardian uncle would gladly set her off in a social whirl.

On her own, she planned to talk to career women—nurses and teachers—any who might help her decide whether she wanted higher education. Uncle Erwin had already promised to send her to William Woods College in Fulton if she wished.

But then St. Augustine goosed Grandma and Jemmy found herself chained to an irascible old woman whose favorite phrase was "whoreson beast." Jemmy couldn't so much as invite a friend over for gossip without bringing horror down on her head. She found herself cut off from friends and forced into a rut of unsavory tasks.

In order to tend Grandma at night, Jemmy slept on the parlor sofa. Grandma often waked her by banging her silver knobbed walking stick on the floor. Usually, she wanted to drink water or make it. After helping with the chamber pot or the water jug, Jemmy couldn't go back to sleep. She spent dark hours listening to the hall clock tick away her precious youth and feeling sorry for herself.

Grandma detested the fact that her splinted finger kept her from feeding herself. She fixed her frustration on her caretaker. Jemmy fed Grandma liquids—soup and tea. When Grandma wanted no more, she didn't tell Jemmy. She let her granddaughter know the meal was ended by spitting the rejected spoonful in the young lady's face.

After Jemmy learned to count the number of spoonfuls needed to slake Grandma's appetite, she became adroit at dodging the spray. Granny became cagey. She varied the number of swallows and took to spitting at the back of Jemmy's head when she wasn't looking.

Jemmy longed for an end to the torture. She had never thought she would miss sweeping floors, washing windows and serving meals to the boarders; but she did.

Fifteen-year-old sister Miranda was no help. Well-brought-up nineteenth century girls had no means to be black sheep, but they could be impish. Miranda kept the family in knots with her romantic schemes and her preposterous plans to become someone other than Miranda McBustle.

She was in her "flower phase." She adopted the peculiar belief that changing her middle name to the name of a flower would change her life. She convinced herself that she could live flower power—that if she called herself "Gardenia" she would attract a secret lover. She dreamed up a new flower name for every occasion.

Miranda moaned that because Grandma was ill, she had to do all Jemmy's work. "Miranda Rhododendron McBustle—"

In an aside she explained herself, "'Rhododendron' means 'Beware, I am dangerous'—has to do all your chores. All you have to do is sit and read to an old lady."

Jemmy grabbed a handful of Randy's curls and marched her into the parlor saying, "Dangerous, are you? You think you can compete with Grandma when it comes to danger?"

She pointed to a glass of water and a spoon and said, "Grandma, Randy wants to give you a drink of water." Grandma spat the first spoonful right up Randy's nose. From then on, little sister had no complaints about work.

Jemmy did read to Grandma—hour upon hour—until her eyes itched and her voice cracked. She might have enjoyed reading if only Grandma wanted to hear books Jemmy wanted to read. St. Aug's nose had changed even the lady's taste in reading.

Before the St. Aug goose, Grandma read the Bible every day and several of the weekly sermons printed in newspapers. The only work of fiction she allowed in the house was *Ben-Hur*. Jemmy read General Wallace's novel with passable results. Grandma never screamed an epithet more than once or twice during each chapter. Jemmy asked Uncle Erwin to bring over more historical books. Grandma refused to listen to even the foreword.

Uncle Erwin brought over Biblical books. They received no better reception. Jemmy tried the most popular books in the country, *The Adventures of Huckleberry Finn* and *The Gentleman from Indiana*. Neither Mark Twain nor Booth Tarkington raised a chuckle. She had more success with Sir Walter Scott. Grandma didn't like *Ivanhoe*, but she didn't dislike it either. She said, "Find me more like that—but not about foreigners—I want American."

Jemmy consulted with the man next door. "Mr. Bappel, perhaps you might help me find the kind of books my grandmother likes—adventure books."

"I recommend Mr. Mark Twain. His books have adventure and humor, too."

"Humor annoys her."

"How about *From the Earth to the Moon* or something else by Jules Verne? He's famous for fantastical adventures."

"Fantasy annoys her."

"Have you tried Sir Walter Scott? *Kenilworth* is a grand adventure."

"Foreigners annoy her."

"Do you know of anything which doesn't annoy your grandmother, Miss McBustle?"

"No, Mr. Bappel."

"Well, you might try penny dreadfuls. They are full of adventure and American to the core."

"Do you think the Mercantile Library loans such books?"

"I very much doubt it, but I have a few you might borrow."

And so, Jemmy began reading Mr. Bappel's orange-covered Beadle books. Grandma became almost cheerful when Jemmy read tales about Deadwood Dick, Calamity Jane and Kit Carson.

Dime novels convinced Jemmy that Grandma's old self was well and truly gone. Grandma didn't object when a nice woman married a bum or even when respectable people drank liquor. Jemmy stopped skipping over certain words—words Grandma would have once deemed obscene. In earlier times, Grandma often pontificated that words like "belly" and "vomit" were unfit for Christian women to read.

Jemmy didn't mind reading dime novels—and they were short—forty pages. But these were not books Jemmy hungered to read. She had discovered Wilkie Collins. The brightest spot in her day came when Grandma fell asleep and Jemmy could thrill to the suspense of *The Woman in White*. Too bad Mr. Collins was British.

One June morning Lord Percy Glyde was about to force his wife, the beautiful Miss Laura Fairlie, to sign her entire estate over to him when Grandma's voice broke through the printed page.

"Dave Tutt, I want my Pappy's watch you think you won off me playin' poker yesterday. I told you I'd pay up. You had no call to noise my losin' around Springfield like you're doing."

Annoyed by the interruption, Jemmy snapped the book shut around her ribbon bookmark. She looked up to see what Grandma wanted; but instead of a wrinkled face, she looked straight into the barrel of a cap-and-ball Colt dragoon pistol.

Grandma pulled the hammer back as she said, "Dave, don't you come across here with that watch. I warned you not to show Wild Bill Hickok's watch about. I'll have it now." Jemmy sat frozen in disbelief.

Grandma said, "Dave Tutt, you whoreson rebel bushwhacker, turn over my pappy's gold Waltham." Then Grandma aimed straight at the chest of her granddaughter and fired.

Chapter Two

What a blessing Grandma was weak and nearly blind. Even though she had been holding the pistol with both hands, she couldn't shoot straight because the tongue depressors on her finger ruined her aim. The heavy gun flailed about so wildly she missed her mark by a month. She blasted the belly button of a carved plaster cherub which beamed from the cornice over the parlor room doors. Jemmy had ducked to the floor and rolled under the sofa, but she needn't have bothered.

Mother chalked the incident up to reading Colonel Ingraham's Beadle book *Wild Bill, the Pistol Deadshot*. She struck dime novels from Grandma's approved reading list.

Still, the fact Grandma possessed a loaded firearm caused concern even if it was a pre-Civil War relic. Mother confiscated the pistol and took the precaution of removing Grandpa's saber from over the mantel. She scoured the parlor for anything which could be used as a weapon and even gave Jemmy custody of the silver-headed walking stick.

Two boarders left. From then on, Mother frisked Grandma for firearms or other contraband after every meal.

For the next three weeks, the doctor bounced in twice a week. Bruises paled and scratches became no more than pink lines, but Grandma's broken leg scarcely improved.

After yet another lashing from Grandma's shrill tongue, the young doctor spoke to Mother. "Mrs. McBustle, I am unhappy about the lady mother's progress. I can honestly say I have never stood in the way of a patient's full recovery, and I do not propose to stand in the way now.

"Mrs. McBustle has taken such a dislike to me I fear her ill temper is impeding her return to health. Her right lower limb refuses to heal. I would like to turn the case over to another physician in whom, perhaps, Mrs. McBustle may find a more pleasing guide on her path to recovery. In any event, changing doctors could scarcely make things worse."

Mother said, "Of course, Doctor. If you think a change would help, we'd be grateful for any improvement in her condition—as well as in her disposition. She upbraids all of us at least as harshly as she does you."

The young doctor set his straw skimmer on his head. "I have in mind a gentleman who is more her age. Perhaps my youth is what rankles her so."

A distinguished-looking salt-and-pepper bearded doctor came with hand-holding and sweet-talking of times gone by, but the reign of terror did not end. Over the next four months a succession of doctors—old—young—even a woman—brought their fresh optimism and good intentions. Grandma flattened them all. She wanted her Pinkham's and she wanted to be bled.

Each of the doctors lasted about a week, two visits, before they passed her on to her next whipping post. They tried everything they could think of—scientific or un.

One brought a wicker wheelchair and lifted Grandma into it. With Jemmy's help, the pair toted her and chair down to the sidewalk and began a stroll in the sunshine. She demanded to be taken the other way—in the direction of the pharmacy. When the doctor found out Granny had cooperated only because she hoped to resupply her Pinkham's, he refused her gently.

She said, "Take me back to the house at once. You whoreson beast." When he tried to explain that sunshine is a great healer, she grabbed Jemmy's open parasol and broke it over the only part of his anatomy she could reach, his gluteous maximus.

When he took the weapon away, she began screaming with all her might. "Save me from this whoreson beast. Will no one help an old lady who can't defend herself? Call the police to arrest this whoreson—whoreson—whoreson—"

She screamed the word ever louder as people gathered to stare out their windows at the ruckus on St. Ange Street. Defeated and red in the face, the doctor returned Grandma to the front parlor and left the premises discreetly rubbing his backside. He never returned.

The lady doctor persisted for two whole weeks despite Grandma's tantrums and the new vocabulary Grandma summoned up to revile her upstart female doctor. As a woman in a man's field, the lady doctor was used to being called names. The lady took it in stride when Grandma called her "Mocktor."

Still, she made no more headway than the others. In desperation she pretended to bleed Grandma. When the ruse failed to cure, Grandma demanded that Mother dismiss the Mocktor and bring her something useful—the Pinkham's she had forgotten that she hid in her embroidery basket.

Mother found Pinkham's there and in a dozen other places as well—tucked under hats in hat boxes, rolled up in flannel nighties behind the dressing table, stuffed inside the featherbed, peeping out from boots in the armoire. Mother took satisfaction in pouring the contents of every single one down the drain. She had sworn an oath to ban liquoritous spirits from the house forever because demon drink had killed her dear husband Easton.

Then, Mother did a remarkable thing. She lied—in a good cause to be sure. She told Grandma she had found not a drop of Lydia Pinkham's potion and the only way Grandma would ever taste Pinkham's in the future was to get well and walk down to the pharmacy to buy some for herself. Grandma blew into a rage that made the 1896 tornado a summer zephyr by comparison.

She called Mother a "Hurdy-Gurdy woman" among a dozen other shocking expressions describing women of ill-repute. Even after her recent shenanigans, her epithets surprised the family. Who would have thought straight-laced Granny knew such words existed? And who would imagine she would say them out loud under even the direst provocation? She demanded to be removed from the hussy's custody and sent to live with her son Erwin whom she trusted to look after her properly as befits an eldest son.

The fracas shook the Bricktop and all its inhabitants down to their cornerstones and corsets. Of the remaining boarders, all women of mature years, two more declared their intentions to find more suitable accommodations. While they had always considered the Bricktop their ideal lodging place, they could no longer ignore the spate of foul language flooding forth from the first floor. They didn't much care for gunshots in the parlor, either.

One suggested exorcism because anyone could see that a demon had claimed Grandma's soul. When Mother protested that she could never embrace the Roman church, the lady opined that a few more months of Grandma would make Mother not only a Catholic, but a saint—or at very least, a nun.

Only Miss Hendershot stayed. She was more tolerant, or at least more hard of hearing. She did, however, request to be moved. She wanted to be moved to a back room from her present room with its two big windows, the best room, the front room, the airiest room with the best view. Why did the good lady wish to relinquish the nicest room in the house? The front bedroom stood directly over the front parlor which had become Grandma's shooting gallery.

In tears, Mother telephoned for help from her brother-in-law, Mr. Erwin McBustle. He sent his emissary, his redoubtable wife.

Delilah Snodderly McBustle arrived in a flurry of sage green linen skirt and matching jacket embroidered with irises. The cobalt blue of the flowers matched her kidskin gloves and the feathers of the blue-birds nestled on her wide brimmed hat. Aunt Delilah was a fine figure of a Victorian matron "of a certain station and of a certain age." Imposing and imperious, she and her cronies ruled the second tier of St. Louis society with silver fists inside velvet mittens.

On that Tuesday when Mother told her that Grandma was keen on living with the Erwin McBustles at their home in Compton Heights, Aunt Delilah said, "I would sooner eat fricasseed scorpions and sprout asparagus from my ears. I have just spent a whole year rebuilding our home after the great tornado. I do not plan to invite a cyclone to take up residence.

"I hope to keep the tummies of my plaster cherubim bullet free. Besides, I must spend this summer arranging my son's life. And I must say, Duncan is scarcely more cooperative than Mother McBustle. He spends most of his time and all of his allowance on horse racing.

"I am preparing to orchestrate his transition into manhood. I shall see to it that he transfers his affections from equines to members of his own species. Wife hunting will be a more sensible and much more lucrative pursuit if I do it for him—especially when the husband-to-be has as little grasp of horseflesh or mathematics as Duncan has."

Mother put on her most hopeful smile. "I should think Mr. McBustle would take pride in teaching his son and heir the warehouse business."

"Mr. McBustle won't let Duncan set foot on any McBustle properties. The last time Erwin tried to teach Duncan the ropes, the tangle he made

19

nearly tripped us into bankruptcy.

"No, Mr. McBustle is taking the appropriate corrective action—by turning everything over to me. I mean to marry Duncan off to a suitable wife despite all opposition or obstacle. I have pledged to take whatever measures might be necessary, even if I must sit the wayward pair down in the parlor and read them Psalms until they set a wedding date. Of course, I must locate the lucky bride first.

"Therefore, this summer I shall be hosting picnics and rowing parties and hayrides. I shall insist that Duncan accompany me to salons and lectures and band concerts while I peruse the current crop of debutantes.

"Why, even today, I have scheduled Duncan three hours to practice his elocution. He is to appear in the upcoming debate at the Oracle of Delphi Debating Society this Saturday on the topic 'Resolved: That Bachelors Should be Taxed for the Support of Infirm and Indigent Old Maids.' He is upholding the affirmative."

Mother's silent tears now burst forth in a sob that shuddered her frame. Delilah rose to offer her sister-in-law a white linen square with "Mc" embroidered in green and blue curlicues. "There, there Belinda."

Mother said, "I don't know how I can go on. I weep myself to sleep nearly every night. We have but one boarder left. Is there nothing you can do?"

"Of course, you may count on us to pay the bills. And I'm certain Erwin can find boarders who won't be offended by Grandma's cursing—dockworkers or—or teamsters."

At the thought of having a house full of rowdies around her four virgin daughters, Mother took in a shocked breath. The end result was a series of gasps anyone might mistake for a death rattle.

Aunt Delilah hastened to take back her words. "Oh, of course we won't fill your house with wharf rats. Erwin will find you nice gentlemen, traveling salesmen or ministers."

When Mother gasped even louder, Delilah said, "Do forgive me, I am mortified by how thoughtless you must think me. We will pay the bills for as long as needed."

Mother kept right on gasping and crying.

Delilah paused then said slowly, "There is, of course, another way."

Mother looked up and blinked.

Delilah said, "Erwin and I have discussed one other possibility."

Mother blinked again.

"We thought perhaps Mother McBustle might heal faster under the care of professionals."

"A hospital?"

"Yes, in a manner of speaking. Of course medical hospitals treat the bodies of the patients. I am given to understand that medical science has done all it can for her in a physical way. Now, nature must be given the opportunity to effect a cure of a higher order."

Mother said, "I don't quite see what..."

"I'll speak plainly, then. I suggest that we place Mother McBustle in a lunatic asylum. That's a solution isn't it? She must have lost her reason. Do you think it normal for an old lady to take up shooting at the grandchildren as a hobby?"

Mother blinked a dozen times or more.

Aunt Delilah put her hand over her stomach. "My corset is too tight. It's barely ten o'clock in the morning. I'm not used to getting dressed so early in the day. Ordinarily, I wouldn't think of making morning calls before four in the afternoon."

Mother stopped blinking and stood as tall as her five feet four inches permitted. She said, "I want to hear from Erwin himself that he wants to send his mother to a mad-house."

"Belinda, sit down. I've been too blunt. We have in mind a wonderful

21

place—Dr. Lyman's Sanitarium. Why, going there would be more like a visit to take the waters in Hot Springs, Arkansas, than it would be going into a mad-house."

"You have no words to convince me to put Mother McBustle into a nut-house."

"You've said it yourself. You cannot keep her. She's a menace to every-one. What if she had slain Jemima? You'd feel differently if Mother McBustle had better aim."

Mother opened her mouth, but nothing came out.

Delilah took her arm and wheedled, "Let us take you to see the sanitar-ium. It's a handsome place in the country—way out on Arsenal past the City Poor House. Don't you think she would enjoy the fresh air?"

Mother gently but firmly removed Delilah's arm.

Delilah took Mother's hand and urged again. "Dr. Lyman has a splen-did reputation—most progressive. They say he studied with Dr. Freud in Vienna."

Mother stared at Delilah's hand until Auntie removed it.

Aunt Delilah gave up. "Well at least consider it. It's a fine place with lovely baths. Even the food is good. Tell me you'll think it over."

"When I die, I want to be able to face Easton with a clear conscience. If I cast away his mother as a lunatic, I would have to hide my head in shame. Goodbye, Delilah. Tell Mr. McBustle we thank him for assuming our finan-cial support. I know it is a burden."

Mother and Aunt Delilah's discussion took place in the back parlor while Grandma was napping. Jemmy opened the pocket doors an inch so she could hear every line. Mother's rejection of the mad-house idea crushed Jemmy. Mother was being unreasonable. Surely Grandma wouldn't be any more unhappy at the kind of place Aunt Delilah described—a place with trained medical personnel and lovely baths.

Jack the Ripper in St. Louis

Jemmy wanted desperately to go to the sanitarium and see the place firsthand so she might find a way to convince Mother, but she couldn't leave the house.

She did the next best thing. She asked Uncle Erwin to bring her any books he could find about mad-houses. That's how she came to read *Ten Days in a Mad-House* and why Nellie's words caught fire in her brain. That very day, she drew into her heart a new idol, undercover reporter Pink Cochrane, known to the world as Nellie Bly.

Wonder of wonders, Grandma liked Nellie's stories. She came very near to crying when Jemmy read about Nellie's days working in a box factory sweatshop or being forced to bribe employment workers to give her even the lowly job of servant.

She said, "Count your blessings, child. Thank heaven you don't have to suffer as poor women do. Your mother and your uncle will see that you marry a man who is a good provider."

Grandma liked to listen to Nellie's stories even when she didn't agree with her message. She dismissed Nellie's story on Mexican political corruption—too foreign. She applauded the government for throwing Nellie out of the country.

She broke down and sobbed at Nellie's description of how the city of New York treated unwed mothers. She said, "Let that be a warning, girl. Never be alone with a man you can't trust—and there's no man you can trust—except your husband. So get one. I have that wrong. The only man a girl can trust is her father. Of course, you can't get yourself a father. A husband will have to do. So get a husband—but don't trust him."

Jemmy took it as a good sign that Grandma wanted to hear, over and over again, about Nellie's amazing trip around the world. Grandma nearly almost came rather somewhat close to smiling each time Jemmy read that Nellie's stunt outdid the fictitious Phileas Fogg of Jules Verne's *Around the*

World in Eighty Days. When Grandma heard that Nellie managed the trip from Hoboken and back again in just seventy-two days, six hours, eleven minutes and fourteen seconds, she insisted that Jemmy calculate the difference down to the second.

On occasion Grandma substituted "Seven days, seventeen hours, forty-nine minutes, forty-six seconds"—or a mixed-up version of those times—for "Whoreson" in her rantings at doctors.

Then he came. He carried two canes and a black case. He wore a black wool swallowtail coat with a red brocade vest. He sported a neatly trimmed white goatee and mustache with waxed curls at the ends. He rode a white horse and so did his valet. With a single word from him, his matched pair of elegant greyhounds sat obediently on the front porch like sculptures of gray and white marble.

He called himself Dr. Francis J. Tumblety. He swept into the parlor and shooed Jemmy out before Mother could protest. Mother was aghast at how unseemly it was for two strange men to examine Grandma with no female present.

In short order, he swept out again and the pair ushered Mother into the back parlor. This time Grandma was wide awake and fuming about being poked in the belly so Jemmy heard nothing of the conversation beyond the closed door.

After the doctor and his boy breezed out, Mother stood transfixed in the doorway. Jemmy pumped her for news. "What did the Doctor say?"

"He wants to—"

"Yes, he wants to what?"

"He says your grandmother is hysterical because she needs a hysterectomy. He wants to put her in hospital tomorrow."

"Are you going to let him?"

"I don't know. I'll have to talk it over with your uncle. I don't know whether she'd survive an operation."

Mother called Uncle Erwin who left the decision up to her. When Dr. Tumblety swept in the next day, Mother told him she could never face her dead husband Easton if she had sent his mother to her grave by allowing this surgery. No hysterectomy.

Dr. Tumblety and his assistant shooed Jemmy out of the parlor so they could re-examine Mrs. McBustle and perhaps choose some less recommended, but potentially beneficial treatment. In ten minutes they swept out again and promised to return the next day.

Three hours later, Grandma died.

Chapter Three

The best thing about funerals is that they require a year's worth of organization crammed into a week's worth of days. And one dare not forget a single detail lest one be considered an ingrate. The instant Grandma expelled her last breath, Mother dropped the hand she was holding and stood up to marshal her troops.

"I will telephone the photographer to come as soon as possible—after I speak to Uncle Erwin and the parson. Gerta and I will wash Grandma with rosemary water and dress her in her black bombazine gown, the one she wore to Easton's Funeral."

"Miranda, you are to stop all the clocks in the house. After that, fetch a ladder and cover all the mirrors with black bunting which you may borrow from Mr. Bappel.

"And this is to all of you, and to Miranda especially. Do not look in any mirror. Heaven forbid that anyone should look in the mirror and see Grandma's image standing behind. Another death is sure to follow. And remember, too, that we will have no curls or other adornment for the time being so we will have no need of mirrors.

"Minerva, go to the stationers' for black-edged stationery. You are to address the envelopes while Merry pens the funeral invitations. Of course, we won't know the details until Uncle Erwin has made the arrangements. In the meantime I think Merry might cut butterflies from black paper to symbolize Grandma's soul passing into the next life.

"Jemima, write the obituary; but not until you have taken the black-edged handkerchiefs out of my cedar chest. Air them in the sun. Check them in an hour. If they smell too musty, you'll have to wash them and iron them yourself. We have no time to send them to the laundress."

Mother called upon the Bappels to inform the neighbors. Mr. Bappel brought over his family funeral wreath of willow wands wrapped in black crepe. He installed it on the front door himself. The whole family marveled at his one-footed agility when he hopped up a ladder to drape black swags over the front windows so all who traveled down St. Ange Street might know they should pass by in silence to show respect for the grieving family.

Mother even enlisted Mrs. Hendershot's help. She was to seek out suitable mourning garments and remove the decorations from them. Black for Mother and Jemmy, gray or white for the other three girls. Every spare moment of every female in the house went to basting black edging on hems, sleeves and necklines of anything that wasn't black already.

The whirl of activity stopped when he swept back. Two hours after Grandma died, Dr. Tumblety and his valet returned. The doctor set about examining the body and filling out papers. Then, he took Mother's arm and said, "I am heartily sorry that your mother, that is, your mother-in-law, has passed on. I fear I should have realized how rapidly her diseased organs would claim her life. If I had taken her straight to an operating theatre, perhaps she'd be living yet."

"I do not blame you, Doctor. Nor do I blame myself. Her time had come."

The doctor's face was a picture of sympathetic regret. "Yet I would make amends as best I can. Would you permit me to make the funeral arrangements. I have the services of a most excellent undertaker who will lift all disturbing responsibilities off your shoulders. His female embalmer will personally see to all the intimate details. I could have him take the body away within the hour so you might spend your time consoling your loved ones."

"I thank you for your kind offer; but Mrs. McBustle's son, Mr. Erwin McBustle, has already begun arrangements of his own, with Bromschwig and Husmann. Be assured that I am grateful for your offer."

Dr. Tumblety's smile became pursed lips as he replaced his top hat and took his leave.

Jemmy watched his servant hold a stirrup to receive the doctor's black boot. She could not help admiring the valet despite his peculiar livery. He was well-turned out—a handsome brown-faced boy about her own age who sat ramrod straight in the saddle. His suite of clothes was gorgeous, if strange. The outfit reminded Jemmy of pictures of Zoaves from the Civil War.

The boy wore a dark red fez with a long tassel that whipped him in the nose when he bent over to untie his horse's reins. The fez matched his red wool blouse and baggy-legged trousers that ballooned over his boots. His dark blue jacket came down to brush the top of his gold waist sash. Golden epaulets dripped braid fringe down his shoulder caps.

Jemmy wondered whether Nellie Bly had seen such exotic fellows in her travels. She daydreamed that he might be the disguised son of an Eastern potentate—something straight out of *Arabian Nights*. She thought of him at the oddest moments, while polishing the crystal or sweeping the porch or scraping manure off her shoes.

Between thinking about the intriguing boy in the fez and feeling guilty that she wasn't even trying to pray her own Grandmother into heaven, Jemmy couldn't keep her mind on the her assigned tasks. She doodled all over a page in her tablet, but wrote not a single word of the obituary.

She took a break from not writing the obituary when the photographer arrived. She peeked through the parlor doors as he puffed cotton wool into fluffy clouds to frame Grandma from the waist up. He fussed over her appearance for a good five minutes. Finally satisfied, he folded her hands around a white prayer book, placed a single white lily on her chest and took her picture from four different angles.

He said, "I believe these photographs will come out very nicely. Cloud frames are a speciality of mine, and I always bring the white prayer book for piety and a fresh white lily to symbolize heaven. Too bad she wasn't Catholic. Rosaries make a fine finishing touch, don't you think?"

As he packed up his camera and his clouds, he said to Mother, "I shall bring the prints around as soon as I can return to my studio and develop the plates, tomorrow morning if that's agreeable. As soon as you choose a pose, I will provide the number of pictures you require as my highest priority."

He became all obsequious smiles and syrupy sentiment when he clasped Mother's hand. "You have my condolences, Mrs. McBustle. I hope my humble talents may do justice to your dear departed. Please, keep the lily with my compliments." Mother yanked her hand away and turned on her heel. Mother placed faux feeling somewhere between drunkenness and red hats in the category of things she actively disliked.

Uncle Erwin and Grandma's casket arrived at the same time. A dandy casket it was, too. Bromschwig's best, a lead-compartmented, silk-lined, silver-plate-handled Abraham Lincoln model covered in black velvet. The undertaker beamed as he pointed out the features that had accompanied Abe into the hereafter. Grandma even merited the Presidential prerogative of panels holding blocks of ice to keep her cool on those unseasonably hot October days.

Mother looked relieved. "I thank you, Brother Erwin, for not insisting upon embalming. I know your mother would have disapproved. She was an old-fashioned lady who deserves an old-fashioned funeral."

He smiled and patted her hand as he said, "You were a true daughter to her and a godsend to me. I'm sure she was happy here—far happier, I daresay, than she would have been if subjected daily to Delilah's tender mercies."

While Bromschwig and Husmann installed Grandma in the casket, Uncle Erwin reported on his contributions to the burial brigade, "All afternoon I have been down at Western Union telegraphing the out-of-town relatives. I expect answers by this time tomorrow; then I can finish setting up the event with the parson.

"I'll just sit with her a few minutes, then I'll get started on the obituary."

Mother offered, "Jemmy has been working on one. Perhaps you can work together."

For the next hour, Jemmy and Uncle Erwin sat at the dining room table. He composed while Jemmy took dictation. For the first time, she really looked at him. She saw a kindly man, portly and prosperous with flecks of white in his red-brown hair. Not much taller than Jemmy but with an air of confident self-worth, he looked to be a fellow who knew how to get along in the business world. His clean scent of Barbasol and bay rum made her feel secure in this uncertain world where two souls, who once meant home and hearth to her, had now permanently decamped for regions unknown.

Even though the out-of-town family had wired they could reach St. Louis by Friday, Uncle Erwin had to postpone the funeral until the following Monday because the parson had weddings and Christenings scheduled for Friday and Saturday. The parson would not be so unfeeling as to hold celebrations on funeral days. Of course, Sunday was out of the question.

Jemmy spent hours making copies of the finished obituary. She spent one whole day—her happiest day in months—taking them around to all the newspapers in town. Guilt weighed on her head. She should have been teary-eyed over Grandma's departure instead of wide-eyed with fascination over the wonders she discovered in the inner sanctum of the fourth estate.

Over the next week, a parade of people came to Bricktop with offerings of lemon cake and sweet-and-sour cole slaw. The iceman came often, but on Tuesday Mother began to doubt that Grandma would remain patient outside her grave for a whole week. Uncle Erwin consulted Bromschwig. Husmann said there was nothing for it but embalming.

Bromschwig and Husmann carted Grandma, casket and all, off to their establishment.

Two hours later, Mother walked into Grandma's room to begin sorting out her belongings. She looked into the closet and screeched, "Jemmy, Jemmy come here this instant."

Jemmy ran in with needles of shock running up her back. "What is it?"

"Her tartan. She can't be buried without her tartan—or her prayer book either." Mother put her face down in the soft blue plaid of Grandma's tartan shawl and began to weep. For the first time, Jemmy realized that her Mother really did love the old lady. Then pangs stabbed her own eyes. Her lips quivered as she held back the tears.

Mother folded the plaid and stroked it. "I don't know what happened to her prayer book. You must look for it. When you find it, take the book and the tartan to Bromschwig's. Don't forget her six-thistle brooch. Their funeral parlor is on Eleventh, I think. Yes, Eleventh and Biddle."

To get them out of the way, Jemmy had taken all of Grandma's books, religious and un, to the third floor dormitory where she and the rest of the McBustle girls and Gerta, too, had been sleeping since Mother had begun taking in boarders. Jemmy had planned to sort them for return to the Mercantile or Mr. Bappel.

As she picked up Grandma's prayer book, a dime novel slid to the floor, one she had not read aloud prior to Mother's "penny dreadful" ban. Thomas Rascoe's sensational *Belle Starr, The Bandit Queen*. Jemmy slipped it inside the back cover of the prayer book on the off chance that in eternity Grandma might prefer Belle's company to St. Paul's. In any event, the old lady deserved a choice.

Jemmy wrapped the items together in brown paper and tied the package with string. Then a peculiar thing happened. Just as she was wrapping an end of string around a loop and sticking her fingers under the string to pull it into a bow, her vision blurred. A fat tear splashed a dark circle on the tan paper. Jemmy discovered she was crying.

Was it seeing mother weep? Jemmy had not witnessed her mother shed a tear since Father's funeral. Was it the tartan, the Celtic pin, the prayer book? Did Belle Starr betray Grandma's secret vice and remind Jemmy how frail and human the old woman was?

Jemmy never knew. She only knew that a tidal wave of love and regret rolled through her body and out her eyes. She remembered Grandma driving in a dog cart behind a Shetland pony while the girls waved to envious friends on the sidewalk. She remembered the streetcar rides to Barr's department store and the cherry phosphate treat before the ride home. She remembered Grandma's flute-like treble singing a lullaby about the fourteen angels who watched over Jemmy while she slept.

She remembered her own lack of feeling. Every time she had dribbled soup down the old lady's chin, every time she had fluffed Grandma's pillows just so she could punch out her anger on the helpless goose feathers, every time she had dropped a book on the floor just to wake her—every petty act of thoughtless neglect or willful spite now tortured and shamed her. She was helpless before the tide of remorse. No power in heaven or earth could let her take back a single act of childishness or selfishness. She faced the solemn truth—Grandma was dead.

Jack the Ripper in St. Louis

She sat on the floor weeping and rocking with her finger still stuck under the string atop the brown paper. She didn't stop crying until the wet paper disintegrated. Even then, the tears rolled on. Not until a good hour later did she replace the soggy paper and tie a new bow with new string.

She had not thought it possible she would miss her irascible old granny. Only the knowledge that Granny was old—her time had come—gave Jemmy the comfort she needed to bear the loss at all.

Drained of tears, Jemmy donned her hat and jacket and took three trolleys to Bromschwig's. On the way, visions of Granny's good deeds and her own hurtful ones pestered her like demons on a spree.

The door sign at Bromschwig and Husmann's read "Closed." Jemmy's grieving had caused her to arrive after regular business hours. Frustration threatened to overwhelm her right there on Biddle Street.

A light glinting off the polished coffin in the window rescued her. A gas jet or electric light from the back room cast rays over the top of the blue velvet portieres. Jemmy hated to go home with nothing to show for her trouble. She'd have the errand to do all over again the next day. She walked down the alley to the back and knocked on the rear door.

When no one answered, she thought she might leave the bundle. She could telephone the next day to explain how to drape the shawl; but where should she leave the package? She tried the back door. When it opened to her touch, she walked inside and started to set the parcel down on the table. Then she heard a noise from the basement. She walked to the cellar door and opened it. "Hello, is someone down there?"

A woman's voice replied, "I can't come up just now. Could you wait a bit?"

Waiting was the last thing Jemmy wanted to do. The sharp sweet smell of formaldehyde made her wretch and pull out her hankie to cover her nose. The sooner she finished her errand and left, the less likely she would be to create a mess on the floor.

As she started down the stairs to explain how to fasten the tartan and where to place the six-thistle brooch, she called out. "It's getting late. I would like to be home before dark. I'll just leave this bundle with you and tell you—"

She stopped with the sentence half finished. The blood drained from her face as she tried to grasp the scene in front of her. On a slanted wooden table lay Grandma, the pale yellow-white color of a fish's underside, stark naked. The woman hastened to stand up and cover the remains with a sheet. But she was too late to keep Jemmy from the most horrifying sight of her life—a foot long gash down the center of Grandma's belly. The woman had been sewing the flaps of skin together.

She said, "I'm so sorry you saw that. You shouldn't have come down, you know. I was nearly finished with—"

With lips quivering, Jemmy ended the sentence for her, "Sewing up Grandma."

Jemmy's vision blurred as salt water flooded out to burn her red-rimmed eyes. She sat down hard on the stair, put her head down on the package of Grandma's treasures and let the tears roll.

The woman flew to Jemmy's elbow to raise her and propel her back toward the upstairs light. In the undertaker's back room which served as office to the establishment, she sat Jemmy down and fetched a damp cloth to place on her forehead. As she made tea, she said, "I cannot apologize enough. What a shock to find your Grandmother so."

"I didn't know you cut them open."

"Oh, my dear, we don't. We wouldn't think of doing such a thing. All we do is substitute a preserving fluid for the blood. My no, we never cut them open."

The denial roused Jemmy's Irish blood. "I saw you sewing her up."

"But that was not our doing. No, no, indeed. Her doctor came to take her diseased organ for study."

"How could you let him?"

"He showed me papers. He said Mrs. Belinda McBustle gave him permission."

"Mother would never allow it. It must have been a forgery. Why didn't you telephone?"

"How could I telephone? No, no, I didn't have the number."

"But I'm sure you do. I heard Mother give it to Mr. Bromschwig himself."

"That doesn't mean he gave it to me, no, no. Neither Mr. Bromschwig nor Mr. Husmann was here at the time."

Jemmy stood and clinked her teacup down in its saucer. "Does Mr. Bromschwig know what you've done?"

The woman's face registered her fear. She shook her head.

Jemmy stood as her face reddened to match her eyes, "I will take great pleasure in telling him."

"Oh, please don't tell him. He'll fire me sure as I'm standing here."

"That's exactly what you deserve. I bet you didn't even read those papers, you just let some quack..." Jemmy couldn't bring herself to say the words.

The woman knitted her eyebrows and apologized softly. "You're right. I didn't read the papers." The woman hung her head and cupped her hands. "I couldn't read the papers. I tried, I really did; but there were so many big words."

Jemmy clutched her parcel to her chest and moved toward the door. The woman's hand found Jemmy's arm to hold her back. Tears welled up in her eyes as she begged, "Please don't tell Mr. Bromschwig. This is the best job I ever had. I can sit down most all the time. When I was little, I worked in a cloth mill until the big loom caught my leg." She showed Jemmy her mis-shapen ankle.

Until then, Jemmy had not even noticed the woman's clumping walk. The woman spoke more softly, "I couldn't go to school, you see, not then. But now, I'm learning to read. Someday I'll be able to understand papers, but..." Her voice trailed off.

Seeing the pitiable leg brought Jemmy once again to the brink of tears. "I won't tell Mr. Bromschwig. I suppose I should be thanking you for... But I don't understand. Why didn't the doctor close the wound himself—if he was a real doctor. What did he say?"

"He didn't say anything. After he showed me the papers, he opened his black case and..." She motioned in Grandma's direction.

"Who was he?"

"Dr. Kumberty, or Tumberty, I think."

"Was he an elderly man? Fine-looking, though, and tall with a fierce looking mustache waxed at the ends? Did he carry two canes and have a boy wearing red pantaloons with him?"

"You know him, then."

Jemmy said, "Yes. Dr. Tumblety."

"Might I be so bold as to ask you to tell no one about what has happened here. I am good with wax. I can make her look untouched. I promise. And I'll sew her gown to the lining. I'll use a thousand pins. No one else will know, not Mr. Bromschwig or Husmann, not anybody. No one will ever see except you and me—you and me and Dr. T."

If the lady embalmer had known how often that phrase would ring in Jemmy's bad ear, she would never have been so cruel as to set it to rhyme. From that moment on, Jemmy could not banish it from her head. It echoed and rang and sparked and trampled—the last thing on her mind when she fell asleep and the first thing she remembered when she woke.

Jack the Ripper in St. Louis

The only thing she dreaded more than beginning the rhyme was ending it. She tried to drag out the vowels in those seven syllables for as long as she could. She fought against seeing again the vision that haunted her nights. Bloodless hands over a dark gash in Grandma's pale sunken body.

Chapter Four

Jemmy didn't tell Mother what she had seen. She said not a word about the gash, the forged papers or Dr. T. She toyed with the idea of telling Uncle Erwin, but such news about his mother would surely give him pain—and what purpose would it serve? She chose to bear the vision alone and in silence. But even if she had wanted to unburden herself, she couldn't have found a quiet moment.

By Thursday, Mother was glad the McBustle townhouse had five unrented rooms to offer out-of-town family. Even the spacious Erwin McBustle place in Compton Heights overflowed. Aunt Delilah called upon her sisters to house the less prestigious members of the horde of house guests.

All relations spent the days at Bricktop performing the usual cycle of storytelling, boohooing and eating. Funeral rites had a well-defined shape. Ladies in black and men with black armbands and black weed bands on their hats moved with soundless steps and downcast eyes through the murmurs of Mother and Aunt Delilah.

They entered the parlor, went straight to the casket, kissed the corpse and dabbed their eyes. Folks already present observed a protocol of strict silence for two minutes followed by a period of decorous whispering and shushing.

Once the newcomers left casket-side and began circling round the room renewing family ties with the kin whom they had not seen since the last funeral, everyone had permission to talk.

In the afternoon blush of warm October days, men drifted outside to smoke cigars, talk business and sip from pocket flasks the whiskey Mother banned in the house. Women were stuck inside. Knitting needles clacked out the minutes like a thousand keys locking a thousand doors.

Only one peculiar thing interrupted the talk-and-eat ritual. The glasses in the china cabinet clinked against each other and the coffee cups on the sideboard danced until two fell off. One crashed on the wooden floor while the other rolled harmlessly under the table.

Mother chastised the help, "Gerta, girls, you must not put the china close to the edge. I would think you would know better. We've already had two tremors this year. For all we know, the next one could be much worse. We must pray never to have another like the big earthquake of 1812."

Even before Mother Nature grumbled over Grandma's death, Jemmy's world was out of joint. The comfort of routine had vanished. Mealtime became meaningless. Gerta did her best to keep the dining room table filled with clean plates and food heavy enough to keep the mourners' minds off their sorrows.

With Mother always playing hostess in the parlor, the girls didn't need to be told to take up the slack. Minerva commenced weeding the garden and shopping at Soulard market each day. Merry wrote nearly a hundred thank-you notes then disappeared for hours as she returned emptied dishes to their owners. To Randy and Jemmy fell the cleaning and dish washing. Of course, when off-duty, they were expected to pose, hands folded demurely, in the parlor.

Randy sat in sullen silence; but much to her surprise, Jemmy found that she liked being around family. At least, hearing the stories chased away the macabre memory of Grandma's violated body. That vision so possessed her waking hours that she ordered her imagination to find some other thought to hold. Just one daydream of a boy in a fez floated effortlessly to the front of her brain. A memory of red trousers as they ballooned against the flanks of a white horse.

She forced herself to stay up nights writing down family stories. She managed to exhaust herself so completely that a few times she fell asleep without once repeating "You and me and Dr. T." She learned more about her grandmother in those three days than she had in the entire seventeen years she had spent living under the same roof with the old lady.

She especially liked Uncle Erwin's story about how the McBustle family got its name. The ancestor who first came to American shores was neither a McBustle nor a Scotsman. He was an Irishman from County Derry who liked the sound of the word "freedom"—especially if it meant freedom from the English and his father's boot. He planned to make his fortune and return to the Emerald Isle in splendor.

He landed in Pennsylvania where he spent on education every penny he had as well as every penny he could earn by swamping out stables at night. He learned surveying at Philadelphia College. When he couldn't find a job, he signed on to be a soldier and won a commendation from George Washington by heroically beating a goodly number of liquor makers into paying their taxes during the Whiskey Rebellion.

1794 began his rise to prosperity—when he changed his name. Any group of immigrants that grows big enough, or bold enough, or brazen enough to want equality with old timers is, as the saying goes, "lustin' for a bustin.'" The Irish in America were no exception.

As Peregrine Bussey, Irishman, he couldn't get a surveying job with the army—or any job at all other than mucking out stables in the city of brotherly love. The word was NINA—No Irish Need Apply.

He sought help from an acquaintance who had a canal survey underway. Arms folded across his chest, Peregrine was standing on the edge of the canal trench while his benefactor hollered at the fifty or sixty diggers within earshot in the bottom of the five foot ditch. At that very moment when the men leaned on their picks and shovels to look up, the embankment crumbled.

In his only clothes, Peregrine slid down the bank and splatted into the puddle at the bottom. Amidst the guffaws, Bussey's sponsor introduced "That Mick Bussey—trying to haul up the dirt on his arse. He'll take any kind of job so long as it is not *manual* labor."

Eventually the crew stopped laughing, but the name lingered on. Every time anyone said, "MickBussey," Peregrine couldn't get a single manjack of them to call him anything else. When he drew his first paycheck, the paymaster listed him as "McBustle." When he protested that his name was "Bussey," the paymaster said he would pay "McBustle" and none other.

Being transformed into a Scotsman made all the difference. The McBustle name let him escape digging with a spade and running wheelbarrows of dirt on slippery planks up the sides of muddy ditches. With a letter from his benefactor recommending "McBustle" and the hope no one would ask for better credentials, a change of name had made Perry McBustle respectable.

The day of Grandma's funeral dawned warm and golden—more like spring than autumn. The parson of Lafayette Park Presbyterian Church spoke at length about Grandma's devotion to religion. He discretely ignored her recent predilection for shooting firearms and spouting obscenity.

As the pall bearers marched in solemn procession to load Grandma into the hearse, the McBustle family, including the out-of-towners, held their collective breath.

They wondered why Uncle Erwin had chosen his skinny twelve year old nephew as a pallbearer. The entire family glued their eyes on no one but him. They were dead certain he would sneeze and drop Grandma on Duncan's foot, or trip over the door sill and launch Grandma down the marble church steps into Missouri Avenue. What else could one expect from a person his own mother called "Hideous Heathcliff"?

But, the six of them tucked Grandma up safely behind the glass doors. The four white horses in black harness and black ostrich feather cockades set off majestically in front of the four family carriages. Behind them marched the bagpipers wearing their distinctive clan tartans and playing their loudly mournful songs. Ironically enough, considering Heathcliff's usual uncouth behavior, the pipers were the ones who caused consternation in the cortege.

Most of the streets to Bellefontaine Cemetery, like most streets in most American cities, were mostly unpaved. Even streets paved with brick or asphalt tended to attract a generous supply of the gifts horses leave behind when they answer nature's call.

A piper marching about midway back among the fifty or so musicians tried to step over one rather fresh and prodigious pile. When he couldn't span the whole mass, his forward heel plopped in the substance.

The heel slipped. As the piper tried to keep his balance and throw his other foot forward, his momentum faltered. He fell into the manure, bottom first, as his kilt floated out in a perfect circle around him. As the unfortunate piper's bag wailed itself out of wind, his companion piper put out a hand to help him up.

When the fallen fellow grabbed the offered hand, he overbalanced the rescuer. Without traction enough to stay upright, the second man fell. He landed on one knee as his pipe let out an eagle scream.

The musician following those two had been so intent on remembering his fingering that he failed to see the roadblock ahead. He plowed into the pair. His legs slid forward which knocked the fallen pipers down again as they tried to stand. His bagpipe flew up and came down on his head like a wheezing hundred pound sack of plaid flour.

The man directly behind the three saw the pile-up too late to avoid it. He tried to hop over the top. He even managed to avoid stepping in some offal. Instead, he stepped on his three downed comrades. The trio resented his clodhoppers on their clan escutcheons. They pulled him down, quite intentionally, and rubbed his face in it. This breach of good taste angered a pal of the attackee so mightily that he pulled the nearest attacker up out of the mire and popped him over the head with his mouthpipe.

Seeing a fight cheered up the rest of the pipers to a considerable degree. After all, what Scotsman would prefer a funeral to a free-for-all? They elected en masse not to go to the cemetery; but to skirmish a while, then refresh themselves at the nearest saloon. It was just as well. After twenty fellows brawl in the dung of the street for even a few seconds, who would care to stand downwind of them at graveside for an hour or more?

Luckily the half of the pipers who were still marching and playing didn't miss their combative brothers. They kept right on marching and whooing. Being at the rear, the drummers couldn't help but notice the melee. They didn't join in though.

Simultaneously, they split their lines in the center with half making a smart ninety degree turn to the right and half making a sharp ninety degree turn to the left. Upon reaching the side of the street, they made right turns forward and marched single file.

After passing the knot of wrestlers, they reversed their maneuvers and rejoined the parade in proper drum lines. They didn't miss a single beat.

Proof positive that practice makes perfect.

In a voice a little too loud, Aunt Delilah commented that the smaller number of pipers was a blessing. She opined that the conductor should consider throwing half his men in the settling lagoon before every concert. She said such a measure might save the hearing of thousands.

And so Grandma was laid to rest in her best black silk bombazine and her blue tartan fastened with a silver brooch. Her hands held her prayer book to read if her eyes were cast up to heaven and *The Bandit Queen* if she had occasion to focus in the other direction.

Back at Bricktop, the family ate cole slaw and lemon cake as they reminisced about the wake.

Uncle Erwin said, "For the first time, I am grateful Peregrine Bussey became a ditch digger instead of a bagpiper. I don't know about you, but I'd rather be called 'McBustle' than 'McTurd.'"

With much stiff-armed embracing and black-edged hankie waving, the mourners and their baggage passed through Union Station and disappeared on trains by Tuesday afternoon. The three-and-a-half stories of Bricktop seemed deserted with only seven people left.

Mother lit into a top-to-bottom housecleaning, and she lit into the girls if they slacked off. By Friday, the place gleamed, right down to Merry's freshly painted sign in the front window. "Room to let. Inquire within."

When Aunt Delilah dropped by to retrieve her silver chafing dishes, the sight of the house and the sign rendered her very nearly speechless; but that condition was too alien to her to last long.

As she entered the front door—minus its funeral wreath—and walked by the un-creped hall mirror and the undraped portrait of Peregrine McBustle in the Hall, she marveled. "My dear Belinda, has the pain of these last months removed your reason? What will people think if you

cease proper mourning after only a single week? I daresay they will con-
clude that we loved the old lady no more than we actually did."

"I am being entirely reasonable, Delilah. My children and I must have
an income if we are to survive. My line of employment is the operation of a
boarding house which, I might add, I do quite well. No one chooses to live
in a funereal house draped with black bunting—at least none I would care to
have as residents. Quite sensible that the trappings of the grave must go."

"I beg you to reconsider. You yourself said how old-fashioned Erwin's
mother was. You know the minimum time for mourning a mother-in-law is
three months. And that's three months whether you liked her or not."

"And so I shall wear black for three months."

Just then Auntie Dee caught a glimpse of Nervy looking pert in blue
plaid. "And the girls. She was their own grandmother. They should be
wearing gray or white with black edging for at least six months."

"Nonsense. They have to work. White is impractical. They will be
wearing funeral badges for six months. That is quite enough."

"And Jemima? She's seventeen. She should be wearing black for six
months."

"Jemima will be wearing black for one month. She has been tending her
grandmother for five. That is a total of six months. Surely you cannot fault
her sense of responsibility or fulfillment of duty when you take that into
account."

"Whatever happened to the good old days when children were not seen,
not heard, and not dutifully responsible for anything at all?"

Mother cocked her head to one side. "Does that require an answer,
Sister-in-Law?"

Aunt Delilah pursed her lips and tried again. "If it's a matter of money,
I'm sure Erwin will..."

"He has been more than generous already. It's time for us to reestablish our independence."

With an upraised hand and a nod of the head Mother silenced Auntie Dee. "Besides, strict funeral customs are no longer in fashion. You yourself, a leader of St. Louis society, could scarcely maintain that you are in deep mourning. Surely you would expect to set the standards yourself to serve as example for others with less knowledge and insight."

Auntie Dee had no reply. She was wearing a solemn black wool gown, but with silver lace at the cuffs and throat. The rest of her weeds were no better suited to deep mourning. Her hat had the appropriate yard of crepe, but gray satin ruching and silver lace framed her face. Her hankie was edged with mauve, not black. And she wore a brooch with her own mother's brown hair plaited and crocheted into a miniature willow tree. And that's not to mention a silver belt buckle and earrings of French Jet.

Mother led her sister-in-law into the dining room as she said, "Thank you for the use of the dishes. Without them we wouldn't have had hot food. Hot food is such a comfort during sad times, don't you think?"

Delilah left shaking her head. Mother expected a visit from Uncle Erwin, but none came, not even a telephone call. Perhaps Uncle didn't think Mother would consider intercession from him any more pleasing than she had from Auntie Dee. Perhaps he secretly agreed with Mother that practicality should take precedence over sentiment. In any event, he let that sleeping dog lie.

Packing away the black brought Bricktop back to life. Pumping new life into the boarding house business brought Jemmy back to life. Going to the newspapers nearly chased away her vision of Granny in Bromschwig's basement. "You and me and Dr. T" ran through her mind no more than a hundred times a day—well down from the too-many-to count of the week before.

Taking copies of Mother's carefully worded advertisement to the newspapers brought Jemmy back into the heady world of journalism. More than ever, she knew what she wanted—excitement—adventure—maybe even to make the world a better place. She wanted to be St. Louis' answer to Nellie Bly. And she was desperate for something to do. Only a busy mind could keep "You and me and Dr. T" at bay.

While running her mother's errands, she asked for appointments to see people in charge of hiring reporters. She spent the weekend deciding what to wear, how to act, what to say. On the first Monday in November, she set out on the first step toward realizing her dream. She asked to be hired as a newspaper reporter.

She first tried the *St. Louis Post-Dispatch*, a paper owned by Mr. Joseph Pulitzer—the same Joseph Pulitzer who owned the *New York World*—Nellie Bly's paper. The Post turned her down. She came to know what editors were going to say before they said it. They all sounded like the first one.

"Miss McBustle, I don't think you have a grasp on how dangerous newspaper work can be. Covering a horse-cart accident or fire poses risk to life and limb. A burning wall could fall. A horse-drawn fire engine could run you over. They can't just stop on a dime, you know.

"But there's much more. Our reporters must speak to many people of unsavory reputation and unacceptable character. I would never be able to sleep at night if a nice young lady like you should be victimized under my authorization. No, my wife would never forgive me—nor your mother—nor myself."

One editor was kind enough to show Jemmy what a real reporter looked like. He pointed through the open door of his office to slim fellow of about thirty with an enormous ice-skate blade of a nose. "That's Amadé Boudinier. That's our crime reporter. He has the best nose for news in town."

As Jemmy stifled a laugh, the editor looked down and said, "Don't bother me again until your nose looks like his." That was his last word.

Most let her down more gently. "I will keep you in mind in case we should find ourselves wanting a women's activities reporter, though we have so few needs in that line and so many real reporters I wouldn't expect an opening if I were you. We might be in need of secretarial help if you are a qualified typist."

Jemmy murmured, "No." And so she spoke with the news editor of all the dailies and weeklies in St. Louis—even the literary ones. More than twenty editors. No success. No job. By the end of the week, depression made her so listless she had to force herself to get out of bed. "You and me and Dr. T" set her failure to music.

The next morning, Jemmy made her way to the kitchen and slumped into a chair.

Gerta, turned from the stove and saw something was wrong, "Vat is it, Jemmy? Gerta help, maybe."

Jemmy answered, "The only job I want in this world is to be a reporter like Nellie Bly. But no one will give me a chance. I guess Uncle Erwin will make me marry some boring old bald guy and have babies and teach Sunday School."

Gerta said, "Sometimes people must make own chance."

"What do you mean?"

"Gerta make own chance. I go out Vest to make fortune in Dakota Territory. I don't find gold to mine, but I find miners to mine." She pointed to herself. "Make own fortune."

"How can I make my own fortune. Am I supposed to go to the Klondike and mine the miners?"

"No, I talk about take chance, make chance, not make money."

"Pardon me, Gerta. But look how you ended up. I mean you're a cook. What happened to your fortune?"

"I not careful. Lose money gambling—take fool chances."

"You must know in here," she pointed to her heart, "if chance is right.

Heart knew gambling vas not right, but I gamble anyvay. Must listen to heart. It tells true."

"But I don't know how to 'make my own chance.'"

"Gerta teach. Ask self vhy no one hire you?"

"Because I'm a girl."

"Then must show girl can do job like man. Better than man, maybe. Do job man can't."

Jemmy thought for a moment. "It's so simple, so obvious. I have to get a story newspapers want to publish."

"Vait, vait. I think you say you vant job—not just story."

"You think I still won't get hired even with a story."

"You need plan—plan to get job after get story."

Jemmy came up with a plan—a long shot, perhaps, but a plan. She made a new appointment at a newspaper. This time she didn't want to see the news editor. This time she had just one person to see—the owner. Only one newspaper in town was owned by a woman. Jemmy went to see Mrs. Celestine Willmore, owner of the *St. Louis Illuminator*.

Mrs. Willmore had given up her social butterfly status when Mr. Willmore died leaving her the paper along with a pile of debts. Mrs. Willmore learned to keep the books herself. She reined in costs and promoted the paper as "free from political influence," and "the friend of the little guy."

After she pushed the paper back on its feet, she installed herself in an office on the top floor. Every day she refused to see anyone until she had read all competing St. Louis products as well as top papers from Chicago, Cincinnati, New York and Boston. She clipped articles and sent them to her staff with sharp notes saying she expected a similar story PDQ.

When she first entered the office, Jemmy could see nothing of the lady except her hands on either side of a *Kansas City Star*. Mrs. Willmore was a little birdlike woman with watery blue eyes. She pulled the newspaper

49

down just below her nose and said, "Yes."

Jemmy started talking as she walked toward the desk. "Mrs. Willmore, I'm Jemima McBustle, the next Nellie Bly."

Mrs. Willmore put down her paper and looked at Jemmy. "What makes you think you could be half the reporter Nellie Bly used to be?"

"I know that I can, and I want you to let me prove it."

"May I see your work references?"

"I don't have any."

Mrs. Willmore said, "Nothing published, I suppose."

Jemmy said, "Not yet."

"All right, then. Because I like you, I'll read your story anyway. Maybe we can use it."

"I want more than that. I want an assignment. Give me a story to do. If you like it, then make me a reporter."

"Isn't that a little previous? How am I supposed to know you have even a little talent for newswriting or getting the story or, for that matter, singing in the church choir?"

"That's what I plan to prove."

"You're bold enough. I'll give you that, but I won't give you a story assignment. In the first place my news editor makes story assignments. What I make are story suggestions."

"Then give me a story suggestion."

"Oh no. If you're a newspaperwoman at all, you know your city. You won't have to ask for story suggestions; you'll smell a story and go after it."

"So you'll give me a job if I get a story."

Mrs. Willmore laughed. "What cheek. You come in here asking for a job with no experience, no references, no story and want me to promise you a job. Why should I?"

"Mrs. Willmore, how will you feel when I prove I'm the next Nellie

Bly; and you, the only woman owner of a newspaper in St. Louis, had first crack at me and turned me down?"

Mrs. Willmore laughed out loud. "I rather imagine you are more likely to come *out* as a debutante than you are to come *up* with a story. Still, I admire your style." She paused and clicked her teeth. "You're ahead of me. I was twice your age before I could get anyone to take me seriously."

"You won't regret it."

"I will most certainly regret it if anything happens to you. You will be careful. You must promise not to do anything so insane as having yourself committed to an insane asylum—like Nellie did."

In fact, Jemmy had toyed with the mad-house idea; but she said, "I promise. I won't pretend to be crazy."

"All right, then. You get a story we can use and I'll give you a job—a six month trial—but my news editor will decide whether you stay on after that."

Jemmy produced a paper and said, "Then you wouldn't mind signing this. You can add the part about the six months here." She pointed to the margin about halfway down the page.

Mrs. Willmore read the paper, put her hand to her forehead and laughed loud and long. She tossed the paper back to Jemmy and said. "You step high enough to take the cake in any cakewalk. I am not about to sign your paper. But you may trust my word. Get a good story, and I'll make you a reporter— for a trial."

Jemmy said, "I'll get a story, a story that will sell ten thousand papers."

Mrs. Willmore chuckled again. "More likely you'll get ten thousand corns on your feet. Goodbye, Miss McBustle, it's been a pleasure to meet you. Might I also wish you a long and productive life since I don't expect to see you again."

"You'll see me again, Mrs. Willmore; or should I say 'Boss'?"

Chapter Five

Jemmy kept her composure down six flights of stairs before giving way to uncontrollable shaking. She collapsed in a flood of joyous, nervous laughter on the bench in front of a hardware store. She whispered to herself, "It's true. I'm going to be a reporter."

A lady with a little boy in tow stopped to see whether Jemmy required assistance. Jemmy beamed, "Thank you, Madam, for your solicitude; but I've never needed assistance less than this very moment."

Jemmy sat basking in the late afternoon sun and basking in her "chance." Then obstacles to her Nellie Bly plan poked their ugly snouts through her rosy haze.

Mother would never allow her to become a stunt reporter—not if she knew what Jemmy was up to. And she needed money. The dollar and thirty cents she had saved to buy Christmas presents wouldn't go very far.

Her biggest obstacle vanquished the pink glow. Where would she find a story? She had promised not to get herself committed to a mad-house— too impractical anyway. If she failed to come home every night, Mother would have half the city looking for her. So where could she find the Nellie Bly story—the story a woman could get but a man could not? Maybe the editor of the *Illuminator* was right. Maybe her nose was too small for sniffing out the news.

She tested her proboscis for talent. She looked—really looked—at the passers-by. When she stared at one man, he sauntered over to the bench, put one foot up, and began to retie his shoe. He smirked suggestively as he said, "I might be interested in buying what you're selling."

Jemmy jumped in shock. The man tipped his hat and beat a retreat. After that, Jemmy didn't dare look too boldly—not even at women. She concentrated on their shoes. Neither her new-found observations about shoe leather in spats nor her untrained nose told her where to find a story. "You and me and Dr. T." The dark rhyme turned cartwheels in her head.

The wind turned chill in the afternoon shadows. She had just about decided to mull the future over at home when she discovered the thing she had been missing—a nose for news. No—not her own nose—the redoubtable beak of the nose-for-news himself, Amadé Boudinier.

He made notes in a little notebook as he waited at the westbound trolley stop across the street. Jemmy vowed to have a notepad just like it and keep it with her always.

The Nose was handsomely turned-out in a brown pin-striped suit and vest, brown bowler and tan spats. When Jemmy saw the trolley pull up to the stop, she crossed the street and took a seat near the rear. When The Nose disembarked at Nineteenth Street, Jemmy followed.

She stayed a discreet distance behind as she followed him three blocks.

She watched him enter an ordinary-looking two story house with blue shutters. She sighed to herself, "Looks like The Nose went home."

She was about to retrace her steps to the Olive Street trolley line when a commotion turned her head back to the house with blue shutters. A burly man hauled out a fellow in shirtsleeves and hat who was pulling up his suspenders. A well-dressed matron tossed the man's vest and jacket after him. The ejected man turned around in circles while putting on his duds. He shook his fist at the house and said some words the wind blew away from Jemmy's ears. After a while, he buttoned up and ambled off.

Jemmy didn't understand what she had seen, but she did think it peculiar that The Nose should have a giant at his home as well as someone deserving of being pitched out on the street.

She walked into the neighborhood drugstore and bought a tin of Woodbury's pimple cream. While the druggist was counting out her change, she said, "Sir, would you be so good as to tell me who owns that house down the street. The one with blue shutters."

The druggist shifted his feet and said, "The only thing you want to know about such places, Miss, is to keep far away from them, for a fact."

"But why?"

"It's not fit for a nice young lady like yourself to discuss such places."

Jemmy teared up and supplied a catch to her voice. "But I must know. My future depends upon it."

"I suppose you saw your father go in there? I mean, for a fact?"

"No, my dear father has passed away. My intended—that's the one I saw. That's why I must know. My whole life is at stake."

The druggist softened. "If I were you, I'd have my brother or uncle investigate. I'm sure they can advise you."

Lies were coming easier now, "But I have no brother or uncle, no one to guide me. That's why I'm begging you to help me. If you don't, I might make a terrible mistake."

"Well, I suppose I have better reason to warn you than to protect some—" He leaned over the counter and whispered, "For an actual fact, the house with blue shutters is a sporting house."

Jack the Ripper in St. Louis

Jemmy mumbled a tearful, "Thank you, Sir, I believe you have delivered me from a life of misery."

Back on the street, Jemmy wiped the tears. The Nose worked. It led her to her story—the story a woman could get but a man could not. She knew what to investigate—the women of the houses of ill repute.

Her guilty conscience shot down her giddy success with a barb in the form of the accusing look—the look Mother would stab through her—if Mother knew. Mother never told lies—well—almost never. When she did tell fibs, compassion ruled her heart and overruled her instinct. Concentrate as hard as she might, Jemmy could find no noble cause in her own lies.

Deep in thought, she walked in the direction of the streetcar line, but soon found herself turned about. She looked up to see nothing familiar, not the two story brick houses near the streetcar line, but dreary little places with grimy windows.

Two tough-looking boys of about sixteen trotted up and squared off on either side of Jemmy. She edged back until her shoulder hit a porch post. One of the boys placed his hand on the post above her head and said, "You're a sight cleaner than most of the scarf trade we get around here."

Jemmy tried not to let her nervousness show. "I don't know what you mean. I'm on my way home."

The other boy took off his cap to expose greasy dark hair. He said, "Colley, show your best manners now. Can't you see this chippy's the kind plays hard to get. Get a better price that way, don't you, sweet meat?"

Overwhelmed by the need to escape, Jemmy burst between them and took off at a run back the way she had come. She heard laughter from the toughs. One yelled. "Go ahead, we'll give you a sporting chance—a whole block's head start."

Jemmy's corset cut off her wind. Her little spool boot heels dug into the soft dirt. No doubt about it. The boys would catch her before she even found out where she was. She teetered on the brink of panic when the fates smiled.

Just as the greasy-haired boy caught up, Jemmy landed in other hands. A tall policeman in mutton-chop whiskers said, "These lowlifes pestering you, are they?"

"She was sportin' with us like sportin' women do, Sir."

In a huff Jemmy said, "I was not and I am not. Officer, I just went to the drugstore. When I came out, I must have turned the wrong way. Then these ruffians accosted me."

The officer pointed his nightstick at Colley and took a step toward him, "Accost her, did you, young buck?"

The greasy-haired boy said, "Accost her? No, Officer. We did not talk about a-cost."

The officer shook his nightstick. "Off with you or I'll see if you still have so much brass in your mouth after I ram this down your throat."

As the greasy-haired boy trotted off, he tossed back over his shoulder. "Sweet meat, I'll tell you what I'll a-cost next time. Bring three dollars—that's a fair price for MY services."

The officer tipped his cap and offered his arm, "May I escort you home, Miss?"

Jemmy took his arm. "I'd be much obliged if you could see me to a streetcar stop on Olive, eastbound."

The officer said, "I thought you lived in this neighborhood."

Jemmy heard the suspicion in his voice and said, "No. I made a special trip to Woodbury's Drug Store." She lowered her eyes and her voice, "...for pimple cream."

"But your skin is clear."

"It's for my younger sister."

"Is there no pimple cream in a drugstore closer to your home?"

56

"Woodbury's is ever so much better than the rest. He makes it on the premises, I'm told." She produced the tin from her reticule. That seemed to satisfy the officer. He saw her safely on the trolley and tipped his hat as it moved away.

After three hours as an almost-reporter, Jemmy took stock. She discovered she had a talent for lying which was just about equal to her lack of talent for sensing danger. She shuddered to think what might have happened if the policeman had not been handy when the toughs caught up with her. She would have to stop daydreaming—no doubt about that. As to the lying—well—

Back home, she began laying plans. First she cut tablet paper into three-by-five inch pieces, punched holes in the top and threaded string through the holes. No money for a proper notebook meant she had to make do.

She looked up Amadé Boudinier's home address in the city directory and wrote it down on the second page of her "notebook." The next step would have to wait until morning. Until past three o'clock that night Jemmy played out in her mind the plans that would launch her into the world of investigative journalism. "You and me and Dr. T" didn't intrude, not even once.

She lied to Mother. She swore dutiful daughter Jemmy was keeping her promise to find suitable employment. She had an interview as companion for a lady confined to her bed by tuberculosis. Jemmy surprised herself by how easily she adapted to the lying life. Her conscience now gave her scarcely more than a twinge. Soon she'd be able to lie without even crossing her fingers.

She went to see Aunt Delilah in Compton Heights. Of course, she knew Aunt Delilah would not be home on a Wednesday morning of Wednesday Club meeting day.

When the housekeeper answered the door, Jemmy asked if she might see

Aunt Delilah. The housekeeper told her Mrs. McBustle was not at home. Jemmy said, "I don't think Aunt Delilah would mind if I borrowed a book from the library, do you?"

The housekeeper let her in and disappeared out back. Jemmy peeked down the hall. Empty. She sneaked to the telephone and winced at the noise as she cranked the bell. She asked the operator to ring the home of Amadé Boudinier.

She was still riding her string of good luck. The Nose had a telephone. Jemmy waited with baited breath, fingers of both hands crossed. She prayed that Mr. Boudinier had a Mrs. and that she was home.

"Hello," came the answer, a bit faint behind the crackling sound of temperamental electricity.

"Hello, am I speaking to Mrs. Amadé Boudinier?"

"Yes, I am Mrs. Boudinier."

"I am Mrs. Victor Kalinowski from St. John Nepomuk Church. You know our church was ruined by the big tornado last year, and we hold monthly raffles to raise money for rebuilding. I understand that you are the winner for November.

"Now, what I would like to do is ask you a few questions so that I might write an article for our parish newsletter. We want to keep firing up interest in our raffles. So would you be so kind as to answer a few questions for me?"

The voice said, "This is the first I heard about a raffle. What did we win?"

"I'm afraid I don't really know. We've had so many excellent awards; I'm sure it's very nice. October's prize was a hundred dollars in merchandise at Scruggs, Vandervoort and Barney Dry Goods Company."

"I think you must be mistaken. No one has told me about a raffle prize."

"Perhaps it was your husband, wanting to surprise you. Oh, dear, I've gone and ruined his treat."

"Well, perhaps. He does try to help Catholic charities."

"Since the surprise is already ruined, what harm could it do to give me just a little information for my article?"

"What would you like to know?"

"What does Mr. Boudinier do for a living?"

"He reports the news at the *St. Louis Illuminator.*"

"I suppose his job keeps him away from hearth and home."

"He works six days a week, but he does his best to be home in the evenings—except Monday nights when he goes to Knights of Columbus meetings."

"Do you and Mr. Boudinier have children?"

"Yes, we have seven children, four boys and three girls."

"What a splendid family. Might I have the names and ages of the children?"

"René , Gaston, Pierre, Marcel, Anais, Denise, and Celine. I really haven't time for the ages, Baby Celine is trying to eat the cat's tail."

Before Jemmy could even offer thanks, the line went dead.

As she copied down names in her makeshift notebook, a baritone voice stopped her in mid-name. "What on earth was that all about? Why should you care about Boudinier children?"

The voice came from handsome cousin Duncan McBustle. He stood on the stairs and grinned down at Jemmy. He wore a rust colored sweater and tan tweed britches. Even though noon was fast approaching, he looked as though he'd just forced himself out of bed. He yawned and said, "Could it be little Jemima has set her sights on a married man? Or maybe, little Jemima was checking up on a beau who said he was single, but now turns out to have—how many children was it?"

"Seven."

"Seven children? My hat's off to a man of such parts."

The joke was lost on Jemmy. She teared up. "Just wait until someone you trusted turns out to be a fraud." She sniffed into her hanky.

Duncan softened, "I'm sorry. I'm not used to thinking of you as anything but my brat cousin."

Jemmy stuck her chin up. Duncan said, "May I offer my services if this married cad needs discouraging though I doubt you need me. It seems as though you are smart enough to find out his secrets. I imagine you are smart enough to deal with him yourself."

Jemmy started to walk toward the door. Duncan said, "Don't be offended, cousin. Come have breakfast with me. Then I'll show you my new race horse. A splendid black filly with white forelegs—wild though. I can't wait until she's old enough to race."

"No, thank you. I have errands to run."

"I'll ask Mother to invite you to some of the winter outings she insists upon planning. Would you like that?"

"You needn't bother. I have better things to do with my time."

He put one hand over his heart and mocked her with a deep bow. "No doubt the mayor is awaiting your opinion before he makes the next important mayoral decision. Or are you the emissary of the governor? I forget."

"I'm trying to get a job—not staying in bed on a weekday morning when I'm supposed to be studying Latin and Greek at the university."

Duncan let that pass. "And just what job does my sweet cousin think she's fit for—breaking bucking horses?"

"I'm going to be a journalist—a stunt reporter—if you must know."

She closed the front door while Duncan yawned and ran his fingers through his hair.

Not until she reached the corner did she realize how foolish she had been to let Duncan goad her into telling her secrets. She flinched when she thought about how he might use that news to mortify her. She'd have to keep a better watch on her tongue and her temper.

With that in mind, she rehearsed the next part of her plan on the trolley rides to the *St. Louis Illuminator*. As she stepped off the trolley, she thought to herself, "Jemima McBustle, how you've changed. What would Mother say if she knew her eldest daughter had taken to lying like a squirrel in an oak tree? What would she do if she knew little Jemima was about to become a blackmailer?"

Chapter Six

Jemmy paid a boy three cents to take a message to the third floor news-room. He took the money, but looked surprised that she wanted it delivered to the very building they were standing in front of. He said, "You know they have an elevator."

She said, "I want the person who receives this to come down to me." The boy jingled the coins as he went inside.

Shivering a little, Jemima replayed the note she had written.

Dear Mr. Boudinier,

If you value your home and family, follow this boy to the one who penned this missive.

A Well-Wisher

If that didn't arouse a reporter's curiosity, nothing would.

Within minutes, the pair emerged. The boy pointed to Jemmy and left. Boudinier hunched up his shoulders and shoved his hands in his pockets as he started walking her way.

Jemmy took a deep breath and braced herself. Icicles of excitement prickled on the back of her neck. She had never felt more alive, or more jittery.

He said, "You have something to say to me?"

Jemmy said nothing. She showed him the page in her homemade notebook which displayed his address.

"My home address is no secret. It's in the city directory."

She turned the page to show him another address—the address of the house with the blue shutters.

He took a sharper tone, "I'm a reporter—a crime reporter. I go lots of places to find stories."

Jemmy shook her head left and right, very slowly, as she stared into his eyes. The effort of keeping silent made her weak in the knees.

His agitation spilled out in a rush. "Oh, for heaven's sakes, what do you want?"

Jemmy said nothing. She tapped her nose with her finger.

Boudinier pulled his hands out of his pockets. "*Mon Dieu*, what does that mean? Are you saying you know something? You can't blackmail me; I have no money."

He glared down at Jemmy, but she stood her ground. He said, "Are you deaf. I have no money. I have seven children. Take one of them if you will, but I have no money to give you."

At last, Jemmy broke her silence. She managed to speak slowly despite her jangling nerves. "I've been told you have the best nose for news in the business."

"Yes, so? Do you expect me to cut off my nose? Give it to you as a trophy?"

Jemmy shook her head. "It's only worth anything to either of us if it stays right where it is."

"Then what DO you want?"

"To share it."

He shook his head and let go a chuckle. "My nose may be large enough for two, but a method for sharing it is not something I care to think about."

"I don't want the stories you do. I want you to tell me stories I can do—stories a man can't get but a woman can."

He snorted, "Woman? You're no woman. Go back to grammar school and stop bothering me. I have work to do."

But he made no motion to leave. Jemmy said, "All I want from you are story ideas and just a little help now and then."

"And if I don't, you'll tell my wife I go to sporting houses."

Jemmy smiled.

He said, "And if I do help you?"

Jemmy said, "You get the satisfaction of helping a damsel in distress."

"You're a damsel in distress like Carrie Nation is a drunkard."

"Do you have a regular timetable for going to the house with blue shutters?"

He pursed his lips. "Most Tuesday afternoons—sometimes Thursday."

"Two o'clock tomorrow?"

"What about it?"

"I'll see you then?"

"Now, wait a minute. I'm not taking a SWEET young thing to a—you know. Go on and tell my wife. I don't know why I'm even talking to you."

"You won't be taking a sweet young thing. You'll hardly recognize me."

"So you plan to look like a woman of the town? Think again. I wouldn't need to go to Mrs. Nanny's if I had my own burlesque woman, would I?"

"I'm not going to be a burlesque woman."

"What, then?"

"I'm going to be your bodyguard."

He laughed out loud. "You, a bodyguard? A little slip of a girl?"

"Not a bodyguard, then. Errand boy—or lookout—or your son."

"I'd never take my son to such a place."

"I'll hold your horse."

"I don't have a horse; and I don't need you to hold my pantaloons, either."

She raised her eyebrows and insinuated, "I understand that you've lately been too drunk to find your way home."

He huffed in exasperation. "I suppose I could say that I sometimes have too much to drink. I suppose you could wear a whistle to call policemen and scare away the riffraff."

"And I could hold your pistol while you were—"

He interrupted with an impatient sigh. "All right, we'll try it tomorrow and see if anybody believes you are a boy. After that, you're on your own. And let me tell you, if you get murdered or worse, it will be just what you deserve. I won't even let on that I know who you are."

Jemmy stuck out her hand, "Agreed. Mr. Boudinier, I'm proud to have you as my mentor."

He threw both hands into the air in a clear refusal to shake hers. Jemmy watched him stomp back inside. She couldn't help feeling smug as she boarded the trolley for home.

Reality intruded. Jemmy had become both liar and blackmailer. What depravity, sin or crime would she commit next? She already had the answer—stealing.

While Mother was entertaining a prospective boarder in the parlor, Jemmy sneaked into the cellar to raid Father's trunk. Mother had no sons to hand the clothes down to; Cousin Duncan didn't need them. She should have given them to the church to send to overseas missions, but she didn't

65

part with them. Jemmy thought her mother couldn't stand the idea of not knowing where those sad remnants of her old life had gone.

Jemmy already knew which clothes to take—Father's forest green sweater and muffler, his business suit and vest. She snatched up summer drawers and undershirt. Winter was coming and the union suit would be warmer, but too awkward. Black gloves and shoes; two white shirts and collars; all the pairs of wool socks and all the handkerchiefs.

She tried to slip through the kitchen unnoticed. No luck. Gerta asked, "Vhere you go with Mr. McBustle's gray tweed suit?"

Jemmy put a finger to her mouth to shush her, then whispered, "I'm doing what you said, making my own chance. Come help me."

Gerta snatched up the sewing basket and followed Jemmy out the back door into the now-unused carriage house. In the drafty building, Jemmy shivered out of her chemise and pulled on her father's things.

When the trousers refused to stay put, Gerta pulled down a length of rope from a nail. She hacked through it with a scissors blade and handed it to Jemmy, "Hold up britches with bit of rope."

Gerta cut off the trouser legs and pinned up the hems, then turned her attention to the jacket. She said, "You don't have man shape." She held up a finger as if to say she'd be right back with the solution. She returned with two clean muslin flour sacks.

Jemmy had to strip again in the cold to let Gerta wrap her, mummywise, breast to waist. Gerta seemed satisfied with the pants and shirt. She pinned the vest down the back to mark where to stitch it in. But the jacket wouldn't do at all. Gerta said, "Get your father's greatcoat."

Jemmy protested, "But that's even bigger than this jacket."

"Good to hide in. How shoes fit?"

"Better than I thought. Three pairs of socks make them fit pretty well."

"Now, vhat about hair?'

"I wish I knew."

"Gerta know." From her bosom she pulled a white skullcap and wig.

Jemmy giggled as she looked at the bright orange hairs sticking out in all directions. "But that's a circus wig."

"Tomorrow it be brown."

"It would still stick up every which-way."

"Vild hair vould cover edge of vig so Jemmy keep her own hair hid avay."

Jemmy tucked her hair under the skullcap and tugged on the clown wig. It fit. Jemmy thought about asking Gerta why she happened to have a clown wig in her cleavage, but thought better of it.

Gerta said, "You need cap."

"Father's gray derby?"

"No, not for boy."

"What then?"

Gerta shrugged her shoulders.

Later that night, Jemmy sat bolt upright in bed. She knew where to find a cap. Grandpa's Civil war trunk. She sneaked down to find it. As she removed the insignia from the kepi, she said, "Forgive me, Grandpa. I'll try to wear it with as much honor as you did." Jemmy knew that was a lie even as she said it.

Jemmy spent the next morning in the carriage house altering the trousers and vest with fingers stiff from the cold. She told Mother she had found a job looking after an invalid. She explained she would be called upon to stay with the poor old lady on nights when the lady's cigar sales-man son was out of town. They did not have a telephone, but Jemmy could go to the drugstore down the street if she were delayed.

When Mother said she would get Uncle Erwin to investigate the home straightaway, Jemmy almost blacked out. Her plans could be ruined before

67

she even got to see the inside of the house with blue shutters.

Mother telephoned the Erwin McBustle home only to find that Uncle was off to Kansas City on business. Aunt Delilah offered Duncan's services, but Mother declined. She had little trust in Duncan's judgment or discretion.

Jemmy made up an address because Mother refused to let her out of the house without knowing where to reach her in an emergency. And so, that afternoon Jemmy was off to her new position as lady's companion—so Mother thought. Jemmy walked out the front door in the direction of the trolley stop, but soon doubled back to the alley to change into Jem McBee, "street arab."

Gerta awaited. When she saw Jemmy, she held up her prize offering. The clown wig had turned out remarkably well after spending the night in a walnut hull soak. Boiling had softened the horsehair, and the hulls had dulled the redness to an almost human color. After Gerta's haircut and a little Macassar oil, it came out the hue of dirty dishwater with just a hint of rust. Not very attractive, but not noticeably phony, either.

Gerta brushed up Jemmy's eyebrows with pomade to make them bushy. Jemmy looked at herself in the mirror and thought her own mother wouldn't recognize her if she kept her mouth shut.

As she put on the greatcoat, Gerta said, "You fool nobody if you valk like girl."

"How does a girl walk?"

"High heeled shoes make little step. Boy take big step."

Jemmy tried taking big strides. It felt good, free. Gerta said, "Keep knees stiff, move side to side."

"This stiff-legged walk feels awkward." Jemmy asked, "Are you sure this is right?"

Gerta nodded as she said, "Cock of the Valk. Like man."

Jemmy said, "I guess the shoes will help me remember."

"And keep arms loose. And not touch face. And not cross legs at ankles." As Jemmy headed out the door, Gerta put a hand on her shoulder. "And Jemmy remember Gerta, yes?"

"Jemmy remember Gerta, yes, if I get the reporter job. But you'll have to be patient."

Jemmy practiced her swagger on the way to the trolley. On the trip she observed how men held their newspapers, how they sprawled their feet into the aisles and how they tipped their hats to ladies.

Amadé Boudinier didn't recognize her right away. She said, "I knew you wouldn't recognize me. I was right, wasn't I?"

"You don't look like the pretty girl from yesterday. Of course, you don't look much like a boy either. Rather you don't sound much like a boy."

Jemmy tried to sound gruff. "How's this?"

"Best not talk. Children should only speak when spoken to anyway. Just say, 'Ma'am' and "Sir.' That should get you by if you say it fast."

A trolley ride and walk brought them to the house with blue shutters. Jemmy squared her shoulders and took a deep breath. She was about to enter a place where respectable young ladies of her age never ventured. She was about to go in a place that would ruin any hopes she might have of marrying well and living a respectable life in St. Louis—that is—if anyone found out.

Jemmy McBustle, at the tender age of 17, followed Amadé Boudinier up the steps of a middle class bordello in what was otherwise a genteel neighborhood. Whether the shivers down her back came from the cold, from fear of being exposed as a reporter, or from the pure excitement of entering a forbidden world she would never know. She only knew she was crossing the most momentous threshold of her life.

Chapter Seven

What a let down. The interior of the house with blue shutters disappointed Jemmy because it was so blindingly ordinary. She had halfway expected a Chinese opium den replete with veiled slave girls in see-through harem trousers. Instead, she saw only a prosaic mirrored coat rack with shelves added for hats. The hall looked like a hall in any middle class home in the city. A telephone hung on the wall by the parlor doorway. A basket for walking sticks and umbrellas bespoke nothing but bland normalcy.

In the alcove under the stair, the burly fellow she had seen two days earlier was playing solitaire on a chess table. He stood and greeted Mr. Boudinier. "Pleased to see you back, Mr. Bo. If you'll just come this way." He motioned toward the back of the house and asked, "Shall we have the boy come, too?"

Amadé snorted and waved him off, then started down the hall. He pointed to Jemmy to stay put as he said, "Take off your cap, boy. Mind your manners in front of Mr. Nanny."

While they were gone, Jemmy scanned the parlor in hopes of finding some oddity, some identifying mark that the world would understand to mean "bordello." Nothing. No naughty pictures on the walls, no nude statuary, no half-naked women sitting about smoking Egyptian cigarettes. The room was spectacularly ordinary—expensively furnished—but ordinary.

From the rectangular piano in the bay window, to the corner what-not shelves crowded with knickknacks, to the plush upholstered chairs with crocheted doilies on arms and backs to the oriental carpet on the floor—the room even smelled middle class—stale kerosene smoke and lemon oil furniture polish.

Furniture crowded the room with two too many sofas. A game table took the place of honor in the middle. The parlor looked ready for a Sunday afternoon family gathering. The only unusual thing she saw was a glimpse of a billiard table through the pocket doors in the place where a dining room table ought to be. She tried to memorize the scene so she'd be able to describe it down to a fare-thee-well in her soon-to-be-written brilliant series of articles.

In moments, the burly man came walking back in front of a matron who was wearing purple watered silk and Amadé who was wearing an expression of disgust. He fumed, "I don't see why I have to undergo that examination every single time. I was just here day before yesterday."

The pleasant-faced matron patted her piles of graying blondish hair finished off in peacock feathers as she hooked her arm in his.

"House rules, Mr. Bo." The burly man said the words as if he had said them often. "Nanny says it's for your protection as much as for the girls."

Matron chimed in. "What kind of a nanny would I be if I let my girls get diseases? What kind of business would I have if my customers, like you, couldn't trust your valuables in my establishment?"

Amadé said, "It's damned humiliating."

Matron said, "It's a small inconvenience to spend time with Lord

Murphy, wouldn't you say?"

Jemmy was too surprised even to move. What did that mean? To imagine this house might be something other than the kind of establishment she had been so sure it was—well, this was a revelation beyond anything she had bargained for. She said nothing.

Amadé began climbing the stairs. He barked at Jemmy. "Stupid boy, get up here. I want you outside the door for the next two hours. I'm not paying you to be underfoot in everybody's way."

Jemmy raced after him. He pointed to a the wall beside a door with a placard on a string hung over a nail. The placard read "Lord Murphy."

As Amadé disappeared into the room, he said to the person inside, "You look more glorious every time I see you."

Jemmy sat on the floor to consider what Amadé might be doing with Lord Murphy. She didn't have long to ponder. The door to the front bedroom opened. A plump and pretty girl with her hair in a turban stuck her head into the hall.

She called to Jemmy. "What's your name, boy?"

"Jem." Jemmy almost forgot to add, "Ma'am."

"Well, Jem, go downstairs and tell Mr. Nanny to bring up Annie's bath water."

"Please, Ma'am, my boss told me to stay right outside his door."

"That door? Fifi's door? Mr. Bo, is it? He'll be there his full hour."

"Two hours, Ma'am."

"Go on then, there's a nickel in it for you if the water is good and hot."

"Thank you, Ma'am."

Jemmy went downstairs to the burly man and said, "Annie says she'd be obliged to have her bath water now."

The burly man stood and said, "Come on then—and be sure you call her 'Spokane' when Nanny is around. She don't like nicknames for the gals unless she gives 'em out herself. She says soft names make gals too soft-hearted for good business."

In the kitchen sat a coal stove with a big pot atop and a strange contraption where the stovepipe ought to be. Jemmy asked, "What's that?"

Mr. Nanny's burly chest puffed with pride. "That's me own invention. Stove pipes are hot. I thought putting one inside a boiler should make for some hot water at no extra expense. Took me some time to make it all work. I had to build my own stovepipe out of tinker's tin—with no leaks. All I have to do is turn that spigot there and fill the bucket."

Jemmy pumped two buckets of cold water from the cistern while Mr. Nanny tapped two buckets of hot water from the contraption. The pair toted their four buckets up to Spokane's room where they dumped Jemmy's water, and some of Mr. Nanny's, into the round galvanized tub.

Annie dipped more hot water into the bath until the temperature suited her, then set the chamber pot lid over the rest to keep the heat in. Mr. Nanny took the empty buckets away and Jemmy started to leave. Annie called again, "Come here, boy. I need a hand."

A rush of whiskey breath convinced Jemmy everything she had heard about fallen women and hard drinking was true. Annie steadied herself with a hand on Jemmy's shoulder as she slipped off her mules and untied her rose velvet wrapper. She stepped into the bath as she dropped her robe. Jemmy gasped to see her back.

As Annie sat down in the water, she said, "Fetch that sponge from the table. I want you to bathe my back—gently though. Don't break anything open. Better roll up your sleeves. You don't want to go out wearing wet clothes and catch your death."

As Jemmy began to rinse Annie's back, she tried to think of some way to begin asking questions, Annie seemed to read her mind. "Go ahead and ask."

"Ask what, Ma'am?"

Annie's slurred speech suggested she had a lot more than a little to drink. "The question everyone wants an answer to—what's a nice girl like you doing in a place like this."

Jemmy practiced keeping her voice pitch low. "Ain't my business, Ma'am."

"That's right. Well, maybe for now, because I won't be going back to sportin' for a while—maybe now because I've been two days without company and I'm feeling lonely—maybe because the drink is not enough to ease the pain—maybe now I'd like to talk to somebody who knows how to mind his own business. Is that you, Jem? Can you mind your own business?"

"Reckon so, Ma'am."

"Well, here it is, Jem. The answer to what a nice girl like I is doing in a place like this. I'm a farmer's daughter, Jem. Don't listen to the jokes, Jem. Nobody's more respectable than a farmer's daughter. Up at sunrise, dig potatoes until you can't stand up straight, shuck corn until your fingers are too blistered to pick up a needle, eat squirrel-and-turnip stew day in, day out. The only rest is Sunday sermon and the only pleasure is a—funeral."

Annie turned to look at Jemmy and winked, "I bet you though I was going to say the only pleasure is a wedding. Well, a wedding is no pleasure—at least not for the bride. She turns over her whole life to a man. He owns her—her children. Even the money she earns by her hands is his by law. Folks say slavery is dead. Don't you believe it.

"Jem, go over to the table by the front window and pour me a shot of bourbon—make it a good two fingers."

Jemmy followed directions, then returned to sponging Annie's back.

Annie took up the story again. "Then came the Panic of '93 and we lost the farm. We took our goods and ourselves to Chicago. Everyone in the family started looking for work, but jobs were hard to come by. I worked in a hat shop—for three dollars a week. Not even enough to feed the family—

not that we used it for food. Father took it for drink. When I wouldn't give it, he beat me until I did. I think I'd be dead today if I hadn't run away. I had to be clever, though, so they couldn't find me.

"I offered to do favors for a notions and ribbon salesman if he would take me off somewhere far away. He brought me to St. Louis—to Nanny." Annie held up her glass, "So here's to my notions and ribbon salesman. Long may he sell buttons and thread." She drained the tumbler. "No other man ever did as much for me.

"You know, Jem, without him I might have been a streetwalker—risking my health out of doors in all weather—getting diseases from clap-ridden johnnies. Here I'm well-fed and a doctor sees me once a week—even if he is a strange old bird.

"In truth it's Nanny and the soapy water in her peter pan keeps us from the poxes. I don't know why she keeps that old leech coming around. I know for a fact that he's killed at least two females with his mercury fumes and doses.

"Take my word for it, Jem. If you should get the syphilis, don't let some old quack kill you with salversan. I know a female on death's door from a doctor's treatment. Her mouth rotting and her teeth falling out from the mercury. Went home to the country to die—and started using herb poultices and teas. Came back from the edge of the pit.

"But what am I doing complaining about doctors? Doctors are the best job insurance I've got. Yes, Jem. Doctors say men are apt to get diseases if they don't have relations with women once every four days. But women risk diseases if they have relations more than once a month. That means that for every time a man enjoys his wife's favors, he enjoys mine..."

She began trying to make calculations on her fingers. Jemmy helped out. "Six or seven."

"Right you are. So you see, doctors give me steady employment. I have my own room—fine as a princess in a palace. Nanny takes care of all expenses—and I get a quarter of the price she charges for me. Nanny takes care of everything else—fancy clothes, food, even ticket money so I can work the theaters when times are slow.

"You're getting a rare treat, Jem. That old bird doctor once paid me to tell him my life story. I'm giving it to you for free."

She winced when Jemmy touched an open sore. "Want to know about my back, Jem? Why my back looks like a skinned rabbit?"

Annie paused so long Jemmy felt obliged to say something. "Fall from carriage, Ma'am?"

"No, Jem. A man did this. A special event, Jem." She gave a hard edge to the word "special."

"This particular gentleman—who is anything but gentle—has lots of money. You may not know this, Jem, but many of the men who come to me are quite respectable married men.

"They just want to have a good time and no strings attached. You see, at home, they have children pestering and bills to attend to and modest little wives that won't even let their husbands see them naked in the daytime—much less indulge their more unusual fancies.

"But there are also men who find pleasure in pain. Luckily for me, most of them want to receive the pain—perhaps to make up for all the pain they cause others every day. But a few want to give pain. Even fewer have enough money to buy that pleasure.

"It took some doing for Nanny to persuade me. She promised not to let anything too bad happen. Mr. Nanny stood right behind that bed curtain." She pointed to the rose velvet drapery behind the bed. I was to keep my cameo box under the pillow and open it if I needed him. You can look at it on the dressing table. It's a tiny music box. If he heard the music, he was to rescue me—though it never got quite that bad. And afterwards I was to have a whole week off.

"And I was to keep all of the price. Do you know how much he paid? One thousand dollars. So, yes, Jem. It was worth it."

Neither spoke. Then Annie asked, "Did my story disgust you, Jem?"

"No, Ma'am."

She added several dippers of hot water to her bath. "Do you think I'm drunk, Jem?"

"No, Ma'am."

"Well, I am. You know I don't drink, not as a rule—that would cut into my nest egg. But just for now Nanny is giving me all the liquor I want and not charging extra for it. So you see, it's my duty to drink. My duty and my right—and little enough for what I went through to earn the privilege.

"Have you noticed I have the best room in the house—biggest and best—overlooking the street—two windows? That's because I'm the tip-ster's choice—odds-on derby favorite.

"Do you know Nanny gives us all professional names—the names of horses? Kentucky Derby winners."

Annie chuckled. "Yes sir, I'm the Derby winner for 1889—Spokane. Oh, don't think I've been here since 1889—no I've been here three years. Three down and three to go. Yes, this is the halfway point. Three more years and I'll have the money I need. Would you like to know what I plan to do with my life, Jem?

"If you want to say, Ma'am."

Annie dumped in the rest of the hot water. "I have plans, big plans. I've already picked out the perfect spot. A little shop right on the trolley line. Wonderful spot for a millinery. I can do hats—one-of-a-kind hats—better hats than the big stores.

"The shop will be grand. And it is in a four-story building with not one, but three fine big apartments upstairs.

"As soon as I am able, I'm going to get a loan from a banker I know for the rest of the money to buy the place. If I can keep the apartments rented, that by itself would be enough to pay off the loan. All I would need then is money for showcases and buckram and feathers.

"Maybe I can get the money in two years or even one. Wouldn't that be fine? My own home, my own business—and a legitimate business it would be—all by the time I'm twenty-one years old."

She shivered a little. "The bath is getting cold and there's no more hot water."

"Should I get another bucket, Ma'am?"

She pointed to the bed "No, get that Turkish towel and help me up."

As Annie patted herself dry, she walked toward the old-fashioned four poster bed with its crocheted tester. She handed a piece of faded flannel to Jemmy as she lay face down on the feather bed. She pointed to a jar of Sayman Salve on the bed table and said, "Will you dress my back with salve, then cover it with this cloth? I don't want the whole bed to smell like sulfur."

No sooner had Annie relaxed than she began to snore softly. Jemmy felt an odd mixture of sadness and admiration. This was a girl with ambition, a girl who knew what she wanted and was finding a way to get it—even if the way was strewn with pain and heartache—a girl not unlike Jemima McBustle.

Jemmy was pulling the bedclothes over Annie when she heard a drunken shout from the hall. "Boy, good-for-nothing boy. Where are you?" It was the voice of Amadé Boudinier.

She ran into the hall to see him staggering a bit as he turned in her direction. "What were you doing in there? I told you to stay right here by this doorway. Come here."

Head down, Jemmy walked to the place he pointed out. He backhanded her so hard she hit the floor. She was too stunned to get up right away.

No one had ever slapped her before, not in her entire life.

Lord Murphy turned out to be a girl who called herself Fifi. She said, "Bo, *mon cher*, the boy was just helping Spokane—she's been under ze weather."

He raised his hand as if to slap her, too. She took the hand, kissed it and wrapped it around her shoulder. She motioned for Jemmy to take the other arm. The pair turned him sidewise and dragged him down the stairs between them. Amadé blubbered, "I don't pay you to help whores. I pay you to see I get home by six o'clock."

Mr. Nanny opened the front door. Fifi dropped her shoulder and walked back upstairs as she said, "*Au revoir*, Bo, see you next week."

As Jemmy dragged Amadé onto the front stoop, she could hear someone, Nanny perhaps, playing a concertina and singing "My Darling Nellie Bly." Sniffing out a story was posing more problems than she had expected. She might just have to reconsider the newspaper line of work.

Amadé leaned heavily on Jemmy as they made slow progress for the next two blocks. A half block from the streetcar, he stood up straight and began walking quite normally. Jemmy's mouth fell open. "You weren't drunk at all."

"I thought all you were after was the illusion—not the fact."

Jemmy felt anger rising like pressure in a steam engine. "You were perfectly sober when you slapped me."

Amadé took his signet ring from a vest pocket and put it on with great ceremony. He said, "You should be grateful, my dear, I took great pains not to leave a permanent scar. That might dim your marriage prospects."

"You've been planning to hit me all the time."

He said, "Well, somebody ought to slap some sense into that noggin of yours. A little slap is the least of the troubles you're going to have if you persist in this stupidity."

"Little slap? You knocked me across the hall."

"What do you think someone like Mr. Boo would do if he caught you trying to get a story on him? You wouldn't live long, I tell you."

"Who is Mr. Boo?"

"Forget I mentioned it."

"A good reporter never forgets."

"All you need to know is that he's the one who did what he did to the person in the front bedroom."

They had arrived at the trolley. He said, "Get on. I'll take the next. Our association is at an end."

And so Jemmy had found a font of information—more than she could have hoped. And yet, she didn't see a story in it. How could she write an exposé of middle class bordellos when she might well be the girl in Spokane Annie's bed right this minute—recovering from whip marks on her back.

The only difference between them was that Annie's family was poor—dirt farmers displaced from a meager existence. Country poor who came to the city but found no job that paid a decent living. The only hope for a girl like Annie came from the life she could wrest from an inhospitable world.

Jemmy now had a second picture to haunt her when her brain insisted she listen to "You and me and Dr. T." The pictures in her brainpan snapped back and forth between hands sewing the gash in Grandma's belly to hands holding a whip over Annie's bleeding back.

Chapter Eight

At dinner, Mother announced that Aunt Delilah had delivered the Christmas pageant costumes. Jemmy moaned inwardly. A stunt news reporter had no time for Christmas pageants. How would she get out of it? When Aunt Delilah summoned, only the foolhardy gave even one thought to thwarting the command.

Aunt Delilah was planning a nativity pageant to eclipse all pageants. Lafayette Park Presbyterian Church held its annual Christmas program in the park on the Saturday before Christmas. With its combination of spectacle, song and merriment, the event always drew a grand crowd—not just churchmen, but heathens, too.

The ritual had become a fixture in the events of the Christmas season in St. Louis. The procession followed a time-honored pattern.

With the addition of a bit of straw, the band gazebo in the center of the park turned into a stable. A feed trough became the manger to cradle the Christ child.

A boy with a lamp in the big oak tree served as the Star of the East. No one was supposed to notice that the tree stood west of the gazebo.

The pageant breathed life into the traditional story in the traditional way. First arriving from the church across Missouri Avenue came a choir of angels in white robes and fluffy white angel wings singing "O Come, All Ye Faithful." Four sturdy men in white choir robes, minus the wings, carried Mary on a palanquin.

The procession stopped near the statue of Thomas Hart Benton for the Annunciation scene. The choir set down the palanquin, and the singers knelt as they held their candles aloft in a halo of light around the virgin. No sooner did the Angel Gabriel tell Mary she is with child than Augustus Caesar's tax man burst through the circle to proclaim that all must go to their place of birth to be taxed.

The choir re-formed into columns while singing "O Little Town of Bethlehem." Joseph emerged from behind the senator's behemoth bronze girth with a donkey, lifted Mary upon its back, and led the procession to the gazebo.

The innkeeper announced that he had no room, but they might bed down in the stable. The choir formed a double semi-circle round the back of the bandstand behind the assorted cows and goats tethered there. Joseph spread a blanket on the straw for Mary to lie upon and produce the baby Jesus—a pre-swaddled doll hidden under the hay. The choir angels sang "Silent Night."

While the choir soared on the notes of "The First Noel," the boy in the oak tree lit the Star of the East. Shepherds brought their sheep to the gazebo/stable where both species fell down on their knees to the tune "While Shepherds Watch Their Flocks."

Then came the three wise men following the Star of the East as the choir sang "We Three Kings of Orient Are." This was to be Aunt Delilah's shining moment. Usually the wise men, dressed like Arabian emirs, trotted in on horseback. This year, they were to ride real camels—three of them—rented by Aunt Delilah especially for the occasion.

When Jemmy had first heard the word "camel," she whispered into cousin Duncan's ear, "Camels—one lump or two."

When Aunt Delilah wanted to know the cause of Duncan's horse laugh, he told her. "My cousin and I want to know whether the camels have one lump or two."

Auntie Dee gave him a false smile in front of a freezing stare as she said, "One of each."

Auntie's dubious math sent the wise-cracking wise men into laughter which turned into coughing as they tried to get themselves under control.

From that day forward, Jemmy and Duncan had a new catchword. Whenever the McBustle cousins heard about enterprises large and daring, one would query, "Camels? One lump or two?"

The other replied, "One of each."

The pageant continued apace. After the wise men offered their gifts, the choir sang "Hark! the Herald Angels Sing"; the rest of the schoolboys in the trees lit their mirrored lanterns of cut tin to provide twinkling star sparkles to light up the night.

The procession sang "Joy to the World" as the choir led onlookers away from the bandstand to a jolly bonfire built in the intersection of Lafayette and Mississippi near the police station. Then the minister gave his blessing and invited the crowd to share the joy of the moment with hot mulled cider, molasses popcorn balls and frosted sugar cookies.

Jemmy liked pageant night better than any other time of the holiday season, but this year she would gladly sacrifice her part, if only she could manage.

Mother held costumes up to the girls as she described the roles Aunt Delilah had assigned. The choir needed Miranda's brazen alto to balance the current crop of tinny sopranos. Mother sent Randy to the basement to fetch the family's set of angel's wings—a wire frame covered with buckskin and pasted over with white chicken feathers.

She returned with the same sorry pair used since the very first pageant. They now looked like a chicken with the mange.

Accompanied by gestures too theatrical even for melodrama, Randy wailed, "Miranda Anemone McBustle bets Gerta hasn't saved enough white feathers to make these wings fit for an angel." She pouted like a grief-stricken monarch as she said, "Like the fragile anemone, Miranda is forsaken."

When that elicited only giggles, she changed her tactics. She stomped her foot and said, "If we have to open a pillow, it's not going to be mine."

The white cotton robe didn't please her either. When she shook it out, she poked a finger right through the moth-eaten material.

From its storage in brown paper, Mother took Esmerelda's costume—a plain, soft blue gown and delicate white wool shawl. Merry was to play Mary—not just because she was the sweetest natured—but because she was light enough for Nervy to lift onto the donkey. Minerva was to wear a rough brown wool gown for her role as Joseph.

Aunt Delilah had slated Jemima as Balthasar. Jemmy had to admit that she liked the idea—wearing purple silk and a crown—carrying a chest full of wooden slugs painted gold to shine like Roman coins.

Even so she stood her ground. "Mother, you must tell Aunt Delilah that I have a job—a responsible job. I may not be available, so she should not count on me."

Mother looked wistful. "I hope you'll be able to manage. The family has never been apart on pageant night."

The next day, Jemmy found herself part of a pageant—though not a pageant like the one to be presented by the good folk of Lafayette Park

Presbyterian Church. Still, a naughty person might call it a tribute to the virgin.

When Jemmy reached the house with blue shutters, a group of men were shivering as they waited on the steps. Mr. Nanny would allow only one in at a time. When he saw Jemmy, he said, "Mr. Bo isn't here."

Jemmy scuffed her foot on the walk. "I made Mr. Bo angry."

"So what do you want, then?"

Jemmy hung her head as if ashamed. "Please, Sir, Miss Spokane promised me a nickel; but she fell asleep."

He smiled. "Go on up, then."

Jemmy walked past the well-dressed men and climbed the stairs. She rapped on Annie's door. Annie opened it and pulled her in as she said, "You'll be perfect. I've been wondering how I would pick up my money with this stiff back. I'm sure I can dance, but I'm afraid to bend over lest I break something open."

Jemmy gathered that she was to pick up Annie's earnings. Annie breezed on, "But you need a costume. Here, take off that greatcoat."

Annie popped a plain white nightgown over Jemmy's head. "Heavens, it smells like sulfur." She fumigated it with dabs from a crystal perfume stopper. "Like it? It's real perfume from Worth's of Paris." She dabbed a drop on Jemmy's chin. "Jay Rev-ee-ens. It means 'I will return' in French."

Over the nightgown, Annie stuck Jemmy's arms through a kimono of green and gold striped silk. A black velvet ribbon fastened a white scarf around her head. Jemmy looked into Annie's pier glass and saw the reflection of an Arab chieftain—not that Jemmy had ever seen an Arab chieftain.

Annie nodded. "Perfect. Now what I want you to do is carry my veil as a train, then pull it off as I start dancing. I'll be offering scarves to the customers, but I want you to remember who takes them and make sure you get all the scarves back. I don't want the expense of replacing them."

Annie dumped the jewelry from a treasure chest into a pillowcase and tossed in the ring from her own finger, a gold peacock in profile with aquamarine and lapis tail and a single ruby eye. She hid the sack in a hatbox which she placed atop the wardrobe. She handed the empty chest to Jemmy. "Put the money in here. There's a quarter in it for you—fifty cents if I get all thirty scarves back. You know, those scarves cost fifty cents apiece."

Jemmy kept her voice low as she said, "I'm glad you feel better today."

"I feel worse; but I'm not going to miss the chance to make a pot of money for fifteen minutes' work—not even real work—dancing."

Jemmy helped Annie with her costume—pink boots and pink striped stockings with white bloomers and a peasant blouse. She said, "Usually I would wear my pink corset and a chimmy, but today I need to hide—you know—and I can't abide the thought of wearing a corset."

Around her waist went a red taffeta sash with the ends of thirty scarves in rainbow colors tucked underneath. As a train, Annie's pinned a ten foot length of white organza in her hair. She picked up her tambourine with its pink and white streamers, admired herself in the mirror, and pronounced herself ready.

She said, "After I dance, I'll be playing the tambourine and singing. Keep an eye out for what you can do to make a dime. Tips are easy to come by on a day like today."

"What's the excitement?"

"A virgin auction."

Jemmy's voice cracked. "You mean there really are such things?"

Annie chuckled. "Don't tell anyone, but the girl being auctioned off today—this is the eighty-seventh time she's been a virgin."

Jemmy blinked her eyes. "I thought once someone was not a virgin—"

Annie winked, "Luckily for us, that's what most men think. But I know how to make someone who's been in the business twenty years seem like a virgin—leastways, enough to fool a man if she had a paper bag over her head. A little alum, a bit of pigeon blood, a trembly voice and a good loud shriek at the right time—virgin deflowered."

Jemmy may not have been getting her newspaper story, but she was getting an education. "Don't men wise up sooner or later?"

"Professional virgins move from town to town. The last time this one was in St. Louis she was sold for almost two thousand dollars at the Piedmont Club—very plush—very luxurious. Here she might go for five hundred. Next year, she'll be back in town and go to a different house. Anyway, horny men are drunk—and who really looks at a fallen woman? Not the man about to push her down. You can bet on that."

With a rap on the door, the professional virgin herself appeared. She looked quite the height of fashion in blue-green velvet under black wool cape. She wore a matching hat gaudy with silk roses in orange and purple. She pulled up her veil to reveal more greasepaint and rouge than Jemmy had ever seen on one human being.

A bandy legged fellow in a checked suit set down her carpetbag and said, "I'm going to the saloon we passed back on the trolley line. Be back when it closes."

The virgin nodded as he shut the door behind him. She took off her hat as she said, "Mrs. Nanny is ready to start the show. She said that I'm to have this room for as long as I want. I hope I don't put you out too badly."

Annie shook her tambourine, "No. I'm a part of the band, so I'll be staying downstairs. You won't forget to use a rubber sheet will you?"

The virgin pulled one out of her bag and held it up for Annie to see. When they shut the door, she was taking off her hat. Jemmy picked up Annie's train and followed her into the hall. The place seemed a swarm of women. Jemmy said, "Are there enough bedrooms for so many?"

Annie said, "Besides the six rooms on this floor, Mrs. Nanny puts a girl in her own room. She puts down mattresses on canvas in the sheds out back. Then she hangs curtains on ropes to make cribs. She expects to do good business today so she's brought in a batch of some-timers. She hired two musicians, too; and a Negro couple to serve drinks and food."

Annie walked to the top of the stairs and signaled Mr. Nanny that she was ready. He motioned to Mrs. Nanny who started the fiddler playing "Camptown Races"—but playing it so slowly and melodically that Jemmy could barely recognize the tune.

As Jemmy walked solemnly down the stairs holding the end of Annie's organza train, she looked at the faces of the men—already flushed from drink. They looked perfectly ordinary—as ordinary as this house itself. They possessed slicked-down hair parted in the middle, well-shined shoes, and watch fobs dangling from vest pockets.

As Mrs. Nanny, on piano, joined the fiddler and upped the tempo to slow march time, Annie pranced to the center of the parlor—now free of the card table—and began her dance. Jemmy scooped up Annie's train when she dropped it and watched the dance in wide-eyed wonder.

As Annie did a whirling jig, the banjo joined in and the trio came up-tempo. Jemmy thought Annie's prancing little steps across the room to flip a hip against her tambourine in some fellow's face looked just plain silly—until she looked at the faces of the men. They salivated. They didn't care whether the girl could dance or not. All they wanted was to take a bite out of Annie's plump rump. Jemmy saw raw greed, not softened even by desire.

Jemmy ducked her head when she recognized the face of a young swain. She would not have been surprised to see her wastrel cousin Duncan, but he was not in the place. The customer elbowing a couple of young swells and taking in every bump of Annie's pivot dance was a handsome young baseball player she knew from Sunday School, Peter Ploog.

Jemmy had, on occasion, made his sun-bronzed face the focal point of her girlish daydreams. Jemmy concluded a girl had best not take things at face value—at least not where men were concerned.

The men drank. Annie danced until all the perfumed scarves had been snatched by grabbing hands. Then Annie struck a pose as the music stopped. Coins rained on the center of the floor. Jemmy scrambled to pick them up while Annie took her bows.

When the applause and money stopped coming, Annie took her place in the bay window on the far side of the piano alongside the banjo player and the fiddler. While Mrs. Nanny led a sing-a-long to "There's a Tavern in the Town," Jemmy retrieved the scarves. Most men inhaled their fill of "Je Reviens" and returned them. One stuffed a scarf down his pantaloons. If Jemmy wanted it, she'd have to feel for it. She stuck out her chin and dived in while the room dissolved into a chorus of raucous laughter.

When one fellow decided to keep a scarf, Jemmy whispered in his ear that he must give her a dollar. He returned the scarf, but two others coughed up the coin.

Next on the program came a pair of girls who sang "While Strolling through the Park One Day." They bopped each other over the head with black lace parasols until they ended up rolling on the floor and pulling hair in a mock wrestling match.

Then a fat lady did the slow shimmy to "The Man on the Flying Trapeze." As she rolled her great globs of flesh into motion, she moved past the rows of men inviting them to add a little something spendable to her capacious cleavage.

Three in ruffled red petticoats did a high-kick dance one of them called the Can-Can. The splits they did at the end brought down such a thunder of foot stomping that bits of plaster fell from the ceiling. Jemmy picked up money for all the acts except the fat lady. When she handed the tips to the ladies, they rewarded her with a quarter, sometimes more.

Then came the highlight of the day. Before the sale, Doctor Tumblety appeared and read a certificate swearing that the person in question was *virgo intacto*. As he rolled up the certificate, he sent a probing look in Jemmy's direction. She stared right back in hopes he wouldn't connect Miss Jemima with the wild-haired young lad she had become.

The boy in the fez drilled her with a stare that lasted even longer. Jemmy's heart fluttered and she could feel her face reddening. She felt untold relief when the front door closed behind them. Under her breath she muttered, "You and me and if we could only get rid of Dr. T."

Mrs. Nanny left the piano bench to sing "Beautiful Dreamer" with only the fiddle as accompaniment. The customers rose to their feet in hushed respect as Mr. Nanny carried the virgin on his shoulder atop a huge silver tray adorned with vines and apples. He produced a tense moment when he tripped on the carpet and almost dropped her into the piano. He regained his feet to a sigh of relief by all the buyers as he set her neatly upon the piano bench.

The professional virgin wore a fringed velvet scarf draped across her torso with just one bony white shoulder showing. A white gossamer cloth floated over her and the whole tray from the top of her long dark curls to a few inches below the bottom of the tray. No trace of makeup lingered on her pale freckled skin.

Jemmy could scarcely believe her eyes. Could this tiny waif, so small, so childlike, be the same sophisticated lady she had met in Annie's room? As an actress, she could give lessons to Eleanora Duse.

The banjo player served as auctioneer. The bidding soon shut out all but the fattest and flabbiest of the customers. With a final bid of five hundred and forty dollars, the virgin was sold—for the eighty-eighth time. While Mrs. Nanny played "Bicycle Built for Two," Mr. Nanny hoisted the virgin upon his shoulder and toted her back to Annie's room.

Jack the Ripper in St. Louis

After he returned to his post at the door, he began directing traffic. Mrs. Nanny left the piano to examine latecomers and secure fees. The Negro couple bustled about selling drinks and serving tidbits of salty food to make the customers thirsty.

Annie shoved her tambourine into Jemmy's hand and pointed to a place by the banjo and fiddle. Jemmy took her place and beat time as Annie danced to entertain the customers who were forced to wait their turns. Soon Mrs. Nanny resumed her place at the piano.

In due time, the proper shriek came from Annie's room. Soon after, the virgin's buyer appeared looking satisfied. Annie collected her scarves and treasure chest from Jemmy and went upstairs. Soon, came another shriek—but this one sounded like "Help"!

Mrs. Nanny bolted from the piano and pulled her skirts above her knees as she raced up stairs. She motioned for Jemmy to come with her. When they ran into Annie's room, Annie lay on the floor with the virgin stomping her sore back.

Mrs. Nanny hissed to Jemmy, "Get the little one off her."

Jemmy grabbed the virgin from behind and swung her away from Annie while Mrs. Nanny got Annie to her feet. However, the virgin didn't take kindly to the interference. She uttered such a string of foul language that Jemmy blushed in spite of herself. With skinny legs churning against Jemmy's shins, the virgin reached back to scratch Jemmy's face.

Jemmy, resenting the bruised shins in the extreme, threw the virgin down and fell on top of her. After a scramble, she got hold of the virgin's wrists and sat on her back. The best the virgin could do was kick Jemmy in the behind— and keep screeching a cuss-fest that would cause a sailor to blush.

Mrs. Nanny came over with a handful of Annie's scarves and tied one around the virgin's mouth, then helped Jemmy tie the demon's arms behind her. She asked, "Now. What happened?"

Annie shouted, "She's a thief. Look in her bag. You'll see my carnelian pin and my jet earrings and necklace, and my pearl bracelet, too."

Sure enough. When Mrs. Nanny inspected the carpetbag, she found not only the virgin's piano scarf costume and rubber sheet; she also found Annie's jewelry, her rose velvet robe and her lead-glass perfume bottle of "Je Reviens."

To the subdued virgin, Mrs. Nanny said, "As a fine, I mean to give half of your half of the five hundred and forty dollars to Spokane." The virgin sputtered through the gag. Mrs. Nanny continued, "I'll let you speak if you promise to be quiet and clean up that filthy mouth."

The virgin nodded and Jemmy loosened the gag. The virgin spit out the cloth and said, "You can't take my money. I'll have the law on you."

Mrs. Nanny chortled. "Half of my half goes to the local powers that be. You'd end up in jail—or sent out of town—which is where you're going anyway. But if you go to the law, you'll go without any money at all."

The virgin fussed, "She's got her stuff back. I deserve my money. You madams are the real thieves."

"On the contrary. I supply good clean customers, the place, the protection, the facilities, advertising, entertainment, food, liquor—I arrange everything. Most would only give you a quarter of the price. I'm more lenient than anyone else in the city. And how do you repay my generosity? By stealing. I won't allow it. Now, do as I say or I'll tie you up in the corner and keep every penny of the five hundred and forty."

Mrs. Nanny turned to Jemmy. "Your name is Jem? Well, Jem, I want you to throw her cape over the foul one's head and come with me. Mind no customers see her."

Mrs. Nanny put the virgin's things into the carpetbag and deliberately set her boot down to smash the hat with the orange silk roses. She rammed the ruined hat into the carpetbag. "See. We're an honest house. You're getting back everything you came with—and hardly the worse for wear."

Jemmy pushed the virgin behind Mrs. Nanny down the back stairs and into Mrs. Nanny's study. Mrs. Nanny counted out one-hundred-and-thirty-five dollars in two stacks and recorded it in her ledger. With ceremony and finality, she snapped the ledger shut around a peacock feather bookmark.

She tucked one set of bills in the virgin's carpetbag—the other she gave to Jemmy saying, "After you throw this tramp out the back door, I want you to take that money to Spokane. Here. You'd better take this along, too." She handed Jemmy an unopened bottle of brandy. "Do what you can for her. Later on, I'll give you fifty cents—no, a dollar—for making yourself useful."

The three passed through the kitchen to the back door. Jemmy set the brandy on the table and stuffed the money in her trousers. She took a deep breath and untied the scarves. Jemmy had wised up enough to stay well back from the virgin's feet. When the virgin kicked at her, Jemmy shoved the spitfire out the back door. Mrs. Nanny tossed the carpetbag after her. The virgin wheeled to pick it up and said, "You haven't seen the last of me."

Mrs. Nanny put her hands on her hips. "In ten minutes, you'd best be well away from here and don't ever come back. If you get picked up as a woman of the town, you'll find yourself at the Social Evil Hospital. Heaven help you if you get sent there."

The virgin started digging in her valise. "I'm afraid of nothing and no one."

Mrs. Nanny produced an old-fashioned, twin-barreled derringer from her pocket and said, "Are you looking for this?"

The virgin looked up, then went back to digging in her bag.

Mrs. Nanny held up the long thin blade of an Arkansas Tickler. "...or this?"

The virgin held out her hand. "If you do run an honest house, you'll give them back."

Mrs. Nanny said, "Do you think me a fool? I'll mail them to you—General Delivery—Kansas City."

"If I get murdered, it will be on your head." She looked straight at Jemmy, "...and on your head, too."

Mrs. Nanny offered a matter-of-fact, "More likely you'll get paid, and it will be on your back."

Jemmy shivered. "Was that a curse?" she asked Mrs. Nanny as the virgin stomped off in the falling snow to meet her destiny.

Chapter Nine

Jemmy drew a pail of hot water from the contraption on the kitchen stove and took it along with the money and the bottle of spirits up to Annie. The number of the waiting customers had diminished, but the ones left clapped their hands or did the new craze, the Stomp Dance, as the Ragtime rollicked. Jemmy wondered whether wood and plaster could stand the onslaught.

Annie was standing at the washbasin rinsing blood out of her peasant blouse. When Jemmy held out the money, she said, "That's hardly enough money. That whore stole my peacock ring." She rounded on Jemmy. "She wouldn't get away with that if I didn't have a bloody back."

When alarm registered on Jemmy's face, Annie sighed. "It's not your fault or your problem. You are sweet to bring bath water. Would you please tend my back like you did before?"

Jemmy left the brandy on the dressing table and went back to the kitchen for more water. By the time she had filled the tub, the brandy was a quarter gone. As she sponged Annie's back, she asked, "How did you know the virgin was a thief?"

Annie said, "Never trust a whore. It's a strange sisterhood. They'll tend you if you're sick, feed your child if you can't, pay their last dollar to see you buried proper; but not a one can be trusted with men or money—especially the opium eaters and the stump liquor drinkers." She took a swig from her glass. "I'd best watch out. I'll become one myself if I keep this up."

"How did the virgin fool the doctor?"

Annie laughed. "You don't think he looked at her, do you? That Twom...ble...ton would swear Mr. Nanny was Lilly Langtry if there was money in it."

"Twombleton, is that the doctor's name?"

"In a place like this a quack like him ought to be a 'Tumble-down.'" Annie chortled at her own joke.

"He didn't stay for the auction."

"Doctor Tumble-down is only here for money. He never partakes of anything else. Mondays are slow in this business so he comes every Monday afternoon—to examine us—torture us, more like—and perform other services as needed. If you ask me, he doesn't like females at all."

"Is he from the Social Evil Hospital?"

Annie laughed again, "There's no such place—not any more. St. Louis registered prostitutes about twenty-five years ago. It didn't work, though. They stopped that foolishness a couple of years later. The building is still there—at Sublette and Arsenal—but now they call it the Women's Hospital—for diseased females and unwed mothers. I ask you, who but a man—a crusading reformer of a man—would be so stupid? Putting newborn babies in a house with poxied doxies."

"Do Mr. and Mrs. Nanny have any babies?"

Annie nearly choked on her brandy. "Heavens, they aren't married. Even if Nanny wanted a man of her own, she would never marry and turn over everything she's earned, everything she's built, to some male."

"Even if the Nannies are living in sin, they might have children."

"Not likely. Mr. Nanny is an employee—and good at his job. He makes a handsome living and has a family not three blocks from here.

"Nanny does have a child, though, away at school in Kentucky. She closes this place down for two weeks at Easter. She'll go see the boy then. Nanny is the best madam in the city. Nobody else gives the girls two whole weeks off. Most never get a single day off. I'll wager that's why so many commit suicide or drink themselves to death—or take chloroform or opium to ease the pain—and overdo it."

"Does Mrs. Nanny make a lot of money?"

"My, yes. She owns an orchard somewhere in California—Fresno, wherever that is. When she has squirreled away enough to build her dream house, she's going to leave the business."

"Will someone else take over here?"

"I don't think so. Reformers are closing down brothels left and right. A shame it is, too. Forcing us onto the streets and into the keeping of a pimp to protect us—steal our money and beat us more likely—or leave us victims to murderers.

"Like those girls Jack the Ripper killed. I ask you, would those girls have been better off on the streets of London or protected in a cozy house? And high-minded reformers all the time saying they were saving women—killing them more likely."

Jemmy couldn't hide her surprise. "Do you blame reformers for Jack the Ripper?"

"They didn't ply the knife, but they put those women in harm's way. Reformers made them easy pickings for the Old Ripper."

"So you think reformers will close Mrs. Nanny down?"

"Not Nanny herself, no. She is one of the few true professionals left.

She causes the city fathers so little trouble and brings them so much money they'll help her carry on as usual for as long as they can."

"She must be clever."

"She has her ways. She uses colored paper with a different combination of colors for each girl—you know most of the girls can't read. On the paper she puts a symbol for each quarter hour and other symbols for special things the customer wants. Then the girls know what's expected—and what they'll get paid for. They can't cheat her or fool her with forgeries. They can't even spend too much time with a single customer.

"At the end, the girls turn in the papers to get their money. There's never a quarrel; Nanny is that exact. And generous, too. She never charges for food or coal or kerosene or laundering sheets—only liquor and such.

"And she doesn't miss much in the way of making money. Mr. Nanny sells naughty pictures of the six of us who live here—five dollars apiece. But with masks and fans, so no policeman could tell who we are. Mr. Nanny also sells French postcards and stereographs of demimondes wearing nothing but stockings. He's putting his boy through Washington University on that alone."

After Jemmy dressed Annie's back with salve and tucked her in bed, Annie said. "Bring me the treasure chest. You must have your tips. How much did you make from the other acts?"

Jemmy counted out a dollar and a quarter. Annie asked, "Did you get back all my scarves?"

"No, Miss, I only got back twenty-eight. But I made the two who kept them pay a dollar each."

Annie smiled as she placed money in Jemmy's hands. "Here's the fifty cents I promised and a dollar you earned from the scarf sale, and here's another dollar for taking such good care of me." Annie took a swig of brandy and said, "Turn out the lamp and go back down to the party. There is still time for more tips."

Late afternoon became late evening. Not until very late was the last customer off to a room or cubicle.

Mrs. Nanny paid off the musicians and the Negro couple. With a jolt Jemmy realized Mother would have expected her at home hours ago. She asked permission to use the telephone. Mrs. Nanny said she charged a quarter.

Jemmy called home to hear a frantic mother on the other end of the line.

"Why haven't you called? I telephoned your Uncle Erwin to go to the address you wrote down. He was out of town and with Duncan nowhere to be found, your Aunt Delilah had to go herself. She said the place is a livery stable. Naturally, she couldn't question the men as to whether they knew of your whereabouts."

"I'm sorry, Mother. I must have written it down wrong. Dear Mrs. Panghurst has been so very ill. I haven't been able to leave her side. At last the doctor has come, so I could slip away for a few minutes."

"I would think every shop would be closed at this hour."

"So it was. I had to wake the owner. I thought I'd get arrested for making such a ruckus."

"I thought the woman's nephew would be there to take over."

"I'm greatly worried, too. He's still not here. I have to stay the night. I can't leave her once the doctor goes. Please tell Aunt Delilah how sorry I am that I have the address wrong. I'll make a point of writing it down properly when I come home tomorrow."

"I don't know whether I want you to keep this position. I imagined you had been killed in a streetcar accident or knifed in an alley."

"I'm fine, but I must go back. I'm sorry to have caused such trouble. I'll see you tomorrow."

Mr. Nanny looked up from organizing his stereopticon cards and said,

"Nanny wants to see you."

Jemmy drew in a breath. She hoped he had not heard anything which would give her away.

She rapped on the door of Mrs. Nanny's study where the madam was counting money. "You wanted to see me, Ma'am?"

"Yes, I promised you a dollar. Here it is—and you've been such a help you may also keep the quarter for the telephone. I know you must be hungry. Young boys are always hungry. Go out to the kitchen. You'll find plenty of leftovers in the ice box. Don't eat the ham. It will keep. But have all the chicken salad, rennet pudding, and buttermilk you want."

"Thank you, Ma'am."

When Jemmy didn't leave, Mrs. Nanny asked, "Is there something else?"

"Please, Ma'am, may I sleep on the floor in Miss Spokane's room—in case she needs something?"

Mrs. Nanny nodded understandingly, "No place to go? I suppose you can sleep by the stove in the kitchen. The crib girls will start bringing in blankets from out back before long."

"Thank you kindly, Ma'am."

Jemmy ate chicken salad and counted her money. She had made out surprisingly well—five dollars and seventy-five cents—a dollar and fifty-five cents more than a store clerk working ten hours a day makes in her six-day week.

As the fire burned low in the coal stove, the crib girls piled their musky blankets on her after their trips to Mrs. Nanny's office.

Mrs. Nanny shook Jemmy awake while she was trying to beat her way out of a stifling dream. She flailed her arms to free herself from a net of binder twine in the shape of a mammoth spider web. She awoke sweating and blurted out, "You and me and Dr. T."

Mrs. Nanny took no notice. She murmured, "I want you to take a message for me. I can't use the telephone for this.

"I want you to take this envelope to my lawyer, he lives about a mile from here in Lucas place."

Jemmy squinted, "Is it daytime?"

"Nearly sunrise. You'll be able to see without a lantern. After you give him this and tell him everything he wants to know, I want you to disappear. Don't come back here. If the police don't know about you, they can't ask you questions. But if they should talk to you, all you did was pick up money and tote water and such. You never saw Annie fight with anyone, and you never heard of a virgin auction—never saw that skinny one at all—never."

"What happened?"

"She's dead. Worse than dead, cut up something fearful. One of the crib girls found her in the alley and was too terrified to go home."

The pair looked at each other in silence. Then Mrs. Nanny said, "Never you mind that curse. Probably her fancy man did her in 'cause he thought she was holding out on him. I don't believe in curses, and you shouldn't either. Remember, nobody in this house ever saw her. Not a one of us knows who she is or where she came from."

As Jemmy left, Mrs. Nanny said, "Wait a minute." She came back from her office with a parcel wrapped in newspaper. "Get rid of this in someone's trash barrel far from here, or throw it in the river."

She slipped two dollars into Jemmy's hand, then grabbed both of Jemmy's shoulders. With a stern look, Mrs. Nanny ordered, "Don't you dare try to sell these—you hear me? If a policeman sees you with them, you may find yourself hanged for murder—and no one here would lift a finger to stop it."

Jemmy didn't have to open the package. She knew the paper held the professional virgin's derringer and knife. Jemmy couldn't keep a quaver out

101

of her voice. "Do you think she could have saved herself if we hadn't taken these away from her?"

Mrs. Nanny said, "Maybe so, but I wasn't about to let her shoot me—or you—and you know she would have. We did what we had to do and that's an end to it."

Her voice softened. "Don't blame yourself. Blame me if you want, but I don't blame myself. As I said, it was probably her fancy man getting mad because the girl only brought out half of what he expected—or because she got caught stealing. It has nothing to do with either of us."

Mrs. Nanny ushered her out the front door into the cold December sunrise. Jemmy was glad Gerta had insisted on the greatcoat, not only because it covered her down to the ground, but also because it had big inner pockets where she could hide a package that might be enough to convict its bearer of murder. Jemmy picked her way over the snow-covered tracks in the road. She turned the corner with the idea of doubling back down the alley to see the body. After all, would Nellie Bly miss an opportunity to see a freshly mangled corpse—especially one she knew well enough to fight?

She didn't have far to go. In the alley behind the outbuildings nearest the street, the virgin lay in a heap of white flesh on her black cape. Her blue-green gown had been ripped from chin to knee. Her corset laces had been cut and spread open. Her underthings had been sliced apart and peeled neatly back—no doubt to prepare the site for surgery.

A gash from breastbone through belly riveted Jemmy's eyes. How very like Grandma's gash—but much longer and much bloodier. She didn't know enough about anatomy to tell what was missing, but entrails spilling over the side meant something vital had been cut away.

This spiritless flesh had been a living, breathing, brawling person just hours earlier. But brutal hands had frozen that life into lines and angles and geometric shapes that Jemmy couldn't name.

Jack the Ripper in St. Louis

Jemmy felt oddly detached. The cold had stolen Jemmy's compassion and replaced it with a fierce need to know. Her eyes scanned the body as she sought to fathom the crime, to fix every detail in her mind and file it away for future reference.

Her eyes traveled to the virgin's outflung arm where a tiny pool of dark red stained the snow under the waif's left hand. Her middle finger was missing. On the cinders of the alley peeping up through the snow a line of dark gore thinned to a point, then turned into smaller drops marking the path the hunter took as he left with his trophies.

After staring for what seemed an hour, Jemmy dragged her eyes to the virgin's face. The heavy greasepaint and rouged lips made the soiled dove look oddly alive, but with frost-tinged eyebrows bespeaking old age. A single brown curl lay frozen atop the freckles on her shoulder.

Jemmy would have stared much longer, memorized every inch, but a sound interrupted her trance. She ducked around the corner and peeked back. A blue tick hound sniffed at the corpse. When the dog started licking at the body, Jemmy calmed her churning stomach by trotting off in the direction of Lucas Place.

After half a block, Jemmy lost control of her head. It started shaking and refused to stop. The tremors crawled down her neck, pulsated through her hips and became a fierce trembling. She wobbled on her legs in the powdery snow. The trip to Lucas Place took twice as long as it should have. Jemmy relived the faltering steps of an infant learning to walk.

The sun was well up by the time she reached the impressive townhouse on a street which had once been the home of the city's grandest. She rang the doorbell. She stood on the stoop bracing herself against the door long enough for the shakes to ease a little. She rang the bell again and again. At last she heard a voice through a grate say, "What brings you to my door this uncivilized hour on a Sunday morning?"

103

"Nanny sent me."

"I'm coming."

A bleary-eyed man in a brown wool dressing gown opened the door. He stood in the doorway and eyed her from head to toe, then moved aside for her to enter. "You look half-frozen. Come on back with me and I'll stoke up the fire."

He motioned for Jemmy to follow him to the kitchen where he added a scoop of coal to the embers in the potbellied stove and set a coffee pot atop. He opened Nanny's letter and pointed to a chair.

After reading the letter, he said, "Tell me everything. Don't leave anything out." He shoved an index finger an inch from Jemmy's nose and looked straight into her eyes. "And tell me the truth."

Forcing her mind to remember helped Jemmy to bring her shakes under control. She told about the virgin auction, the attempted theft, Annie's rescue, Mrs. Nanny's justice, and throwing the virgin out. She even told about the curse. She left out the part about visiting the body in the alley.

"What did you do with the package?"

A lie found its way to Jemmy's lips. "Threw it in the trash somewhere on the way here."

He looked annoyed. "Where?"

"I don't know. Just someone's trash-burning barrel in an alley—two barrels, that is. I didn't leave them both in the same place."

"You're not quite as dumb as you look. The river would have been a better place, though."

Jemmy wasn't sure whether to thank him or not, so she stayed quiet. She placed a hand over the pocket to keep the metal of the derringer from clinking against the knife. She vowed to pitch them both in the Mississippi.

"What I want you to do now is go home. Do exactly what Nanny said. Stay away."

Jemmy looked genuinely disappointed because she was.

He said, "You like Nanny's, don't you?"

"It was the best job I ever had." Coffee and coal warmth allowed Jemmy's brain to function well enough to see the irony and truth of her statement.

"Come back and see me in a month or two—after all this blows over. I think Nanny might take you back. A useful young fellow who knows how to keep mum is usually welcome."

Back home Jemmy shivered as she changed into Jemima in the carriage house. Everyone had gone to church. She took a cold bath. Without realizing it, she scrubbed her skin to an angry red. When she looked in the mirror, she wondered what she had been trying to wash away—the curse—the guilt?

Perhaps it was the vision of a girl, a girl not much older than Jemmy herself, mutilated and frozen in an alley. Jemmy's tears blurred that vision into Annie's flayed back and Grandma's violated body. "You and me and Dr. T" hummed in her bad ear like a bee caught under the veil on a hat. You dare not swat it lest it sting. You can do nothing but steel yourself against the pain and pray for mercy.

Then she had a new problem to face, or was it the same old problem? What was she to do if she could no longer visit Annie—her one and only contact in the sporting world? Losing the story popped into Jemmy's brain to deepen her woe.

She thought about Annie's view of Jack the Ripper. For the Whitechapel murders, Annie blamed crusaders who pushed the girls out onto the streets when they shut down the brothels. Jemmy could see what Annie meant, but the logic flew in the face of everything she had been taught about fallen women and crime.

Of course, she couldn't really "get the story" at Nanny's anyway. The place was too nice. She needed a brothel worthy of exposing. Jemmy was still puzzling when the family came home. Mother looked mighty relieved to see her eldest daughter with all her parts intact. In a fit of uncommon sentiment, Mother hugged Jemmy, nearly crushed her. But then spouted off a single stern sentence. "Jemima McBustle, if you fail to inform me in future if you will not be returning home at the expected hour, I shall pack you off to Lindenwood College just as soon as the new semester permits." She marched off to supervise Sunday dinner without allowing any reply from her wayward daughter.

If you had asked her before she smelled the heavenly smells from Gerta's Sunday feast, Jemmy would have said she'd never be able to eat again—not after what she had seen. But she found she was quite able to relish a sizable meal.

Over a substantial dinner of spiced peaches, roast pork with potatoes and carrots, molasses-bran muffins, and red devil's food cake, Jemmy had to weave another tale about Mrs. Panghurst and the nephew. "He was most kind to me. He apologized for being late and gave me the day off. He said he doesn't need me again until Monday afternoon."

That suited Mother. This Sunday afternoon was the appointed time for the pageant rehearsal in Lafayette Park. Jemmy could think of nothing better to do. Maybe a reporter could find time for family life. After all, the best nose for news in the city seemed to find time for seven children and Nanny's Fifi, too.

Come to think of it. She might find a story at the pageant. After all, how many potential debutantes from the Midwest could say they had ridden a camel?

Chapter Ten

With all costumes mended and pressed, new white choir robes, and fresh white chicken feathers covering the bald spots on Randy's angel wings, Mrs. Belinda McBustle set out for Lafayette Park Presbyterian Church with her four young daughters at 2:06 PM in order to arrive at precisely 2:20 PM.

In the church basement since two o'clock exactly, Aunt Delilah had been wielding her authority with surgical precision. At two o'clock on the dot she met with the bonfire bunch.

They assured her they already amassed enough smashed-up crates, old boxes and assorted burnables piled behind the parsonage to make pageant night anticipated with great dread by the firefighters at the brand new firehouse built for Company Number 7 at Eighteenth Street and Park Avenue, just one block away. One wag suggested that the firehouse had been built for the express purpose of insuring that the Presbyterians didn't burn down

Lafayette Square for Christmas.

At 2:05, she met with the cider men. She approved their plan to heat buckets of the sweet stuff at a deacon's house on Mississippi Avenue and employ runners to keep the taps of two ten gallon crocks flowing with the juice of the apple. They also promised that no hard cider would be dispensed—at least not by their hands.

At 2:10, she met with the cookie ladies. To serve the expected five thousand guests at two cookies per person, she estimated the need of eight-hundred and thirty-three dozen cookies. That meant each of the church's seventy-nine households should bake and frost ten and one-half dozen cookies—rounded off to an even eleven dozen.

She handed out jars of popcorn to each of the girls ages twelve through marriage. They were to bring it, nicely popped, to the popcorn balling on Thursday next at 7:30 PM in the church basement.

At 2:15 she met with the menagerie keepers. She directed them to meet in Albion street by the church with animals well groomed by six o'clock on Saturday evening. She instructed them to feed the creatures at seven and maintain all possible efforts to soothe the beasts and keep them quiet. The choir could not be expected to sound angelic amidst a chorus of cow moos and sheep baas.

At 7:30 the wranglers were to lead the sheep and cows to their places around the bandstand. Aunt Delilah would deploy Joseph with Mary's donkey behind the statue of Thomas Hart Benton.

The shepherds were to herd their flock to their bivouac just below the Star of the East so its first rays would fall upon them as they sat on the ground near their sheep. With five shepherds and five sheep, Aunt Delilah was confident the sheep could be sensibly corralled. The wise men and camels would take up their places at the Park Avenue gate.

At 2:20 Aunt Delilah addressed the acting troupe while Jemmy was gluing on her false beard and tucking her street clothes under her silk robes.

Aunt Delilah pursed her lips. "I have most disappointing news. I had been assured that the camels would be here for today's rehearsal. As you can see, no camels. The advance manager of Pawnee Bill's Wild West Show wired me to say that if the beasts failed to appear by Saturday morning, he would not only refund my money, but would also pay a fine equal to their rental.

"I certainly hope he is a man of his word. However, in the event that he should fail us again, we have a secondary plan. In case of need on Saturday and for today's rehearsal, my son Duncan has resurrected our old Arabian tassels and trappings and placed them upon three spirited horses. Jemima my dear, perhaps I should give your role to someone who can control a spirited animal. You could trade with Bunks Bappel. His part is simple—just to meet the wise men and hold their horses while they present their gifts."

Jemima felt the insult and quite forgot she had once wanted to get out of her role as Balthasar. No one Jemmy knew—not even the man's own father—had refuted the proposition that Bunks Bappel was the laziest man in St. Louis. Surely, anything Bunks Bappel could do, Jemima could do.

Besides, Jemmy had taken riding lessons. Aunt Delilah had paid for them because Auntie believed every real lady needed to look elegant while riding sidesaddle. Jemmy had little experience riding astride. But, she had seen boys do it; and if a boy could do it, so could Jemima McBustle.

"Thank you for your concern, Aunt Delilah. But with the benefit of the lessons you provided me, I am quite capable of riding a spirited steed."

"I hope your riding lessons stand you in good stead."

Aunt Delilah told all to take their places. She ordered the practice to commence promptly at 2:30 PM. The rehearsal was perfection itself. Not a line of dialogue dropped, not a sour note in the choir, not a cue missed or an animal braying. All was idyllic—until the entry of the three wise men.

Jemmy took the blame; but the catastrophe wasn't her fault, at least not entirely.

Everything started off well enough. Dressed as Balthasar, she tucked her chest of gold-painted coins under her arm and walked out to Albion Street where Duncan was holding three fine looking horses. One was his own bay stallion; one was a fidgety gray with a black tail; and the last was a small white true Arabian with an elegantly-shaped head.

Duncan would ride his unpredictable bay. He said to Jemmy, "I'm afraid I don't know much about these other two. I borrowed them from a friend who has just bought them both. He plans to race them so they must have some spirit. Take your pick."

"I'll take the little white one. At least it is nearer the ground if I get thrown." Duncan gave her a leg up and handed her the treasure chest. He picked up his empty ginger jar—the presumed repository of myrrh—and mounted the bay.

Not until that instant did Jemmy see a sight that all but unnerved her. She recognized the third wise man's face beneath the beard of Gaspar. A young man Jemmy had most recently seen in a very unsettling setting—the virgin auction at Mrs. Nanny's house of ill repute—the young man she had recognized as a member of her own Sunday School class, Peter Ploog.

He was carrying the most awkward of the gifts of the three wise men— to represent Frankincense, a smoldering silver sensor ball suspended by three chains. Aunt Delilah had borrowed a spare from Holy Angels Catholic Church.

Jemmy champed at the bit to tell the bad boy's secrets. But she couldn't say a single word—not even to him. The one thing she could do, she did. She treated him with open contempt. But the more she rebuffed him, the more he sought her good will.

Jack the Ripper in St. Louis

Jemmy was not Ploog's only problem. His horse challenged him, too. The gray pranced ahead sideways and refused to fall in step. It lurched forward every time the censor hit the animal's shoulder. Jemmy grudgingly admired Peter's riding ability. After every shenanigan, he circled the creature around to talk to Jemmy.

On the first pass he said, "Miss McBustle, may I compliment you on the way you sit a horse."

Since her little white horse plodded up Missouri Avenue at the speed of an arthritic cocker spaniel, she said, "It would be more troublesome to ride a dog cart than this animal, Mr. Ploog."

On the second pass he said, "Miss McBustle, what I meant was that you look most attractive astride that animal."

"How surprisingly candid of you to admit that you find a bearded person attractive. Perhaps you should look for your true love in a circus."

He sneered and chuckled.

On the third pass he said, "Surely you must know I'm praising not the mannish beard but the girlish face that lies under it."

"I hope I'm not too impertinent when I suggest that you might grow your own beard. Then people can wonder whether the face under your mutton chops might be found attractive by some. A female person, that is."

While Peter was dancing off in another circle, Duncan smirked at the banter. He said, "You could do worse, Cousin. His father takes a hand in lots of businesses. I hear he is a silent partner in Witte hardware."

On the fourth pass, Peter said, "Miss McBustle, I'd be most honored if you would allow me to escort you to the Masonic Hall on New Year's Eve. The Masons hold their stuffy waltzes in the Temple's Grand Hall, but they allow us to clear the furnishings from the main lounge and have our own celebration. This year, Tom Turpin has promised us a ragtime band. Ours will be the liveliest ball in town. Duncan will be there; won't you, Duncan?"

Jemima put her nose in the air. "Mr. Ploog, have you lost all sense of propriety? We are here to act our parts in a religious pageant, not discuss profane entertainments."

On his fifth pass, Peter said, "I meant no disrespect. I only hoped to discover whether you would look with favor upon my proposal. I don't like to waste my time asking permission of a girl's family on girls who don't care for my company."

"Yes, Mr. Ploog, I suppose all men like girls who are guaranteed to like them back."

"I'd be pleased if you'd call me by my nickname."

"And I'd be please to oblige, Pet."

For the first time, Peter looked nonplussed. "Pete, if you please. My friends call me Pete."

"How very apt. A fuel from a low lying swamp."

"But Miss McBustle, that is spelled P-E-A-T."

"So, you can spell. I'm sure that must place you in great demand down at Tom Turpin's."

Duncan was chuckling behind his ginger jar when the choir began "We Three Kings."

With Jemmy plodding in the lead, Peter with arm wide out to hold the swaying censor away from the gray horse's shoulder, and Duncan sitting tall on the bay; they soon arrived at the place where they were to dismount. Bunks Bappel was standing in the middle of the path ready to receive the horse's reins. He held up his arm with his slouch hat in it to show the riders where to stop.

Jemmy's little white horse pricked up its ears, then reared on its hind feet. In her panic to stay on the animal Jemmy dropped the reins. She had to use every leg and thigh muscle she owned to stay on the animal's back. She threw her arms around its neck. She even considered hanging on with her teeth, but couldn't find anything worthwhile to bite.

The white horse, meanwhile, performed in a pageant of its own. It snatched Bunks' hat from his hand, pranced three steps forward and tossed the hat onto the ground. When Bunks turned around and bent over to pick it up, the white horse put its nose between Bunks' legs and flipped him neatly into the air. Bunks might well have broken his neck had he not rolled into a ball to somersault away from the equine and land on his own hat. When he turned around to retrieve it, the white horse moved toward him again with teeth bared. Bunks covered himself the way only a coward would and backed up.

The white horse picked up Bunks' flattened hat and stuck a hoof in it far enough to make it look almost normal. Then the white horse bowed on one knee and handed it—teethed it, that is—to Bunks. Through all these maneuvers, Bunks didn't rush. He didn't frown or laugh. In fact, he showed no emotion at all. Perhaps that's why the onlookers thought the whole thing had to be planned.

The crowd cheered at this surprising and delightful addition to what most thought would be the same fusty old pageant rehearsal.

They laughed still more to discover the show was not over. Bunks put the hat on his head then fell back in a crouch so he would be ready for whatever hijinks the horse had in mind.

When nothing else happened, he tried to catch hold of the loose reins; but whichever way he moved, the white horse foiled his attempts to grab the reins as it poked its head under Bunks' arms and nuzzled him all over. Jemmy hissed, "You must have something in your pocket that it wants."

Bunks pulled out an apple which the white horse snatched so eagerly it almost took three of Bunks' fingertips along with the prize. At last he was able to catch the reins so Jemmy could get down.

The only permanent damage happened neither to man nor beast, but to

Jemmy's wise-man crown which had been badly trampled in the perform-ance. None-the-less, she put the battered crown on her head and led the other wise men up the bandstand steps to kneel before the manger.

At last the dress rehearsal was over and all the crews wended their way back to the church basement to drink hot cocoa and to warm cold hands. As they walked by the horses, Jemmy turned on Duncan. "Why didn't you help? Two big men would surely have been able to get the reins of one lit-tle horse."

"You're right. I apologize. I should have done exactly that, but I was having too much fun watching the show to even think of it."

"I'll bet you knew my horse was a trick horse. I bet you planned this whole thing to make me fall off so you could make fun of me."

"I swear I had no idea that was a trick horse. I thought it was a race horse."

"I know practically nothing about horses, but even I can tell that horse is too old to race."

"I thought it might be breeding stock. Anyway, you stayed on. I admire you for that."

"And that Ploog person. You planned that, too, I bet. Throwing us together and telling me he's a good catch. Well, let me tell you..." Jemmy stopped in mid sentence. She had been on the verge of saying much too much about young Mr. Ploog.

Duncan defended himself. "Mother chose him. I had nothing to do with that either. Look, Cousin, I know I used to pester you, but I've outgrown it. You've turned into quite a beauty—beauty with a brain, too." He held up three fingers in the Boy Scout oath. "If anyone tries to embarrass you in the future, I will leap to your defense."

Back in the basement, Aunt Delilah waited. "Duncan, have you no com-mon sense? Your cousin might have been maimed for life if she had fallen off that beast."

"Mother, I swear I didn't know it was a trick horse. Jemmy believes me; don't you, Jemmy?"

Jemmy nodded in the affirmative.

"My dear, you were splendid to stay on the horse. The minister said I should leave the hat trick in. Of course, he also said he was amazed at the speed Bunks achieved. I said, 'Yes, amazing. His rapidity increased all the way from slow as molasses in January to slow as molasses in February.'"

Jemmy took the crown off her head and handed it to Aunt Delilah. "I don't know whether this can be repaired. Maybe if someone would take it to a tinsmith or a magician."

Delilah scowled as she looked at the twisted frame with its broken points. She handed the crown to Duncan. "See that this is repaired or have a substitute come next Saturday. I rely upon you entirely. Don't tell your father until after you've secured the new crown. Maybe it will convince him you are not the feckless playboy he takes you for."

Duncan smirked in his most annoying way. "Feckless? Why mother dear, I'm so full of feck that my friends call me 'fecker.'"

Aunt Delilah sighed, "Thank heaven, we'll not have to worry about trick horses on pageant day. I'm sure camels couldn't possibly cause as much trouble."

Chapter Eleven

Jemmy came down from her lofty Sunday pageant perch as eastern potentate to become a Monday pauper with horsehair. Father's wool great-coat and three pairs of wool socks kept her reasonably warm as she watched the house with blue shutters from a half block away.

She sat on the wooden steps of a brownstone. A trellis of dead clematis leaves hid her from prying eyes inside the house. Privet hedge and wooden gate shielded her from street view both front and side. The only threat of discovery came from people exiting the house. She planned to dive under the steps if she heard the knob turning.

That morning she had raided the kindling bin for old Miss Hendershot's Sunday *Republican*. She scoured the paper for news of the murder in the alley. A single paragraph asked the public for information about the identity of the woman. Below the item was a testimonial from Dr. J.I. Terry of Trimble, Tennessee, stating that "...no other remedy is so prompt and effectual or so pleasant to take as *Chamberlain's Colic, Cholera and Diarrhea Remedy, A Household Necessity*." It bothered Jemmy that the *Republican* deemed an advertisement more newsworthy than a dead girl in an alley. But then, the *Republican* had not seen what Jemmy had seen.

Jemmy watched policemen knock on doors up and down the street. A pair of officers stayed quite some time in the house with blue shutters. Jemmy was trying to think of a way to ask them questions when the pair strode into Woodbury's Drug Store.

She didn't dare talk to the police directly, but maybe she could get some second-hand information. After the policemen left, she walked to Woodbury's where the counterman was arranging Cloverine salve on a shelf.

He said, "What may I do for you this fine day, my lad?"

Jemmy said, "Policemen are all over the place. I thought you might know how come."

"I don't know much for a fact. Just that a young lady was stabbed in the alley last Saturday. I thought this neighborhood was safe from hooligans." He put his hands on his hips in disgust. "Looks like Kerry Patch is moving right in here with its gangs of Irish thugs, for a fact."

"Do the police think an Irish gang killed her?"

He shook his head. "They say they don't know. Just what you'd expect from our police who hale from the old sod themselves."

"Who was she?"

"They don't even know that for a fact. If they ever find out who did her in, I'll turn a cartwheel on the courthouse lawn. But what was it you came for?" He looked expectant.

"I thought you might have some work, deliveries to make or the like."

"Sorry, I already have a boy makes deliveries after he gets home from school—which is where you ought to be, I'd say for a fact."

"Maybe I could sweep up or wash bottles."

"I have a boy for that, too. Both are my sons so they work cheap."

"Maybe you know of somebody who might need..."

He shook his head as he reached into a candy jar and pulled out a licorice whip. "Here. Have this on me. If you don't find something, come back in a week. I'll ask around. See if anyone needs a likely lad."

Jemmy said, "Thank you. I'm much obliged for the help—and for the licorice."

As she closed the store door with the bell jingling behind her, she saw two figures coming down the steps of the house with blue shutters. Dr. Tumblety and his boy set off walking in the direction of Kerry Patch with his pair of greyhounds bracketing the men like porcelain bookends.

Following them seemed the logical thing to do. They might lead her to another bordello where she might just find the story she was looking for. Besides, following a handsome boy in red pantaloons might be a good way to chase off the chills.

She kept well back and stayed near fences or hedges with the intention of flattening herself against them if the doctor or the boy should look back. But soon the hedges and fences disappeared. The buildings shrank from two or three story edifices to one story shotgun houses built right up to the board sidewalks.

Still Jemmy thought she was doing all right until the doctor's boy looked back. She knew he caught sight of her, but the boy merely turned face front. Jemmy had nowhere to hide. She stopped to see what the boy would do. Surely the doctor would look back if the boy told him someone was following. Neither stopped nor turned.

After a few more blocks they disappeared around a corner. When Jemmy arrived at the intersection, she poked her head around just in time to see them disappear into the fourth little row house down the block. The greyhounds settled themselves in a patch of sun near the door.

She took pains to get her bearings at that intersection. Her run-in with the Irish rascals had taught her to keep a good grip on where she was. She looked around for a place to hide until the doctor and his boy came out.

Too late. Two young toughs called to her from across the street about half a block away. The same pair of neighborhood bad boys who had blocked her path when she started her career in surveillance but lost her way.

The greasy-haired boy hollered loud enough for the whole block to hear, "Say, Colley, isn't that a fine coat on the young lad over there. I'd sure like to have me a warm coat like that."

Colley said, "A fine coat it is. Where do you think you might find such a coat as that?'

"Why should I look elsewhere a-tall? That young lad is wearing my coat and bringing it right along to me. Good lad that he is."

Jemmy wasted no more time. She spun on her heel and fairly flew back toward civilization and security—Delmar Street. She could hear running boots thumping hotly on her trail and this time no policeman serendipitously appeared to save her sorry bacon.

She looked back to see them gaining on her. Terrified that they would overtake her before she reached the trolley line, she turned left and raced down the alley. She might have escaped them if she could have reached the end of the alley before they could enter, but she wasn't fast enough. She knew they saw her.

She redoubled her efforts as she reversed her direction and drove with legs pumping back in the direction from whence she had come. Her only hope of salvation was to reach the house Dr. Tumblety had entered and hope he'd be willing to help her.

Panting hard, she flew through the gate and pounded on the door. The greyhounds stood at the ready and growled, but stayed where they were.

Her pursuers had split up. The greasy-haired boy had a hand out to grab Jemmy's greatcoat when the door opened. The boy backed off, shoved his hands in his jacket pockets and rolled his cap down on his forehead as he sauntered off.

A skinny woman with a front tooth missing opened the front door and grinned. "Well, what'll it be, young stud? You look like you might have a quarter to get your wick diddled. That what you're after?"

"Please, ma'am. I have an urgent message for the Doctor."

The woman stopped smiling and stood back for Jemmy to enter. Jemmy heard Colley's running steps rounding the corner down the street as the door closed.

The woman pointed toward the back of the house, "Doctor's back there, through the curtain."

Jemmy looked around. As in most shotgun houses, a person standing inside the entrance could look straight back through several doorways to the back door. The smell of sweat and unemptied slops assailed her nose as she tried to absorb every detail of a working class brothel—bordello was too nice a name. This place was nothing like Mrs. Nanny's place.

The gap-toothed madam resumed her seat to count money at a little claw-footed table. Someone had made the effort to decorate the lounge in homey fashion with lace curtains, faded wallpaper abloom with enormous yellow roses and a framed sampler cross-stitched with the old Irish Toast:

Lift your glass, me boy-o's.
To cheating, stealing, fighting and drinking.
If you cheat, may you cheat death.
If you steal, may you steal your lover's heart.
If you fight, may you fight for the right.
And if you drink, may you drink with me.

A tall secretary with glass doors—locked no doubt—held bottles of liquor. That, along with too many chairs and too many spittoons announced that the first room was both waiting room and office.

Jack the Ripper in St. Louis

The madam said with some impatience, "Go along, then, if you've an urgent message. He's in the kitchen."

Jemmy walked through the first doorway.. Both sides of the room had been partitioned off by canvas curtains. From one came "If that's what you want, it'll cost you another..."

Jemmy heard snoring from one cubicle and wondered how anyone could sleep in such a place. Through the second doorway she could see inside two of the partitioned cubicles. Both had mattresses on the floor. One displayed the kind of mess that bespoke the activity that occurred there, but the other held a neatly made bed—complete with a counterpane and a white flannel nightie with lace around the neck—the kind schoolgirls wear.

Hooks along the solid wall displayed a conservative wardrobe of a brown cape and hat, white shirtwaist and the kind of plain tan gabardine skirt and jacket one would expect to see on a shopgirl. A table in the far corner held a porcelain-headed doll in a yellow velvet riding habit along with a tortoise shell hairbrush and mirror. There was even a doily over the lid of the blue-speckled enameled tin chamber pot.

One half of the next room, the room nearest the kitchen, had been walled off and boasted the only interior door in the house. It was padlocked. Jemmy wondered what treasures or horrors might be stored there.

When she peeked through the slit between the canvas curtain and the door frame, she could see into the kitchen. Jemmy saw nothing of the boy in the fez, but she had a clear view of the doctor's back as he bent over the kitchen table. On it lay the girl who must have been the occupant of the neat crib. She was small and blond—what hair she had left—which was braided and tied in yellow ribbons. The doctor held up her arm covered with patches of black and said, "Have you been using black tar salve to draw the poison from your sores?"

Her voice faltered, "Yes, Doctor, every night and every morning."

"How long have you had the rash on your stomach?"

"A few days. That's why Mr. H called you. My regulars won't touch me no more."

"And the fevers and nausea? How long?"

"Just since yesterday."

"You know it's syphilis, don't you?"

The girl began to weep.

"I can give you a course of salversan treatment. It will be expensive, though—ten dollars."

"I don't have half so much, but if the sores go away, I'd be able to."

He burst in. "Just like a whore to want to infect every manjack in the city. You are in the third stage. The more infected you are, the faster you kill men. Nothing leads to fourth stage syphilis in men so fast as long, violent and frequent times with diseased whores like you. Thank heaven you wear your shame on your skin to keep men away from your rotten hide. You have exactly what you deserve for being a female who enjoys bedding men. You made yourself easy prey to disease. Didn't anyone ever tell you a woman should not have relations more than once a month?"

By now, the girl with the pigtails was sobbing.

The doctor rolled down his sleeves and said, "Without the salversan treatment, you will die. However, if you'd like to try some of the old fashioned methods, you might do yourself some good. In the old days, they purged, sweated and leached—and spit out as much of the poison as they could.

"I am only telling you this because Mr. H is paying me for my best medical advice. I recommend that you go to a Magdalene house or enter a convent. You'll need looking after once the numbness comes, then the blindness, dementia, paralysis. That's the one good thing about syphilis. When the end comes, you'll be too insane to know it."

Jack the Ripper in St. Louis

Jemmy's heart went out to the poor girl. She longed to tell her that Annie had said sometimes herbal treatments can clear up the sores, but she couldn't risk talking to her. The only thing she could think to do, she did. She scribbled a note in her makeshift journal and tore out the page. It gave the address of the house with blue shutters and told the girl to see Spokane at Mrs. Nanny's.

Jemmy hid behind curtains until the doctor and his boy had walked back to the front parlor. She slipped into the kitchen and tucked the note in the girl's hand. She tried to smile some reassurance in the girl's direction, but she feared her teary eyes bespoke only pain.

She doubted the girl could read. But Jemmy could manage nothing more helpful in this confined place with thugs waiting outside to beat her up and steal Father's coat.

While the doctor put on his hat and gloves, Jemmy tiptoed behind him and waited for him to turn around. When the boy saw her, she shook her head in an appeal for silence. He didn't give her away.

When the doctor swung around to look at her, his face brightened. He was no longer brusque or angry. he said, "Aren't you the boy from Saturday's auction?"

"Yes sir."

"You're not apt to find many free-tipping fellows here."

"The Missus says I must stay away on account of what happened out back of her place."

He nodded and started to walk past. Jemmy said, "Beg pardon, Sir. Might I walk along with you and your boy?"

"And why would you want to come with us?"

"Please, Sir, a couple of neighborhood boys want my coat."

The Doctor smiled a little. "I suppose Nipper and I would be able to protect you for a bit. What do you say, Nipper?"

Nipper nodded in agreement, but he was not smiling. Jemmy sensed wariness and hostility—the opposite of her usual effect on boys her age. Still, she had no choice if she wanted to go home that day with coat and skin still on her back.

The Doctor stopped at the Madam's table in the lounge to collect his fee. He asked, "I don't suppose Mr. H will pay for her treatments?"

The madam shook her head. He said, "I wouldn't think so. Better send her away. No man who sees those sores would touch her. I might be willing to take her myself—to study the progression of the disease—if she has nowhere to go."

Jemmy heaved a sigh of relief when the madam said, "She has family here in town. Her mother got her into this business. She came around last week and offered to take her home."

The Doctor scowled, plopped his cane once against his boot, then strode out the front door with Jemmy and Nipper following. He regained his good humor when they reached the street as the dogs took up their posts on either side of the Doctor. He looked around for the toughs. "No savage youths around now. Still, we might meet up with them any time."

The Doctor must have been nearsighted. Jemmy could see the greasy-haired boy and Colley leaning against a fence a few houses down. She pointed. The Doctor and his dogs set off across the street with a purposeful gait. He stopped less than three feet in front of the boys and drilled them with a stare so intense Jemmy could feel their anxiety from ten feet away.

They stood up straight as he poked the greasy-haired boy in the chest with his cane. He said, "If I should find this lad without a coat or with a black eye, I'll see to it that a certain pair of fellows rue the day."

The greasy-haired boy said, "He's naught to fear from us, but you can't fault us if someone else should harm him."

"Oh, but I will. I think you'd be well-advised to see to it that naught

124

happens to him at all." the Doctor emphasized the word "naught" in a scornful parody of the greasy-haired boy's speech. He turned smartly on his heel and strode off.

As she walked behind the Doctor and Nipper, she looked back at the toughs. The greasy-haired boy made an obscene gesture at her. She thumbed her nose in return.

As the human-canine quintet walked in the direction of Market Street, the Doctor said, "I don't think you'll have more trouble with that pair. You should arm yourself, though, just in case. Give him your knife, your kard, Nipper."

Nipper's eyes narrowed as he put his hand on the hilt of the weapon he carried at his waist. He pulled forth a curved seven inch blade that glinted wickedly in the afternoon sun.

The Doctor looked impatient. "Come on. I'll get you another—"

Nipper stuck the knife back in its sheath, unbuckled it and handed it to Jemmy.

"I don't know how to thank you, Doctor. But I can't accept this. Your boy needs it, and I don't know—"

The Doctor interrupted by pulling the kard from its sheath. He gave it a toss in the air and caught it with the other hand. With the blade pointing skyward, he balanced the hilt on his open palm. Then he grabbed the hilt as it fell and demonstrated how to gut an enemy. "Use it like a Bowie knife— thrust in and up. Deep in the belly and rip—or slash across. That will stop the biggest bully on the block."

Jemmy's stomach was turning queasy. She didn't think she could take much more instruction. She took the knife from his open hand as she said, "I'm more grateful than I can say."

As Nipper and the Doctor boarded the Market Street trolley, he said, "Someday I'll teach you a how to express your gratitude." The way he said

125

it made Jemmy pray that her additional matriculation at his hands would not be any time soon.

As the pair rode off on the trolley, Jemmy muttered, "You and me and Dr. T."

Chapter Twelve

Tuesday afternoon saw Jemmy back in the brownstone's yard where she could spy on the house with blue shutters. This time she came equipped with the spyglass Grandpa had used during the Civil War. Nothing untoward happened until a group of four arrived at Mrs. Nanny's door—a far cry from the kind of group Mrs. Nanny was accustomed to entertaining. To begin with, three of them were female.

Mr. Nanny refused to let them in. He stood smack in the doorway, barring the entrance with his sizable frame. Then he shut the door with a "thwack."

The rejection failed to dissuade the quartet. They knocked again—and again—and again until the door opened once more. This time Mrs. Nanny pulled her shawl around her shoulders and came outside to chat. Jemmy could only guess at what she was saying by the vexation written on her face.

Eventually, Mrs. Nanny went back in the house and shut the door with an even louder "Thwack." Still the four would not be denied. Jemmy discovered them to be the anti-vice voice. They began loud singing—hollering, in fact—the grand old hymn "Rock of Ages."

Mrs. Nanny tromped back out and stomped her foot.

The group showed no sign of leaving or making less commotion. At length she waved a defeated arm toward the door in invitation. Goes to show how tough life is for both sinners and sin-stoppers. Jemmy learned a lesson though—persistence pays.

In a quarter hour, the quartet emerged. In front of them, they drove a small herd of fellows doing their best to keep their faces covered with their hats as they skedaddled in all directions.

The second floor front window, the one in Annie's room, shot up. Unrepentant girls poked out their heads and began throwing things at the reformers. Jemmy couldn't make out exactly what they were throwing, but she could hear bits of shouts, "Hey, you unsoiled doves, is that feller with the turned-round collar your fancy man?"

"Better watch out. He'll leave you flat busted. I ought to know. He was my pimp five years back."

Annie put her hands beside her mouth to amplify the sound as she yelled, "Now girls, don't be so hard on the man. Anyone with such a little cock is only good for one thing—finding big cocks for us professionals to whittle down to size."

Pretending oblivion to the catcalls, the quartet stuck their noses in the air and walked on. Mrs. Nanny walked out around the tiny yard picking up the shoes and garters and drawers the girls had thrown. She waved a corset to shoo them back inside, then tromped back in the house and thwacked the door so hard it shook the windows next door.

Jemmy itched to talk to the girls. When would come another time when not a single customer was on the entire premises? But how to get around Mrs. Nanny's interdiction posed problems. Jemmy had nearly decided to risk Mrs. Nanny's displeasure when the police returned—and stayed—and stayed. Jemmy gave up. Mrs. Nanny was having a singularly bad day. Jemmy could expect no welcome from her.

Wednesday's vigil was little more productive until late afternoon. A person Jemmy recognized—the bandy-legged man, companion to the virgin who had been murdered in the alley—arrived in a light carriage pulled by single sedate sorrel. In trying to climb out, the man fell flat which startled the horse into running down the street where it stopped and began nibbling at some dead chrysanthemums in a yard at the end of the block.

The man didn't go after the buggy. He struggled a good five minutes just to raise himself upright. Then he wobbled toward the door like a toddler on bedsprings. He knocked; Mr. Nanny let him in.

Jemmy made up her mind to follow him when he came back out. This might be the story she had been looking for—the story that would make Nellie Bly proud. She slipped behind a fir tree across the street from the buggy and waited. She was close enough to hear the words fly between the man and Mrs. Nanny when he exited the house after only a few minutes.

He growled, "If you don't give me my money, I'll make you pay. She earned that money fair and square and she'd want me to have it."

"I already told you I gave half of her half to one of the girls—the one she stole from and beat up. I don't even have your money."

"Get it back."

"You talk about fair. Here's what's fair. It's fair the girl who got beat up is the one who got the money. In our line of work, we expect to get paid for services rendered."

"I'll get it back from her. Which girl is it?" He stumbled back toward the door until Mr. Nanny stepped outside.

Bandy-legs stopped and wavered as he raised his voice. "You better pay me my hundred and thirty-five dollars, right now."

Mrs. Nanny narrowed her eyes. "You didn't stay for the auction. The only

129

way you could know the exact amount she was supposed to get was if you took it off her body. Was she holding out on you? Is that why you killed her?"

"I want my money."

"Get out. If you're still here in ten minutes, the police will be here. I understand they've not been able to locate you because they don't know who you are. Get off my property or I'll see they find out."

"You're bluffin'. You don't want the police no more than I do."

"Not usually; but in your case, a case of murder, I'm prepared to make an exception." In triumph, she turned on her heel and walked into the house.

The man teetered a while and kept looking at the front door as if some magic would open it and furnish him with his hundred and thirty-five dollars. He wrapped his muffler around his neck and turned toward the street. He stood bewildered for some moments as he looked at the place where the horse should have been.

He scanned up and down the street. It took him another two minutes of staring at the buggy before he committed himself to toddling off in the direction of the mum-munching horse.

Jemmy was waiting for the man to climb aboard so she could hitch a ride on the footplate under the livery stable's advertising sign at the back of the buggy. It gave an address and the phrase, "Servicing the Lindell Hotel since 1888." But the man didn't toodle that far.

Midway between the house with blue shutters and the buggy, he stopped and took a long pull at a bottle from his overcoat pocket. Whereupon he lost his balance and fell over backwards. Well, not so much fell over as sat down, then crumpled forward with upper body listing to the right. When Jemmy reached him, she thought he looked like a capital letter Q with his bow legs forming the circle and his torso the tail.

She first made sure the door to the house with blue shutters was closed and no one was looking out the upstairs windows. She pulled the drunk's body to an upright position, then hoisted him to his feet. He woke up enough to say. "Good horse. Back at the hotel already. Wonder how you'd do at the track?"

Jemmy said, "You're still at Mrs. Nanny's. She sent me to see you get home. You're staying at the Lindell Hotel; am I right?"

He mumbled something Jemmy couldn't understand, but she took it for an affirmation.

The man wasn't big, but he was bigger than Jemmy and with muscles made unreliable by liquor. After considering the problem, she tucked her shoulder under his rump and pushed until she had steered him to the buggy and leaned him against it.

Then came the hard part. She placed his foot on the step a half dozen times, but it kept slipping off. She finally tied the wayward foot onto the step with his muffler. Then she was able to boost his behind more or less onto the seat.

She rested for a minute, then gathered up the reins and climbed aboard. She then had another prickly task in front of her. She had never driven a horse in harness. She had seen boys do it; and if a boy could do it, so could Jemima McBustle.

She pulled on the reins to back the horse out of the chrysanthemums, but the creature wasn't ready to leave. After a few futile attempts, she clambered down and walked over to the horse to discuss the necessity for greater cooperation. The horse continued munching. Jemmy gently pulled the beast away which earned her an ear-splitting neigh. Jemmy had enough. She yanked the head with all the strength she could muster.

She had to lead the horse a good three blocks before it stopped bobbing its head in protest. A voice came from down the street. "Well, Colley, did you ever see the like of that? I've often seen a horse pull a buggy, but I've never before seen a boy pulling a horse pulling a buggy. What do you make of it?"

"I'd say the one in back has the both the looks and the brains."

The pair slapped one another on the shoulder and guffawed at their wit. Jemmy climbed into the driver's seat, took up the reins and smacked the horse's rump with the buggy whip. The horse took off at a smart clip and stayed to the right side of the road on its own initiative. Good thing it needed no guidance from Jemmy because she hadn't the vaguest notion of what to do.

Apparently, Jemmy's masterful horsemanship impressed the boys. The - haired one said, "Now, how do you think a common boy learned to drive like that?"

Colley said, "Maybe he is a stable boy."

"We'd probably find out if we got close enough to smell him, but I wouldn't want to risk it." The pair slapped and guffawed until Jemmy was out of earshot.

The horse slowed down to a plodding walk. Jemmy tinkered with the idea of flicking the whip again, but decided not to tempt luck two times on one trip. On Lindell, she managed a left turn without being run over, and a U-turn to stop in front of the hotel. She was pleased at how smoothly she managed the turn. She cut off dozens of horses and drivers, but only three men shook their fists and swore at her.

The doorman helped her get the drunk down from the buggy. Jemmy asked him to see that the vehicle was returned to the livery. She and a bell-boy half-walked, half-dragged the man to the elevator. They stopped and leaned him against the wall. The bellboy said, "You'll need the key. I'll get it while you hold him up."

Jemmy was grateful he hadn't asked who the man was. She mentally kicked herself for failing to go through his pockets to find out his name—not to mention finding out whether he was armed and dangerous.

Once in the room, the bellboy helped take off his coat and boots and dump him in bed. Jemmy tipped him a quarter of her own money as he left.

Keeping one eye on the known-pimp, probable-murderer, Jemmy locked the door then surveyed the room. She began searching for she knew not what—something that would prove his guilt. The hundred and thirty-five dollars he had talked about would be a start.

She opened the wardrobe and touched the soft wool of a dark blue ladies' traveling suit with fox fur muff and neckpiece. A hatbox held the matching hat and a pair of dainty boots of buttery soft kid leather. These petite clothes ought to convince police the man knew the murdered girl quite well. Jemmy wondered why he had not rid himself of them.

The clothes were the most telling clues she found in the room. Yet they proved only that he knew the virgin, not that he had killed her. His overcoat held a small pistol and four loose bullets—and a pewter liquor flask.

There was nothing for it. She would have to search the body. He was snoring quietly on the bed. Jemmy began with vest pockets and turned up a watch and fob. From his trouser pockets she pulled a pocket knife, tobacco, a well-used handkerchief and coins. Jemmy took fifty cents—for her services—and a quarter to repay her tip to the bellboy—and another fifty cents she meant to give to the doorman.

The man had to have more money than that. She found sixteen dollars in his shoe. Then, she remembered his hat and struck pay dirt. Tucked in the grosgrain ribbon inner band of his black derby were five and ten dollar bills, some with bloody edges. No doubt about it; he had taken the money after the virgin was dead. He was a stone cold killer.

Just then the stone awoke enough to know that he was not alone. He struggled to his feet just as Jemmy was cramming the bloody money back in the hat. He said, "You're a thief."

Jemmy held out the hat to him as some of the bills fluttered to the floor. The man pulled a wicked-looking knife from what must have been a sheath in the middle of his back. Jemmy stood mesmerized for a moment by the point of the wavy-bladed knife—the twin of the virgin's that Mrs. Nanny had given to Jemmy. This glinting metal must be the same half-foot of steel that ripped open the virgin's belly and left her bloodied in the alley. Jemmy stood transfixed by the enormity of it.

The man moved forward, menacing her with the knife in his right hand. He stuck out his left to grab at the money hat. Jemmy shrank back along the wall toward the wardrobe. Once in the corner, she shook herself out of her stupor and flung the hat at the knife hand as she tried to bolt towards the door.

The man lurched back and dropped the knife, then lunged toward Jemmy and grabbed her shoulders. Jemmy shoved him and he twirled away in an attempt to keep his balance. Even though he was facing away from Jemmy, he still blocked her way to the door in the small room. Jemmy hit the floor and crawled on all fours between his bow legs. He was too surprised to move until she stood and toppled him backwards. He yelped once as he hit the boards.

She raced for the door as he began to mutter swear words. The door was locked. She had locked it herself and left the key on the nightstand.

He staggered to his feet and came at her again, without the knife. He flung her banging into the wardrobe. She crumpled to the floor and pretended the knock made her pass out. He turned his back and began to search for his knife.

Just as he bent over to pick up the knife, Jemmy scrambled up and booted him in the behind so hard she thought she would break her toe. He howled and turned to face her as she was heading for the nightstand.

She snatched the key and raced to the door. In fumbling to turn the key, she was seconds too slow. The man reached her and slung her back into the wardrobe yet again. This time he watched her steadily as he felt for the knife with his foot. He picked it up and smiled.

Jack the Ripper in St. Louis

Jemmy picked up the nearest things she could find to defend herself. She hoisted the wash basin with her left hand as a shield, and took the heavy stoneware water pitcher in her right hand and prepared to do battle.

The man laughed out loud. He shouldn't have done that. The laughter turned to coughing. The coughing made him shut his eyes. Jemmy saw her chance. She swung the pitcher against the knife to dislodge it. Next came the water which she tossed into his face with an elegant backhand motion. Last she flung both basin and pitcher with all her might. The missiles buffeted the man back onto the bed before they rolled down to smash on the floor.

Jemmy was halfway out of the door when she heard a cry of anguish. She turned back to see the man sopping wet from the waist down and pointing to his foot. Jemmy could scarcely believe her luck. The knife had fallen from his hand into his own foot. It was sticking straight up between his toes and, no doubt, delivering deep discomfort to his pedal digits.

Jemmy shut the door and locked it. She composed herself and walked down the hall—a little surprised that no more yells were coming from the man's room. Perhaps he was preoccupied with his skewered foot. Maybe he was using his flask to pacify the pain.

Out front, she handed the room key to the doorman along with fifty cents as she said, "The gentleman in room 305 appreciates the services you rendered him today. As you know, he was somewhat besotted. He wishes to conquer demon rum. So he has asked me to give you this key and to request that no one open his door, no matter how he might beg, until tomorrow noon at the earliest. At that time, I am sure he will show his gratitude in a generous way."

The doorman tipped his hat and nodded. Jemmy couldn't help feeling a bit smug. She toyed with the idea of calling the police right away. But, tomorrow morning would be soon enough for them to get his confession. She needed time to think of just the right method to put this vile fellow away without giving up her disguise.

Just then, Jemmy realized that during the struggle upstairs, neither the drunk nor she had said a single word. What kind of a journalist was she? Why didn't she get him to say something—anything that would make a good quote? When, oh when, would she start to think like a newspaper-woman?

Chapter Thirteen

By Thursday morning, Jemmy looked as haggard as she felt. When she was awake, "You and me and Dr. T" churned over and over in ceaseless whispers in her bad ear. She awoke with hands in front of her face to fend off nightmares of jabbing knives.

Jemmy's conscience could stand silence no longer. She walked to Mississippi Avenue with a shawl wrapped around her face. In Lafayette Park she gave a boy a nickel to take a note to the Police Station at the park's edge.

He shot her a quizzical glance since the station was only a half block away, but he wasn't silly enough to point out that fact to a woman so rich and retarded she would give him a nickel to walk a hundred yards.

Jemmy's note to the police read:

"If you want to find the killer of the girl cut and murdered in the alley last Saturday night, look in room 305 at the Lindell Hotel.
A Well-Wisher"

She slipped back home to hide in the carriage house where she tried to write *the story*—the scoop of her life. She sat rubbing her hands in the morning chill and discovered she had nothing to say. She had spent the better part of two hours with a stone-cold killer and never asked him a single question except, "You're staying at the Lindell Hotel. Am I right?" And that was a question for which she had already guessed the answer.

The only advantage she possessed to set her apart from every other reporter in town was that she knew where to find the action. And she had just been stupid enough to deliberately and willingly give up the single best chance she might ever have to land a newspaper job. With a nose for news like that, she was a lapdog, not a bloodhound.

She transformed herself into Jem the roustabout and raced to the Lindell Hotel. The police were already there—as was Amadé Boudinier and other men with notebooks—all milling about interviewing people. Too late, she had thrown away her big chance at big league journalism.

Doubling her self-disgust, she kicked a lamp post. She had seen boys kick dogs and fences in anger. Afterwards, they always seemed happier, at least for a little while. Looking like a boy gave her license to follow their dim-witted example. Thanks to her disguise, extra socks took the blow instead of her toe. She concluded boys gave themselves almost as much unnecessary pain as she gave herself.

A wildly gesticulating man in a gray tweed overcoat had drawn twenty or more people across the street from the hotel. Jemmy reached the fringe in time to hear him titillate the crowd, "...of course, the police didn't have to beat down the door. The maid had a key.

"And so did the doorman who told a cock-and-bull story about a boy who gave him the key and said the man locked himself inside room three-o-five didn't want to be let out until noon today. Said the man meant to give up drink. I never heard of a man wanting to give up drink—not a married man, anyhow."

When the laughter died down, the speaker lowered his voice and upped the drama. Jemmy strained to hear. He said, "So the police unlocked the door, and what do you think they found?" He looked around at the rapt faces, then boomed out the answer on their upturned heads. "Nothing—the man was gone. Vamoosed out the window and climbed down the fire escape. He never even tried to get out the regular way—through the door—not very hard, anyhow.

"He never pounded on the door or hollered for anyone to let him out. I know, because I would have heard him. I'm in room three-o-six and that's right across the hall."

He rocked back on his heels. "Something horrible happened there yesterday afternoon. My wife said she heard the most terrible smashes and crashes coming from that room. Thought a murder must be going on in there. She was too scared to even peek out the door. Hid in the wardrobe. To get her to come out for supper, I had to promise not to say a word if she drank too much wine."

The crowd nodded their sympathy. One fellow asked, "I hear he stabbed some girl in an alley. That right?"

"Well, a policeman told me persons unknown sent the authorities a note telling them to look in room three-o-five at the Lindell. I'm sure they'd be real eager to speak to that woman. She paid a boy to take the note to the Lafayette Park Station. The boy said he thought she was looney paying him to take the note when she had two good feet of her own. The boy was too simple to see that the woman didn't plan to let the police ask her questions."

The speaker pulled his coat lapel up and ducked his face behind so that only his eyes were showing. "The boy said the woman had red-hair and wore a shawl covering her face." He knitted his eyebrows into a sinister scowl.

139

Before Jemmy took time to consider the fact that the whole city would probably be on the lookout for a red-haired woman, she blurted out, "Did they find any incriminating evidence?" Fortunately, at that moment she happened to be a scraggly, greasy-haired boy instead of a red-haired woman.

The man dropped his coat lapel. "He left behind some clothes the police think might fit the dead girl."

A woman put her hand to her bosom and said, "Lawsy-me. I won't sleep peaceful in my bed knowing there's a knife-murderer on the streets somewhere just waiting to slash my throat in an alley."

The speaker said, "He doesn't just slash throats, he cuts open their bellies, too."

The crowd gave a collective gasp. The soon-to-be-sleepless woman put her other hand to her belly and said, "Lawsy-me, just like Jack the Ripper."

At that, the crowd fidgeted and looked at one another. When no more news came forth, the knot of people unraveled. They broke away muttering and pulling their coats closer about them to hold in what warmth they could on this day that had suddenly made their lives much colder.

Jemmy yearned to stay, but she did not want the doorman to notice the boy who had told him to keep a man locked in three-o-five until noon. She walked several blocks before turning in the direction of the house with blue shutters.

She kept a sharp lookout for Colley and the greasy-haired boy, and breathed a sigh of relief when she arrived at Mrs. Nanny's street without meeting the young toughs.

She took up her usual post in front of the brownstone and hunkered down to wait. The residents nearly caught her deep in thought when they turned the doorknob to leave the house. Only a well-made plan kept her from betraying herself. She dropped down and scrambled under the steps as the feet of two people thundered overhead.

Jack the Ripper in St. Louis

She trembled for a good ten minutes before crawling out to assess her damages. She had barked her middle knuckle even though it was inside a mitten. She had muddied the knees of her pants, and her seat was wet from the damp ground. A ringing sound brought her away from the indignities perpetrated on her person by her precipitous dive under the porch.

Fire bells coming from Delmar Street were growing louder. She looked toward the house with blue shutters and saw dark smoke rising from the middle of the second floor. Mrs. Nanny's bordello was on fire.

First came a repeat scenario of the exodus of customers from the day before. Of course, this time no reformers were chasing the men away. This time, the ouster was more sinister.

Jemmy recognized one of the patrons and shook her head. She muttered to herself, "Peter Ploog. How dare you have the nerve to court me when you spend all your free afternoons at Mrs. Nanny's. I'll bet you're going to the popcorn balling at church tonight, too." She scrunched up her face at the thought of eating a popcorn ball molded by Peter's tainted fingers.

Her disgust mellowed into snickers when she looked at him again. Besides his drawers, he wore only red and white striped stockings that made his legs look like candy canes. Jemmy giggled as snide remarks to use on the sinner slipped into her brain.

Jemmy alternated between laughing over the wit she would use on Peter and fuming that her own need for secrecy wouldn't let her expose him for a cad and fraud.

Sudden inspiration struck her forehead. Out loud she said, "The virgin's fancy man. He started the fire. Who else could it be?"

Jemmy bolted out the gate into the street lest more bodies should come charging out of the brownstone to view the excitement. Up and down the block, heads popped out of doors so residents could see how close the conflagration might come to their rooftops. The heads disappeared only to reappear in minutes wearing hats.

The street began to fill with neighbors come to relish some excitement at the expense of Mrs. Nanny's establishment. Some brought blankets to warm the dispossessed or to beat out sparks if that should be the better use.

Not all brought comfort for the troubled. Less practical or more malicious folks gossiped. One elderly lady grabbed Jemmy by the shoulder and commanded, "Help me, boy." She pointed to the brownstone with her walking stick. "Go in my house and bring out a chair. You don't expect me to stand up, do you? Not with this bad leg."

Jemmy followed orders and emerged with an ornately carved dining room chair of heavy walnut. She set it in the road and received a smack on the shin from the elderly lady's cane for her trouble. "Not there. Carry it down to the fire. And give me your shoulder to lean on."

Jemmy obliged, and the pair limped down the street with folks rushing past on both sides as a second pumper arrived from the direction of Lindell Avenue. The Delmar pumper had a full head of steam and was just beginning to pump water from an iron hydrant a half block away when Jemmy and the elderly lady arrived.

Jemmy planted the chair in the street, but the elderly lady sniffed her dissatisfaction with that location. "Take the chair around to the side. You don't think I can see anything but fire engines from here, do you? Besides, I might get run over in the street."

They walked around the hose cart and into the front yard before the policeman blew his whistle and motioned for them to stay back. Jemmy recognized him as the same tall policeman in mutton-chop whiskers who had rescued her from the ruffians. Jemmy started to escort the lady off the premises whether she wanted to go or not.

Just then, Annie noticed Jemmy and her charge. She threw a dazzling smile at the policeman. He returned the smile and nodded in the direction of the yard next door. Annie came over to help lead the elderly lady while Jemmy carried the chair over to a little knoll where the sight lines were good enough to satisfy even the imperious personage.

Annie smiled at Jem, "I see you found another job."

Jemmy flashed her eyebrows. "Not anything as good as with Mrs. N."

"Why don't you come back then?"

"Mrs. N won't have me on the place. Afraid of what I'll tell the police."

Annie caught the policeman's eye and blew him a thank-you kiss. He winked in reply.

Annie looked toward Mrs. Nanny who was staring at Annie's exchange with the policeman. Her glare warned Annie, "Don't let the policeman catch you talking to that boy."

When Annie started to go back to the others, Jemmy took her arm and said, "He started the fire, didn't he? The virgin's fancy man?"

"I don't know, maybe. Everything is such a mess."

Annie walked back to the knot of girls. Mrs. Nanny stood straight and began a spiel. No doubt she was telling the whole group not to talk to Jem lest the police should become curious about him.

Jemmy wanted in the worst way to talk to the girls. For the second day in a row they were without a single customer amongst the whole batch of them. But, Mrs. Nanny knew best. Jemmy wanted to avoid police questioning. Not on account of revealing what she knew about the murder, but fear that she would be unmasked. If that happened, everyone would revile her—from the females at Mrs. Nanny's to the females in her own family.

The second floor hall window shot up to reveal a rotund man wearing nothing but a faded red union suit unbuttoned halfway down the front. His eyes sought about frantically for a way to get down. He spotted two firemen unstrapping a telescoping ladder from the side of the pumper and yelled to them. "Hurry up with that ladder. She's chasing me with a—"

Just then something unseen straightened his back and brought his head up with a start. He finished his sentence. "...chamber pot."

Chivalry be damned. The man had his foot on the ladder even before the fireman locked the brace. No chamber-pot wielding woman was going to beat him to safety. He paid no attention to the warnings of the firemen, much to his dismay.

The firemen, in order to keep him off the ladder until they set the locks, had pulled it away from the house—unfortunately—with the man still on it. Fortunately—the ladder feet sank into the water-softened ground so it stayed more-or-less upright.

The resulting scene looked like a performance by circus clowns. The upper ladder slid to the ground with its passenger barely clinging to the outer rails. With his precarious toehold gone from the crossbars, he plummeted down as various parts of his anatomy hit rungs on the way.

By sounds, his paunch took the worst of the punishment as his rolls of fat slapped themselves against every rod of wood all the way down. By looks, his nose suffered the most damage. Blood flowed freely. It plopped in red blotches on the union suit from his twisted schnoz. His only garment looked like a vat of calamine lotion with roses painted on. But neither the flapped flab of his belly nor his painful proboscis seemed to bother him half as much as his soggy behind.

He shook his fist up at the girl coughing in the smoke-filled window. "You had no call to do that. I wasn't on fire, and you know it."

Between her coughs, she tossed him an obscene gesture, "You monster, you. You nearly killed me. You wouldn't stop even when I promised you two free ones. I couldn't breathe in that smoke. Now you know what it's like. Now you can't catch a decent breath either."

The crowd exploded in laughter.

The firemen pulled the ladder from the mud and set it against the house.

This time, they set the locks and one climbed up to rescue Fifi, alias Lord Murphy, with a fireman's carry down the ladder.

The audience applauded when the fireman set Lord Murphy on terra firma. She coughed as she made a curtsy in her yellow silk kimono with a blue cat embroidered on the back. She presented the fireman to the spectators like a girl changing the signs in a vaudeville show. The fireman bowed from the waist.

The girls welcomed Lord Murphy to their ranks with a warm blanket. The crowd turned cold shoulders to her rotund customer. In his soaked union suit he had to be feeling the bite of winter, yet not a one of the neighbors offered a blanket to warm his soggy backside.

At last, a fireman took the remnants of a moth-eaten blanket from under the seat of the pumper and handed it to his rotundity. "It's Boomer's, I'm afraid." He pointed to the company's mascot, a sad-eyed red-bone hound. The man threw it round his shoulders and soon became preoccupied with picking Boomer's hairs out of his mouth.

Jemmy was reminded of her petty place in the scheme of things by a smack on her rump from the elderly lady's cane and the words, "Get out of my way, you lummox. I can't see through you."

Like a footman on call, Jemmy took up a position behind the lady's chair. The firemen quenched the fire in minutes and began back-slapping to congratulate each other on a job well done. Mrs. Nanny sandwiched the Fire Captain's hand between her two hands in a gesture of gratitude.

The captain beamed as he announced loudly that the thanks should go to his men—and to the city fathers who were replacing the old wooden fire hydrants with new iron ones. He looked around at the spectators and said even louder, "Iron hydrants give us all the water we need—much easier to pump to upper floors in fires like this one on the second story."

Some firemen were unbuttoning their fire shields from the triangle of buttons on their shirts. Others were laying out the rubbered canvas hose into the ditch while two men cranked the hose reel to bleed out the water. The entire fire-quenching process seemed to be satisfactorily concluded until Mrs. Nanny re-entered her house and screamed so loudly Jemmy's elderly lady nearly fell out of her chair from shock.

Mrs. Nanny came storming out shrieking that everything in her parlor had been ruined by water. "I can dry out the carpets, but the brocade drapes—the piano—ruined—all ruined."

The captain said, "Now there, the piano will dry out, too—probably only need a bit of tuning. Anyway—better to lose one piano than a whole house."

Mr. Nanny said, "It's not so bad as all that. At last you're getting some good out of all those fire premiums you've been paying."

That calmed Mrs. N. She squared her shoulders and addressed her troops. "We'd best get busy, girls. We have a mess to clean up. Carpets to bring outside. I think they'll dry all right as long as it doesn't snow again."

Like a lieutenant urging stragglers forward with the flat of his saber, Mrs. Nanny shooed her brigade inside with peacock feather and ledger book. She turned to Mr. Nanny and asked, "What was the name of that company who fixed the roof last year? I wonder whether they can send someone out today. We can't go through the winter with sleet falling on the beds."

The elderly lady told Jemmy to fetch her chair back home because the excitement was over. Jemmy longed to stay, but duty called.

She toted the chair back to the brownstone with the elderly lady keeping herself upright by leaning on Jemmy's shoulder. She replaced the walnut chair in the dining room, then helped the old lady up the steps and onto the settee by the fire in the parlor.

The old lady said, "Stir up the fire a bit and put on another log."

Jemmy complied. "Go out to the kitchen and draw a kettle of water from the boiler and make tea. You'll find butter and gooseberry jam in the icebox. There may be a few raisin cookies, too."

Jemmy fretted that she could not get away from this testy, irksome, demanding old crone. Still, she had been brought up to obey her elders, so she found herself making tea and rolling it on a teacart to the old lady who was all cozy by the parlor fire.

"Why didn't you bring a cup for yourself?"

"I didn't think I was supposed to, Ma'am."

"You deserve a reward for your assistance. You may have as much bread and jam as you can eat."

"Yes, Ma'am." Jemmy would have much preferred a more metallic and less edible reward. But, she did as she was told.

When she had returned to the fire with a cup and plate, the elderly lady asked, "What do you know about the house that was on fire?"

Jemmy stammered, "M-M-Me, I don't know anything."

"Of course, you do. You know at least one of the girls. Remember? I'm sure she came to talk with you, not to help me."

"You must be mistaken. I don't know her."

"Come now. I know better."

Jemmy jammed a whole slice of toast with gooseberry jam into her mouth and slurped tea after it. Through the wad of food she offered gestures suggesting that she had to leave post haste because she had just noticed the late hour.

She was out the front door and tripping down the steps before she realized that the pair who had caused her to dive under the porch were coming through the front gate.

She tried to wipe the sticky jam off her mouth with the back of her hand. The man chuckled, "I see Mother has impressed you into joining her for tea."

147

Jemmy nodded.

The man nodded, too. He said, "Let me guess. You ran an errand for her, but she didn't pay you—except in bread and jam."

Jemmy nodded.

"So, tell me what you did for her."

"She leaned on me while I toted a chair down to the house with the fire. Then we came back."

"It was good of you to stay with her. I know she can be difficult." He reached out his coin purse and handed Jemmy a fifty cent piece. "Thank you, young man. I'm sure my mother is grateful, too. She doesn't have much understanding of the fact that a young fellow like yourself needs a few coins to rub together."

Jemmy nodded and started to walk around them to leave by the gate.

The man stopped her and pressed another fifty cent piece into her hand, "By the way. If you should find yourself performing additional services for my mother, please do as she wishes. Then come see me."

As Jemmy walked out into the road, then took off in a dead run—with Colley and the greasy-haired boy right after.

Chapter Fourteen

Jemmy gave a fleeting thought to seeking refuge in the brownstone, but decided to take her chances on foot. She came close to regretting that choice when she imagined she could feel hot breath on the back of her neck.

Gasping for breath and slowing down, she remembered her hand still clutched two fifty cent pieces. She wheeled and threw the coins as far as her strength would take them. The clinking sound of their colliding with each other drew off her chasers in a frantic scramble. Each tried to beat the other to the prize. She said to herself, "It was worth a dollar to see this."

Colley and the greasy-haired boy reached the coins locked at the hip like contestants in a sack race. As each tried to push his rival away from the prize, the twosome tumbled into a rolling wrestle in the street.

Jemmy didn't wait for the tussle to cool down. Ignorant of the fact that the scene was being watched by an unseen pair of eyes, she took off toward Delmar at a solid, but not panic-driven, trot. Had she known the name of the one who was gazing as she outwitted her pursuers, she would have had far more reason for panic than Colley or his pal could ever cause.

Back home and dressed in a nearly-new green plaid, she tried not to think back on the fire and the disappearing fancy man. She half-listened as Mother asked the sisters to hold up the items they were expected to take to the popcorn balling.

"Jemmy, I expect you to show some gratitude to your sister. Merry spent all afternoon popping corn in the big kettle. She was kind enough to pop your jar as well as her own. All her own idea, too."

When no words, kind—unkind—or any kind at all fell from Jemmy's lips, Mother ordered. "*Jemmy*. Stop daydreaming and tell your sister you appreciate her popping your corn."

Jemmy smiled at Merry. "Of course, Merry. You were most kind to pop my corn. I don't deserve such a sweet sister." She looked at the smirking face of Miranda and said most pointedly, "I know Randy could never be accused of having her own idea when it comes to helping me."

As Mother named each requisite item, all four girls held up their crockery for inspection. "Large bowl and big spoon." In a boarding house, large bowls and big spoons are in good supply.

"Four quarts popped corn. Remember now, that is enough for two batches—only half the corn at a time."

Four hands presented four cornflower-printed flour sacks half-full of popped corn. The sisters settled bags and spoons inside the bowls.

"Show me your aprons."

Three hands held up three aprons. Jemmy had none. She said, "I don't need one, Mother. I'm quite neat."

Her sisters tittered. Jemmy's protestation of neatness caused much mirth. Mother cast Jemmy an exasperated look. "You don't need an apron like a two month old doesn't need a breech-cloth." Giggling, Gerta handed Jemmy an old fashioned pinafore.

"Do I have to wear that?"

Mother sighed. "It seems to be the only thing available. Minerva washed and ironed hers and persuaded the others to do the same. Unlike you, they have their own clean aprons."

"I don't think it's fair that I have to do every little thing. I have a job that keeps me away from home and these pleasant little chores."

"You're not being penalized for working. You're simply being reminded that if you don't do your chores, you have no right to expect anyone else to do them for you.

"Get your wraps, girls. We must be on time. Your Aunt Delilah expects us to set a good example."

The five McBustle females were off in a rush with Randy chattering on about the looks of various boys from church. When she arrived at "Jemmy's own particular beau—that dreamy Peter Ploog," Jemmy could stand no more. "The day I fall for a Ploog is the day I'll bring you breakfast in bed and not even consider slipping a fried egg down your back."

In the church basement, a half-dozen mothers were busy stirring water and vinegar into molasses, sugar, and salt. A half-dozen others were stirring big pots with long-handled wooden spoons.

Aunt Delilah directed the flood of young people to their stations. The Sunday School classes sat together at long tables. For a change, they would be allowed to talk to each other—and not just about Jesus either. This evening was designed for wholesome interaction and socialization of the offspring—as much as for preparing goodies for Saturday.

Jemmy's group was the oldest—unmarried upper teens—who had balled many an orb of molasses and popcorn before. Adults relied upon them to model proper behavior for the younger ones.

Before Mother could notice that she was not wearing her ugly pinafore, Jemmy rushed to be the first in line. Once she had buttered hands, not even Mother could expect her to tie on a pinafore, could she?

Jemmy poured half the popped corn from her flour sack into her big bowl and began walking toward the molasses mix bubbling on the stove. The instant she arrived, a pair of hands supported the bowl from the other side—hands that belonged to none other than Peter Ploog. She returned a pinched smile in exchange for his winsome grin.

The captain of the molasses mothers said, "Now hold the bowl up to the rim of the pot—and keep your thumbs outside unless you want burned fingers." She poured four dippers of the bubbling treacle over the popcorn.

As Peter took the bowl and nodded toward their table, he said, "May I?"

Jemmy swished to their table and began to stir the molasses to coat the corn before it cooled. When she stopped stirring, Peter swiped his hand into the butter. When Jemmy didn't follow suit, he used his unbuttered hand to grab hers and stick it inside his buttered one. When he tried to fetch her other hand in the same way, Jemmy flung it up and out of his reach.

Clearly, this was a game Peter relished. He clung tightly to her one trapped hand as he lunged at her free one. The result was disaster. His elbow tipped the bowl of molasses corn all over Jemmy's almost new green-plaid dress.

A cataract of popcorn spilled down the plaid and stuck there like ocean foam washing dirty sheep onto the shore. Jemmy yanked her hand out of Peter's buttered one and began batting at the corn sticking to her skirts. The procedure worked not quite as she had hoped.

Some of the kernels did fall. Jemmy stepped in them—crunching them underfoot and causing them to stick to her shoes.

Randy was the first to notice her sister's predicament and to laugh and point—which brought the whole room to its feet roaring in delight because they themselves were not the current objects of derision. Peter, gallant that he was, bit his lip to keep from laughing and tried to help Jemmy beat off the sticky wads of corn.

Jemmy did not appreciate his kindly gesture the way one might have had reason to hope. She grabbed a double handful of the corn and settled it like a crown on Peter's head. Peter took his coronation like a king. He laughed out loud and waved the wooden spoon scepter-like to bless the multitudes.

Bested in every way, Jemmy turned on her heel to stomp off and promptly slipped on the single dollop of dropped butter. She abandoned her dignity as she slid down sideways on one hip. Peter hastened to rescue her. She yanked at his arm and tried her best to bring him down, too; but only managed to make him slide a bit.

When he succeeded in hoisting her to her feet, the crowd applauded. One voice yelled out, "Hail to the prince of the popcorn balls! Hail to Peter Ploog!"

Another voice—Randy, of course—yelled out even louder, "And hail to Jemima McBustle—the popcorn princess!"

Jemmy took a step and would have fallen again but for Ploog's supporting arm. She would have stomped out the door and all the way home had it not been for Mother—who did not share the general glee. She stood tapping her foot and pointing to the mess.

Jemmy and Peter knew what she meant. He managed to return the tainted corn to the bowl and dump it in the trash. Jemmy set about cleaning the table and benches with a pan of soapy water and a half-dozen huck towels.

By the time she had fetched the mop from the broom closet, Peter was on his hands and knees to dry the floor. She took a most unladylike pleasure in flipping mop rags in his face. He dodged most of them. To his credit, he never stopped smiling.

At length, everything returned to normal except the prince and princess of popcorn. Jemmy tried to pat down her dress. The green plaid grabbed her hand. Peter tried to pull it free and butter it. Jemmy brought her other hand round to slap him. He caught it and buttered it instead.

Every movement of the pair infuriated Mother more. "Jemima McBustle! Stop that shameful exhibition. Go home at once and soak the molasses out of that dress before it is hopelessly stained."

Jemmy threw off Peter's hands and shook out the ugly pinafore. She put it on with great ceremony.

Peter smirked, "A bit late for preventing spills on your gown, isn't it?"

"I don't want to get molasses on my cloak."

"Very sensible, Miss Jemima. I approve." Peter made a slight bow and said, "May I have the privilege of walking you home? One never knows what ruffians might be lurking about the streets."

Mother said, "Quite unnecessary, Mr. Ploog. You should see to your own attire. I'm sure Jemima's uncle will escort her. We wouldn't want to compromise her reputation, now would we?"

"No, indeed, Mrs. McBustle. However, since I feel much to blame for these unfortunate events, I wish to offer my humble apology. Would Mr. McBustle object to my walking along?"

Jemmy muttered under her breath, "I'd rather be drowning in beer."

Mother asked, "What did you say, Jemima?"

"I said, Uncle is frowning I fear."

Not until she felt the weight of her cloak on her shoulders did she realize that Uncle Erwin was behind her. He said, "Nonsense, my dear. I would be more than happy to take you home in my carriage." To Peter, he said, "And I'd be happy to have you accompany us. After we see Miss McBustle safely home, I'll take you round to your house."

And so the three trooped out the door and into Uncle Erwin's carriage. The silver bud vases on the door frames held holly in honor of the Christmas season. Peter whispered to Jemmy, "I wish those were mistletoe."

Jack the Ripper in St. Louis

With the words, "I'm so glad you reminded me." Jemmy ground her heel on his toe. "I wouldn't want to risk your displeasure. I try never to miss-a-toe."

Peter cringed, but offered no resistance. When Uncle had given orders to the coachman and settled in beside Jemmy, he said, "You two must be quite fond of each other to get involved in such hijinks in front of the whole Sunday School."

Peter said, "May I say that I have the greatest admiration and the tenderest regard for your niece. I do but hope it may be reciprocated in the smallest measure."

Jemmy said, "Even a monkey may hope, I suppose."

Peter said, "I'd gladly be a monkey if you were my cage keeper."

Jemmy tossed him an arch look. "I do not plan to take up organ grinding as an occupation."

Peter's repartee didn't extend far enough to answer that—at least not with anything other than an obscene rhyme—which he most certainly dared not offer.

Uncle said, "Would being a street performer be so much lower than being a stunt reporter, Jemima? Duncan tells me you have aspirations in that direction."

Jemmy was startled that her uncle had knowledge of her wanting to be a reporter."

"Perhaps you'd consider a different sort of career—one that doesn't require you to spend time begging strangers for coins on the street or ringing strangers' doorbells to beg for stories."

"Why Uncle, you're surely not suggesting I should take up an occupation where I'm likely to see just any man's red and white striped stockings."

Peter gave a little start and lowered his head to contemplate Jemmy's cryptic words.

Uncle Erwin scratched his head. "No. Marriage is what I had in mind, not garment factory work."

Jemmy said brightly, "Well, home at last."

Uncle Erwin told Peter to remain in the carriage while he escorted Jemmy to the door. He said, "You know, young Mr. Ploog seems quite smitten with you. He is well-situated to become a scion of St. Louis society."

"So cousin Duncan tells me."

"But there are other young men if he's not to your liking."

"Uncle, before I look for a young man to my liking, I think I need to find a young Jemima to my liking."

Uncle Erwin smiled, patted her hand and closed the screen door after her. "I'm sure you'll find both the Jemima and the young man. I recommend you take ample time for both." Jemmy watched the carriage move away along the gaslit street.

As she put her green plaid in a bucket of cold water to soak overnight, she wondered why the house with blue shutters kept drawing her back. Would she ever find a story in it? What kind of coward was she to be idling away every day when a murderer was on the loose? What would Nellie do? And how, oh how, would she chase away the sights and sounds—Grandma naked in Bromschwig's basement—Annie's bloody back—the body of the virgin in the alley, and "You and me and Dr. T"?

Chapter Fifteen

Jemmy didn't let her misgivings keep her from returning to haunt the street of the house with blue shutters. She thought long and hard, then concluded that she just plain didn't have any better idea. The fancy man wouldn't go back to the Lindell Hotel, but he might come back to Nanny's to finish venting his spite.

When she arrived at her spying post in front of the brownstone, roofers were already pulling up damaged shingles at Mrs. N's. A wagonload of lumber set at the ready to replace the burnt boards. After a few minutes, Annie and Mrs. Nanny appeared at the door. They spoke with a fellow who must have been the foreman. He nodded, and the women set off toward Delmar.

Jemmy followed at a discreet distance. But only after looking around most carefully for the pair of ruffians who seemed to get their jollies by attacking her—regardless of whether she happened to be a male or female. None lurking about—not this time.

When the pair of women queued up for the downtown trolley, Jemmy crossed the street. She kept the line of horses and buggies between the streetcar and herself as she ran to keep up. She panted, hands resting on knees as the women waited for a southbound car on the Seventh Street line. Jemmy dogged them to their stop at Chestnut. She leaned with one foot back against a brick building as she waited for them to emerge from the brand new Lincoln Trust Building.

After a half-hour or so, Annie came out alone and began walking back toward Delmar. Jemmy dodged the horses and wagons as she crossed the street. Annie looked more than pleased to see young Jem.

"Jem, look at this." From a large manila envelope she pulled a certificate with ornate letters vouching that the four story building on the northwest corner of Olive and 20th Streets belonged with no "liens or encumbrances" to one Annette Jerome Milton.

Annie bubbled and beamed. "Look at it Jem. Clear title to my own building. I only hope I can make a success of the hat business."

"I thought you would have to wait a year or more—until you had the money."

"I finally got a break, Jem—two breaks. A windfall of money I never expected and tenants for both my apartments."

"That's wonderful. What happened?"

"Peter Ploog set the house on fire." Annie shocked herself, "Oops! I should be calling him Mr. P."

It was Jemmy's turn to look shocked. "So it wasn't the virgin's man?"

"No. Mr. P took a notion to smoke Egyptian tobacco for the first time. The minute he inhaled, he coughed so hard he kicked over the hookah. The hookah hit the floor—right under the bed curtains. Hindoo Hannah was already too far gone to do anything but laugh. They both just stood there and giggled while the bed went up in flames.

"The smoke finally sobered them up enough to open the door and call for help. Mrs. N called the fire department. Mr. N started a bucket brigade with kitchen pots and chamber pots with water from the bathroom and from the kitchen tap and from the big boiler and from the rain barrel. He and the customers put out the inside flames by the time the fireman came. The fire department had an easy time of snuffing out the burning shingles on the roof.

"Mrs. N was in a fair rage that Mr. P set her house on fire. She read him out proper and said she'd have the law on him. Mr. P begged her not to do that. He said he'd pay for all the repairs to house and furniture, too.

"Mrs. N would have none of it. Said it wasn't just the repairs, but also the lost work and the lost income for herself and the girls. He said he'd pay for that too and asked how much it would cost. Mrs. Nanny said nothing less than a thousand dollars for herself and five hundred dollars for every girl in the place except Hindoo who deserved what she got.

"Mr. P didn't even argue. He said he'd give her thirty-five hundred dollars right away and would pay her back for the repairs when all the receipts were in. This very morning he brought the money."

Jemmy said, "I didn't think another five hundred dollars would be enough for you to own the shop."

"That's the best part. Mrs. N is closing the house and giving everyone a bonus. After the repairs, she's going to sell the place and move to Kentucky—two years sooner than she had meant to. She's planning to live the respectable life as a rich widow.

"You should see her. Giddy as a new bride to set up a virtuous household. Her son will be out of school in two years and ready to establish himself as a legitimate businessman. I imagine Mrs. N's cool head and business experience will stand him in good stead, don't you?"

"So Mrs. Nanny is selling a going concern. That should make her even richer."

"No, she says she's an honest businesswoman who wouldn't recommend anyone to keep a sportin' house anymore. What with the city officials cracking down because the reformers won't let them alone.

"She said the reformers singing hymns on the front stoop spelled the end of her place. The neighbors might tolerate her as long as she caused no fuss—but with reformers about, the kind of clients she wanted would stop coming. At very least, she'd have to move to a different neighborhood—and keep on moving whenever the reformers caught up to her. She swears she'd starve before she'd keep a low-class cat house."

"So what will happen to the girls?"

"That's the best part. Two of them are setting up for themselves and renting out my third floor."

Annie took exception to Jemmy's arch look. "Yes, I know I said I meant to have respectable renters, but factory girls and laundresses can't afford apartments like these—with indoor plumbing. Besides, I know plenty of respectable landlords who not only rent to their sort—they charge them twice the rate they'd charge anybody else. I would never do that. I will charge them exactly what the flat is worth."

Jemmy said, "You don't have to explain..."

Annie continued her tale in a rush. "Fifi is advancing her five hundred dollars from Mr. P which will pay their rent for two years—and means that I am now a property owner. And don't worry that Hannah is going to burn the place down. She already sold her hookah."

"And you still have another flat to let on the fourth floor."

"But I've rented that, too—at least for the rest of the winter. Dr. T and his boy have paid up to the end of March. That gives me enough money to buy buckram and feathers and ribbon to make hats. If I work hard, I'll have the shop open at least a few days before Christmas. Think of it. My first sale."

Annie beamed with anticipation as she said, "Come work for me, Jem."

"What?"

"I need a boy to work. I want to open for business on Monday—in three days. I don't have a moment to lose if I'm to catch any buyers before Christmas. I can't be painting walls, oiling floors, cleaning glass. I've got to make signs and get advertisements printed. You can paint, can't you, Jem? I mean every boy has dipped a brush in a can of paint, right?"

"Well, I..."

"I'll pay you three dollars a day—while the work is hard. Now that's as much as I would pay a professional painter. And later, maybe you can work for the girls. Who knows, you might make more than with Mrs. N."

Jemmy didn't see how she would get out of it so she nodded and said, "Thank you, Miss Annie. I'd consider it a privilege to paint your walls."

Annie cocked her head as if she had another thought. "And you know what? You can live in the apartment with me. I have two bedrooms—only one bed though. Mrs. N is letting me buy the items from my room cheap. But I can make you a pallet on the floor. What am I saying? My bed is big enough for two—two at the very least."

She wagged an admonishing index finger and giggled. "No hanky panky though."

In a serious vein, she laid a light hand on Jemmy's shoulder. "Wouldn't working for me be better than what you're used to?"

"Thank you kindly, ma'am. But I have a place to sleep."

Almost before Jemmy knew it, Annie was unlocking the door of the shop on Olive Street. The shop boasted three tall front windows—soaped on the inside to fend off nosy stares.

Near the solid wall set a long counter with a glass front to display wares. On top, a wrought iron reel for wrapping paper was bolted to one end, and a handsome brass cash-register anchored the other.

The last owner had been a purveyor of boots and shoes. Tiers of shelves behind the counter would show off hats with even greater panache.

161

The former tenants must have left in a hurry—perhaps to stay one step ahead of a process-server. Behind black linen portieres separating the shop from the workroom in the back, they had left a work table and a squat black safe with yellow filigree round the door. A bit of paper stuck between the hinges kept the door from closing.

Annie said, "I'll write to the maker to ask for the combination. I'm not sure they'll give it to me. A safe would be a nice thing to have. I'd like to be able to put my deed in it.

"I'm going round to the hardware store and will be back with cleaning things. You can make a start on the trash. They must have thrown all these receipts and bits of paper around. Looks like a cyclone hit. Well, I can't complain. They left chairs and a good many things I can use."

As she walked out the door, Annie said. "When you finish here, go up the outside stairs to the apartments. Here's a key to each." She broke the string holding a batch of keys and handed the ones with 'back door' tags to Jemmy.

Jemmy took off her greatcoat and began piling together the papers and bits of leather spilling from the safe. She idly looked at them—unpaid bills for tacks and a leather knife. One scrap of yellowed paper caught her eye. She opened it up to find a series of numbers with dashes between—maybe the safe combination. She tucked it in her vest pocket.

She tossed the larger items outside in the trash barrel and set about exploring the upper reaches of Annie's empire. The apartment on the second floor reeked. Jemmy gagged as she kicked food tins of half-eaten and fully rotten sardines and potted ham into a pile. She breathed the foul air through her mouth as she folded the cans into yellowed newspapers.

Plentiful evidence suggested that rodents had enjoyed a better lifestyle than humans in this domicile. Jemmy saw neglect and abuse everywhere—cracked plaster on the dividing walls, iron stains around the sink. Their place had not so much as a stove for cooking or heating. Jemmy was still hauling junk out back when Annie met her at the trash barrel.

Jemmy said, "I haven't been above the second floor, but I've gotten the worst of the stuff from there."

Annie said, "Well. Let's brave the third and fourth. The Doctor wants to move in tomorrow and the girls have only until Mrs. N's house repairs are finished before they will be here too."

They climbed the stairs and opened the third floor door with trepidation. To their great relief, the place was utterly bare—and bone clean. Annie said, "Too much trouble to walk up here, I guess."

The top floor was equally clean and spare. Both could use a coat of paint on the plaster dividing walls, but Annie declared that clean windows and oiled floors would have to do for the time being. She said, "Thank heavens all the outer walls are brick and will never need painting."

The pair set to work on the Doctor's apartment and had it looking quite presentable by suppertime. The arched windows sparkled and the floor and woodwork smelled of linseed oil and vinegar.

On the streetcar home, the hackles on the back of Jemmy's neck kept warning her that someone was watching. She snapped back her head more than once, but could see nothing definite. Once she spun back just as a boy rounded a corner. It might have been Colley or the greasy-haired boy. The only way to know for sure was to run after. Jemmy had neither the inclination nor the energy for that.

That night, she fell in bed and, for once, had no nightmares. She slept the dreamless sleep of the world's overworked and underpaid.

Chapter Sixteen

The next morning, despite the aches of a few muscles newly brought into use, Jemmy was back at Annie's shop early. In an unusual fit of foresight, Jemmy had dug up a faded flannel shirt of Father's to keep varnish off her only suit of clothes.

Annie must have been working late into the night to clean the second floor apartment. Today Mr. N would be bringing her furniture. He had even turned up a secondhand ice box to keep outside on the back stair landing.

Annie went off to buy shellac and left Jemmy oiling the apartment floor.

Jemmy wondered whether she would have the strength to help Mr. N bring up the heavy furniture. She needn't have worried. Mr. N brought his own assistant—none other than the virgin's fancy man. The pair of them made short work of setting up the heavy bedstead and installing the cookstove on its iron plate.

Jemmy noted that bandy-legs had a slight limp—a lingering souvenir of their set-to at the Lindell. She wondered whether he might have been sober enough to recognize the boy who escorted him back to the hotel—and whether he remembered who had locked him in, smashed his water pitcher, and caused him to stab himself in the foot.

From the third floor window, Jemmy watched them leave. Mr. N gave bandy-legs some money. The man looked up at Jemmy, pulled his hat down over his brow and left. Something about that look left an unsettled feeling in Jemmy's stomach—as if she had swallowed a safety pin and was stewing over whether it might open to stab her in the gullet. She tried to dismiss it. After all, Peter Ploog was the one who set the fire. He said so himself and was paying a not-so-small fortune to keep it quiet.

Jemmy didn't look up from her work again. She finished oiling the floor and toted the tools downstairs to the back of the shop. She set about sweeping the shop floor.

She heard a key turn in the shop door lock. Annie arrived like a drum major leading a parade. Behind her came a delivery man from the hardware store wheeling a barrow with shellac, plaster, brushes, ladder, and canvas drop cloths. Jemmy felt that unsettled feeling in her stomach once more when she saw who was bringing up the rear—the virgin's fancy man.

Annie said, "Look, Jem. Everything is going right for me today. I have another pair of hands. Isn't it a stroke of luck that he was leaving just as I returned. I know the three of us will finish today so the shellac has a whole day to dry." She turned to the man emptying the wheelbarrow. "That will be enough drying time, won't it?"

"Yes, ma'am. Even in cold weather, should be good and dry come Monday morning."

Annie donned a loose smock which already boasted a few dozen stains.

The fancy man did just the opposite. Even though the room was cold enough to show vapor clouds of breath, he peeled off his outer clothes until he stood in boots, white undershirt and pants. He slapped his biceps and said, "A person who works hard enough doesn't feel the cold." He pointed up at the embossed floral patterns on the tin ceiling tiles which someone had unaccountably painted red. "You want me to start on the ceiling?"

Annie said, "Yes. White paint will make this shop much brighter, don't you think? I want you to paint while Jem shellacs the counter and woodwork."

Throughout the rest of the day, the fancy man worked with great energy and a fair amount of skill. Whenever he finished a section, he asked Annie whether she could find any spot he had missed. During these breaks he never missed an opportunity to flex his muscles while he paid her a compliment or told a joke.

At lunchtime, Dr. T and his boy surprised Annie with eight roast beef sandwiches and beer from the tavern. When Annie asked who else was coming since the group totaled only five, he pointed to his two greyhounds. "And the greyhounds make seven."

He used a long bladed pocket knife to cut the string from the package of brown paper wrapped sandwiches. "But even if I had no dogs, I'd still buy eight. Eight is my lucky number."

He looked straight at Jemmy as he said, "A person is doomed to failure who doesn't appreciate having a lucky number. And everyone must know his unlucky number and beware. Why, some people don't even know they have one of each. They are the unluckiest—and the most foolish—of all."

Jemmy vowed to consider which were her lucky and unlucky numbers just as soon as she could find a spare hour or two to think on it.

The Doctor sent the Nipper back for ginger beer for Annie and her painters. When bandy-legs made a face, she said, "I'll have only sobersides working in my place."

The three grownups sat around the Doctor's round oak table newly moved to the fourth floor. The Doctor told a story which held his little audience too spellbound to eat.

He looked straight at Jemmy with eyes that skewered her to her seat. He began with the visit of Charles Dickens to St. Louis in 1842. "I hope the ghost of Mr. Dickens comes a-haunting to St. Louis. He'd find the place much changed and much more to his liking. The only thing about St. Louis he had a kind word for was the luxury and comfort of the Planter's House Hotel—not the one at Fourth and Pine now, the old one that burned in '87.

"I feel a close kinship with the great writer. Like me he was a poor boy who made good, an idealist whose illusions of love were shattered, a man sometimes embraced and sometimes persecuted by society. Of course we hated different countries and for different reasons. I abhor England as much as he ever despised the United States.

"He and I share the same fascination with death. Have you noticed that every one of his stories is most profoundly about death?

"Well, why not? Life is profoundly about death, isn't it?" The Doctor looked around at the three pairs of wide eyes for confirmation and found it. Even well-brought-up middle class Jemima McBustle forgot the great social taboo. No person of refinement should ever speak of death during mealtime—bad for the digestion.

Eyes fixed in the beyond of the past, he continued. "One true story held special intrigue for Mr. Dickens—the story of Sir John Franklin and his aptly named ships, the *Erebus* and the *Terror*. How delicious those names. How accurate the prophecy—face the terror of the ice—then the darkness of perpetual purgatory.

"Like many an explorer, Sir Franklin tried to find the fabled Northwest Passage. Think of the fame, the riches for anyone who could link Europe and the Orient in trade by water. Now we know that he was right. He proved a good captain can sail around Greenland and thread his way among the northern islands to the Arctic Ocean. Still, ice doomed his quest—as it can today whenever it chooses.

"The *Erebus* and the *Terror* were last sighted in July of 1845 at the

Entrance of Lancaster Sound, north of Canada.

"Three years later the British Admiralty offered a ten-thousand pound reward for news. Three years after that, Inuit hunters told Dr. Rae of Hudson's Bay Company they had seen white men dragging a boat southward along the shore of King William's Island."

The Doctor's voice turned shrill and thrilling. "Imagine it—men pulling a boat. What must they have thought as they tried to pull a mammoth ship through ice with their frozen fingers? Can you feel the ache in the back, the slip of leaden feet on ice under two inches of frigid water?"

The Doctor struggled to gain control of his quavering voice as he went on with the tale, "Rae traded with the Indians for things the white men had given them. When family members of the crew saw those poor bits of clay pipe and the salt-soaked letters, they wept. White bone and cheap souvenirs were all they had left of the men they cherished.

"When *The London News* printed Dr. Rae's story, all of England whispered the word 'cannibal.' Mr. Dickens wrote his article to refute any notion that English gentlemen could ever be so crude as to eat the host upon finding the larder bare.

"But did Dickens believe his own words? I don't think so. I believe the specter of that doomed expedition festered in his mind. Why else would he and Wilkie Collins write that play, *The Frozen Deep*, set where Parry conquered and Franklin died?"

The Doctor pointed out the irony that seemed to follow Franklin, "Fifteen years and forty expeditions after he set out, Captain Franklin's fate came to light. Captain McClintock of the *Fox* solved the mystery. He found the log of the *Terror* and the crew's skulls and bones at—where else?—Point Victory.

"Franklin's men had abandoned the two ships. What could they do? The hulls were frozen solid in the ice. Franklin was already dead. Eaten? I don't think so. The bones would have shown marks from the butchering. Do you know why the expedition failed?" A sly grin stole across the Doctor's face. "Too much food—8,000 tins of food. Food canned in a rush and badly sealed with lead solder. Franklin killed his men with poisoned food. He killed them with kindness.

"Mr. Dickens lost interest in the story when he discovered the truth. I feel much the same way—though I do wish I had one of Captain Franklin's bones—a femur would be nice, I think—to show when I tell this story."

The Doctor cocked his head to the side as if listening to unseen critics. He leaned closer to Jemmy—so close she could feel his moist breath on her face and smell the beer on his tongue as he rasped in a lower voice. "I even have the same high regard for money as Mr. Dickens.

"Do you want to know a secret? Shall I tell the real reason why Mr. Dickens had not a single good word to say for Americans? Money—old Dickie Bird loved money—just as much as Americans loved his stories— which they enjoyed without paying him a single penny—all quite legal, mind you. Even ten years ago American publishers could steal anything they wanted from foreigners. Now, I guess the United States is joining the world of nations. How commonplace. I much prefer a country to be a bit of a rogue."

He leaned back in his chair in apparent satisfaction with the effect of his story. He chided them in a good-natured way. "But you're not eating your sandwiches. I hope you don't fear food poisoning. The tavern keeper told me his wife prepared the beef fresh this morning—cooked it herself—no lead solder."

The grownups let go their pent-up breath in a rush of chatter and praise over the tavern keeper's wife's roast beef. Bandy-legs said, "That's quite a story." He looked around for appreciation of his oh-so-clever remark.

Annie ignored him. She shuddered, "Freezing to death or eating poisoned food. Either way is a horrible death."

The Doctor looked at Jemmy and said, "Freezing was a risk they freely took, but poison—they didn't deserve to die by poison—too uncivilized even when it's accidental. If I were a murderer, I would leave poisoning to women. I'd send my chosen ones to the nether world with grace and dispatch."

Jemmy shivered, but not because she was cold. Nipper returned with the ginger beer to sit next to Jemmy on the coal bin by the cookstove. After ten minutes or so, Jemmy felt warm for the first time all day.

The boy broke into to her thoughts. "How would you like to make a mint with just a half day's work?"

The Doctor's boy struck Jemmy as being very different from the furtive and hostile person she thought she knew. Today he was all smiles and joshing—despite the fact that he had just come back from an errand he probably resented.

Jemmy said, "I'm working for Miss Annie."

"It's only a half day—tomorrow—Sunday. She don't make you work on Sunday, do she?"

"I don't know."

"Ask her then."

Jemmy raised her voice as she looked up toward the grown-ups table. "Miss Annie, do you need me to work tomorrow?"

Annie considered it, then said. "I'm sure I can finish oiling the floors today. If we get the ceiling and plaster painted, and wood shellacked. We can't do anything else until it dries. So, chances are, I won't need you until Monday."

Jemmy turned back to the Doctor's boy.

"What's the job?"

"Rat race."

"What's a rat race?"

"Boys go down to the big warehouses—you know—the ones along the

170

riverfront on the other side of Market Street. 'Bout this time of year, the owners figure all the rats have gone inside and are just waiting to eat their way through the grain and such. So the owners set up the rat race.

"They pay five cents for each dead one and three cents for each live one. They have a grand supper afterwards—of baked ham—not rats." He nudged Jemmy in the side for a reaction to his wit. When Jemmy edged over with a start, he went on. "They give bonuses, too—an extra ten dollars for each thousand rats. Every boy on the winning team gets a big bag of oranges to boot.

"Last year the warehouse boys won. I'm on the errand-boys team." The boy leaned over to Jemmy's ear. "This year, I have a plan. I know how to get more rats than you can count."

"Tell, then."

"Huh-uh. But I'll show you tomorrow. That is, if you want to be my partner. My plan takes two."

Jemmy was intrigued. Uncle Erwin owned several warehouses, but he had never mentioned a rat race. She asked, "What do they do with the live ones?"

"Search me. I don't kiss 'em; I just catch 'em. Are you in?"

Jemmy nodded. "Where and when?"

"Second and Chouteau at one o'clock."

"My name's Jem."

"The Doc calls me Nipper."

They shook hands to seal the partnership. And so Jemmy volunteered to enter the rat race. Who knows? There might be a story in it.

As the three of them descended from the fourth floor to return to work in the shop, bandy-legs uttered the most outrageous statement yet. "Miss Annie, I'd be much obliged if you would allow me to escort you to church in the morning."

171

Annie said, "I'm not planning on attending services in the morning. It's true that sinners like us need to do serious penitence, but mine will have to wait until after my shop is open for business."

Jemmy thought Annie's words had a hidden meaning. They didn't dissuade bandy-legs, though. He kept up the charm. Nothing could induce him to put on his shirt—not coming back to the chill after eating nor working after the coal man delivered fuel for the shop stove.

By now, Jemmy was pretty sure the fancy man was wasting his time. Sure, Annie was a fine catch—and a terrific replacement meal ticket. True, she was not the virgin type, but a woman with a fine build and a fine building would give a fancy man good security—the kind of security that meant he would never have to do another day's honest work in his life—as if he had ever done an honest day's work.

Jemmy thought him truly insane if he believed Annie would hand over the future she had won by pain and heartbreak. Still, Annie needed to be very wary of this man—this murderer. Who knows what he might do if thwarted? Jemmy looked for an opportunity to warn Annie that she believed he had already killed one girl.

Jemmy had to do something. She couldn't just drag Annie out the door to chat. The hour grew later as Jemmy became more desperate. Very well, if she couldn't think of a way to get Annie to leave, maybe she could think of a way to get bandy-legs to leave.

When Annie's back was turned, and the fancy man was just placing his paint bucket on the fold-down platform atop the ladder; Jemmy pretended to stumble as she threw her weight against the ladder. She sidestepped fast enough to elude the paint which plopped harmlessly on the canvas drop-cloth, but bandy-legs was too busy trying to keep the ladder upright to protect himself. The paint slopped down one arm. Most ended up in his curly underarm hair which now resembled bayberry bushes after an ice storm.

Jack the Ripper in St. Louis

"Look what you did, you..." Looking at Annie kept him from adding what, no doubt, would have been unpleasant words. Instead, he held his right hand aloft and climbed down the ladder.

Annie handed him some rags. "Take the turpentine out back. Bandy-legs strode off mumbling.

"Jem, clean up the mess you made on the drop-cloth. We don't need anyone stepping in it and making white footprints all over the floor.

While Jemmy was sopping up the white paint, she said, "Annie, I'm scared of him. He killed the virgin. I know it."

"If you know he killed her, then you must go tell the police."

"I have no real proof, but I know it. I saw blood on the money. He had the virgin's money—after she was dead—with gobs of her blood on it—so much blood I don't see how any bank would take it."

"Maybe he took the money after she was dead. Did you think of that? If he took it from her before...it wouldn't have gobs of blood on it, would it?"

Annie's stubbornness reduced Jemmy to pleading. "Please, get him out of here. I couldn't stand it if he killed you, too."

Annie gave a sad smile. "You don't think I've lived this long with his kind without being cautious, do you? I've thought he might be the killer."

Annie pulled a pepperbox pistol from her apron. "You're sweet to worry about me, but I know how to take care of myself." She held out the der-ringer, showing it off with pride. "Like the virgin's. That's where I got the idea, but this one is better. Five barrels—five shots. Surely I could manage to hit something important by bullet number five."

Jemmy bit her tongue to keep from remembering that she had stood by in silence while Mrs. Nanny deprived the virgin of her defenses. Her stomach knotted in the knowledge that she had no excuse to stay longer than bandy-legs. She had finished all the woodwork, shelves and counter. He still had the short wall around the portieres to paint.

Her dismay and fear must have registered on her face. Annie said, "Don't give it another thought. Get on out of here before he comes back. After all the gray hair you gave him, I think he's more apt to come after you than to try to kill me."

Annie propelled Jem into father's greatcoat and out the front door. Jemmy pulled the safe combination from her vest pocket and tucked it into Annie's hand. She took Annie's wrist with the other and looked into her eyes. "Please."

Annie shook her off. "Really, now. Don't worry. I'll see you Monday morning—bright and early. And thank you for this—it must be the safe combination. I'll try it out." Annie waved and closed the door. She became nothing more than a dark movement on the soap-frosted front windows.

Jemmy lingered a while, caught in a limbo between responsibility for allowing a killer to remain on the loose and fear that Jem's artificial world might come tumbling down on poor Jemmy's real-life head.

She toyed with the idea of marching back in the shop and taking Annie up on her offer to sleep in her bed; but this night of all nights, she had to go home. Mother was still suspicious of the last time she had failed to return home. Uncle Erwin had returned from Kansas City two days earlier. His backlog of work was the only dam keeping all her lies from bursting forth to drown her.

This night of all nights, she would not be excused. This was the Saturday night of the Great Pageant. Her camel awaited.

Chapter Seventeen

Jemmy had stayed too long at Annie's. By the time she reached the carriage house behind Bricktop and changed back into a girl, she had missed dinner. As she came up the front steps, Mother opened the door with the words, "You're about to miss the lighting of the Star of the East."

Mother shooed the dilatory daughter into her own bedroom behind the kitchen and helped peel off clothes. While shoving an arm into its Arabian robe, Mother touched a spot still sticky with drying shellac and asked, "What on earth is that?"

Jemmy mumbled, "Honey. We had bread and honey for tea."

Mother ignored the fact that honey doesn't belong on an arm as she said, "So the old lady has afternoon tea, does she? Well, I'm glad you ate something not long ago. You have no time for so much as an apple. We shall have to run to reach the church by seven-thirty.

"But first you must put on this head scarf thing and these bands." Mother held up a checked cloth and some coarse ties of braided horse tail strands. "Oh, leave it. We don't even know how to put it on. Fussing over it will make us late for sure. But you must remember to wear it—and for modesty's sake be sure to cover up the back of your neck."

As Holy Angels' bell rang the half hour, Mother and Jemmy hit the bottom stair in the basement of Lafayette Presbyterian. Aunt Delilah cast a critical eye in Jemmy's direction and waved her back up the stairs. "Albion Street—at the alley—go."

Soon, Jemmy found herself under the gaslight looking up at an animal that seemed at least two stories high. Strangers' arms grabbed her around the middle to fasten the buckle of a leather belt. A boy in a fez prodded the shaggy beast's knees with a rod and the creature folded itself onto the ground. Jemmy puzzled over what the Doctor's boy could be doing here. To her relief, the boy turned around so she could see that this was a different boy entirely.

The strange arms now shoved her toward the beast, then boosted her onto a pillowed platform with four sideposts and a canopy atop the dromedary's back. She could now see the fellow who seemed to have more arms than an octopus as he hooked straps from the four corners of the roofed platform to metal rings on the leather belt. He said, "No way you can fall off now." Little did Jemmy know just how right he was.

As the camel lumbered to its feet, Jemmy panicked, "But I don't know how to ride this thing."

Octopus hands reassured her. "You don't have to do a thing. The boy here will lead her. All you have to do is enjoy the ride—and don't unhook until the boy has her lying down on the ground." As they took off, he yelled after, "Hold the straps on the front of the howdah. That'll keep you from getting seasick."

Jemmy tried to make her checked cloth and horsehair bands look like the headgear on the camel drover, but she dropped the bands. A sort of turban was the best she could do. She could hear the strains of "O Come, All

Jack the Ripper in St. Louis

Ye Faithful" as boy and camel with unnerved passenger atop ran to catch up with the two lead camels. Peter Ploog and Cousin Duncan were already well down Missouri Avenue. Jemmy lurched wildly from side to side as the camel ran, not in the four-legged trot of a horse, but seesaw fashion with both legs on one side at a time.

Jemmy wrapped her hands around the straps attached to the front of the platform and prayed for the ordeal to be over. She wished the camel drover had not mentioned sea sickness. Before the threesome even rounded the corner onto Park Avenue, Jemmy was thanking her personal angel that she hadn't eaten anything since roast beef sandwiches at lunch.

By the time the new fez boy stopped the beast at the park entrance to await their cue, Jemmy was casting her head about to decide which way to direct the flow. Salt water bubbled into her mouth like sour lava. Only the fact that her stomach was completely vacant kept it from spasms of seismic proportions.

As the camel stood motionless, Jemmy began to regain her equilibrium. She became conscious of lowered voices from the riders in front. Apparently, Duncan reveled in the newfound power of riding an exotic beast in the shape of a gigantic teapot with six-foot-high legs. He said, "Wouldn't my new lady have a thrill to see me in charge of this animal? Better yet, to ride it with my arms around her?"

Peter said, "Do you think I could persuade Miss Jemmy to join me on this one?"

"I saw her face—chartreuse. I doubt you'd get her up on your camel once she gets down from her dromedary."

Jemmy piped up, "I resent your discussing me as if I weren't here."

Peter said, "I was hoping for a more agreeable answer if I gave you time to think."

Duncan chimed in, "Where's your sense of adventure? I thought Jemima

McBustle was always first in line when it came to breaking rules—or is that only when you get to personally choose which rules to break?"

"What are you planning? Stealing three valuable camels that Aunt Delilah, your own sweet and gentle mother, went to great lengths to bring here for the most important pageant of the season?"

At the words "sweet and gentle" both Duncan and Peter chuckled into their glove leather. When Duncan's laugh subsided, he said, "Pete and I just want to get our money's worth by taking these doozies for a little joyride. That's all."

"Don't you mean you want to get Uncle Erwin's money's worth? What are you thinking, anyway? You're sitting up there discussing stealing camels when the camel herders are standing right below you." She said the word "stealing" loudly enough to turn all three fezzes on all three drovers.

"Cousin, dear, you're always so literal. You never know when I'm making a joke. Of course we're not planning to steal the camels."

Just then the choir took up the carol "While Shepherds Watch Their Flocks," the signal for the triple trio to move into the park. They lumbered to the edge of the crowd in order to be ready the moment the choir started "We Three Kings of Orient Are."

But Jemmy never heard anything past, "We three..." Her first intimation of impending disaster came when she felt her howdah slip. While she tried to pull herself and the ungainly structure back up the camel's back, she felt another slip. Then the whole platform with Jemmy chained to it slid slowly down and under the camel's belly.

Jemmy screeched a medium-loud "Aagh" as she found herself upside down and dangling from the underside of a camel. As she toppled, she knew she was leaving her stomach all by itself in the rider's seat. Under the beast's belly she thought she caught a glimpse of Bunks Bappel in the dim light, though she wasn't sure since he was upside down.

As might be predicted, the startled beast did not care to be ridden from underneath. The camel jerked the reins from her herder, knocking him down in the process. The animal then set off at a bone-jarring run.

It didn't take Jemmy long to discover that the only way she became sea sick faster than by lurching wildly from side to side on a camel's back was lurching wildly from side to side dangling under a camel's belly.

With maddening helplessness, Jemmy remembered that the Lafayette Street side of the park had a sizable gap in the wrought iron fence—a gap filled with yew hedges. The beast was heading toward that very spot.

Jemmy wrapped her arms even harder around the straps attached to the front of the platform and tried to pull herself closer to the wiry hairs on the camel's scraggly belly. Pungent camel smell gagged her and brought her as near to a faint as she had ever been. She could hear galumphing hooves on the path and stifled shrieks and grunts of spectators trying to avoid being trampled.

From behind, she could hear even more hoof-thunder drawing closer. She heard Peter's voice call out "Whoa."

Duncan yelled, "That's not the right word."

"What is the right word?"

"Ball—ball something."

"Balli?"

"That's it."

"That can't be it. That's what the head camel man kept saying to your mother. I think it means 'yes.'"

"Well, try to catch up to the head."

"I don't see anything to grab onto."

"There's a rope dangling from the head. I can't reach it."

"I can't either."

"Try to get the camel between us to slow it down."

That seemed to be working. At least they all slowed down from a gallop to a trot to a clop. Jemmy could tell when they left the park path for Lafayette Avenue by the camel's splayed out feet shooting up clods of icy mud to choke her and make her sling prison even less pleasant—something she had not thought possible.

The other two had nearly brought the renegade under control when the three camel boys caught up. With as much noise directed at the riders as to the camels, the boys brought the animals to a halt.

Jemmy felt a flood of relief to be brought to safety without being hedge-battered, but that feeling was fleeting. The minute the camel stopped moving, it sent out a back foot to scrape the nuisance named Jemmy off its middle. It missed the first time. It kicked higher with a remarkably flexible foot that got hopelessly hooked in the howdah. This brought the animal sprawling and braying as it collapsed on its side.

By the sheerest of chance, the beast fell in the ruts of the road instead of atop its underbelly rider. Jemmy fumbled to unhook herself, but Houdini himself could not have escaped what happened next. The camel's amazingly flexible head poked squarely into Jemmy's howdah and bellowed an ear-splitting roar into the back of her neck. Accompanying the bellow was a gigantic glob of the substance all mammals have in their mouths.

The glob sopped Jemmy's uncovered neck. It glued the turban and silken robes to her neck hair and reached all the way around to her ear on the right side. Now it was Jemmy's turn to howl.

She tugged loose the last hook and crawled out of her prison with the support of the sturdy arms of Peter Ploog. Both he and Duncan busied themselves beating the globs off her Arabian robes while trying their darndest not to succumb to gales of laughter.

Jemmy stood motionless, shoulders upraised and head tucked down into her neck as far as it would go. Her face wore an expression of horror.

Jack the Ripper in St. Louis

It's to his credit that Peter delayed not a second, but unwound his sash and began the task of sputum removal. When he had done his best, he looked as apologetic as he could under the circumstances. "You'd need a bath to get the rest off. Let me take you home." He motioned for her to stay put. "Stay right here. I'll get our coach."

Jemmy grabbed his arm. Between clenched teeth, she said. "I'm supposed to take a gift to the baby Jesus and come spit or come shine I mean to do exactly that. Where's my gold?"

Duncan said, "I heard it fall on the path before the camel spooked. We'd never find it in the dark—not in time, anyway."

Jemmy held out her hands. "Give me all the coins you have."

The boys pulled up their burnooses and fished a few nickels and dimes from their pockets. Jemmy tied them in her handkerchief and said to the boy in the fez, "Well, what are you waiting for? Get that platform off my camel."

The boy looked at Duncan for guidance. Duncan nodded. As the boy pulled away the useless girth strap, he said, "Somebody cut this on purpose, you know. When I cinched it up, it was fine—not even frayed."

With the platform off, the camel wore nothing but a single strap just behind its front feet. Jemmy climbed astride and said in a masterful voice, "Get her up. We have presents to deliver." Jemmy's camel was up before the other two and she set off leading the way.

Despite the racket of galloping camels running clean by their planned stopping place, the choir had soldiered on. The director had sent a runner to find out whether to expect a return of the wise men in minutes, hours or not at all. When the runner returned, pointing at the oncoming camels, the choir kept right on repeating verses and choruses. In the middle of the choir's ninth rendition of the song, the wise ones appeared.

Jemmy didn't wait for the camel to kneel. She swung her leg over and eased herself within two or three feet of the ground and dropped the rest of the way where she waited for her companion kings to get their feet on terra firma. With gold, frankincense and myrrh properly presented, the pageant could, at last, proceed to its grand finale.

Relieved to be singing a song shorter than an oratorio, the choir led the spectators off to the cookies, molasses popcorn balls and hot cider as thousands of voices joined in singing "Joy to the World."

Aunt Delilah bustled about dousing the players with effusive congratulations—at least until she reached the woebegone Magi.

Jemmy expected a tongue-lashing or at least a dressing down for being a "girl whom Aunt Delilah should have known better than to trust to ride a foreign beast in the first place."

Duncan wouldn't let her utter a single syllable. He leaped in with, "Mother, no one deserves more congratulations than Cousin Jemima. Even after the camel ran away, she got right back up and insisted that we go on with the show."

To Jemmy Auntie said, "My dear, are you unhurt? I am to blame for hiring those beasts. Do forgive me."

"It wasn't your fault, Aunt Delilah. The cinch was deliberately cut."

"Was it Carmen Dale of the Pageant Committee? She opposed every improvement I suggested."

"It was Bunks Bappel. I saw him when I slid under the camel."

Aunt Delilah waxed angry. "I'll have the law on that good-for-nothing. You could have been killed. You don't suppose he resented you because I replaced him as camel director—after the problems at rehearsal."

Jemmy said, "I didn't know you dropped him from the pageant. Maybe he was embarrassed."

Duncan said, "Didn't you know, Mother? Bunks has been mooney-eyed for Cousin Jemima ever since she kicked him in the shin because his dog dug up Aunt Belinda's hydrangea bush."

All this came as news to Jemmy—not that Bunks might be interested in her. She had sometimes caught him looking at her with the same look he gave watermelons in July. But why would he take a hard kick in the shin as an act of endearment? Jemmy concluded she didn't know much about men. She said, "That's ridiculous, cousin. A kick in the shin is not a love pat."

"To Bunks, maybe it is."

For the next three-quarters of an hour, Jemmy refused to pay attention to her soggy neck. She would not go home because of a silly little inconvenience despite all urgings that she "...really should if she didn't want to catch her death."

Jemmy tried to ignore the clammy feeling at the back of her neck as she stood in the receiving line. Even as ice crystals formed to send little pricks of steel digging into her flesh, she kept up the smiling as young people came to say how awestruck they were by her daring.

Riding a camel bareback gave her new status with youngsters. Of course, their parents were less enthusiastic. They wasted no time in telling her that such shenanigans might be forgiven of hooligan boys—but girls were supposed to know better.

She warmed herself by drinking hot cider. Still, she felt a rush of gratitude when Mother entrusted the other girls to Uncle Erwin and escorted Jemmy home. Mother even heated water so Jemmy wouldn't have to bathe in cold water. Of course, being a mother, she wasn't above lecturing her eldest, "I told you to wear that checked thing on your head. Maybe next time, you'll listen to your mother."

Warm at last in a flannel nightgown, Jemmy floated off to sleep without remembering a single haunting phrase or vision. She even managed a flickering smile as she recalled Aunt Delilah's parting words. "Next year, I'll use elephants."

Jemmy was pretty sure that elephants didn't spit. Still, her brain echoed a cautionary note.

"Camels? One lump or two?"

Chapter Eighteen

Randy shook Jemmy awake. Still in a dream of camels, she mumbled, "What time is it?"

"Breakfast time, then church time, then Sunday dinner time."

Jemmy moaned and slumped back on the pillow. "Don't I deserve a little extra sleep after nearly getting killed by a camel last night?"

"The fact that you didn't die last night means Mother is dead set that we all must go to church. If it were up to Miranda Ranunculus McBustle, I'd prefer to let you sleep yourself all the way to that hot place most people wish to avoid—and I don't mean Chicago."

"Ranunculus. That's a good one. We could call you Uncle Randy. Even better—Runny Randy. Runny Randy the uncle. Good choice."

Randy walked off in a huff saying, "I still like the meaning of ranunculus." She turned back to spit the words at Jemmy. "It means, 'I am dazzled by your charms.'"

Jemmy yelled after her as she slammed the door. "It's a good thing you're dazzled by your own charms. From all reports, they seem to have no effect at all on anyone else."

At Lafayette Park Presbyterian, Jemmy could not keep her mind on Joseph's tax troubles or Mary's Bethlehem-bound trip on a donkey. She didn't even have to work to hide her face from the stares and snickers of the grownups who had seen the events of Saturday night's festivities—that included just about everybody.

The minister said a prayer of thanksgiving that no one had been injured. Peter Ploog offered smiles and solicitude. Cousin Duncan joked, "Remind me never to share the stage with you again. You're a born scene-stealer."

Jemmy put her nose in the air in an effort to rise above the slings and arrows of outrageous camels. She would rather tromp through a trough of spit than let any one know a beast got the best of Jemima McBustle.

The other reason why the congregation failed to faze her was that she kept seeing faces—the camel boy in the fez who turned out to be a stranger, the virgin's fancy man with white paint down his armpit leering at Annie, a girl in a cold basement sewing skin together in a dark line down Grandmother's belly.

Not until Sunday dinner wash-up did she remember she had a promise to keep to another boy in a fez. She barely had time to change into Jem before she was off to the races—the rat races. Her body, aching from unused muscles recently forced into service, protested even the short walk to the streetcar stop.

When she arrived at Second and Chouteau, she barely recognized the boy in the fez. He wasn't wearing one. Instead of his usual flamboyant get up, he looked more-or-less normal in brown brogans and newsboy's cap. He wore a plaid flannel shirt under a black suit that was a bit too small.

He looked relieved. "I thought you might not come."

Jemmy flashed her palms up as she said, "Here I am. I hope you're the pied piper of Pestalozzi Street so I don't have to do much running. I'm stiff and sore from a little run-in I had with a camel."

The boy's eyebrows shot up as he hoisted a clanking gunny sack over his shoulder. "Camel? Does St. Louis have a zoo I don't know about?"

"No, this camel was especially hired for..." Jemmy realized that her lowered energy had already resulted in a lowered I.Q. She hoped she had not given away too much.

She backpedaled "...catching rats—by drowning them in camel spit. But I couldn't get the beast to spit at anything but me—not even with a bribe of a plug of chew from the Weisert Tobacco Company."

By now Nipper was laughing at Jemmy's far-fetched story. They were both laughing when they rounded the corner and saw hundreds of boys lining both sides of the street. The boys joked and jostled as they played mock combat with baseball bats, spade handles, brooms and assorted cudgels. Men collected the lads into groups of twenty or more and told them the location of the warehouse they were to cleanse of vermin.

When all the groups knew their targets, a man with a thin line of a mustache announced the rules through a fire captain's brass megaphone. "No one is to start until your team's target warehouse is called. We will allow transit time both ways for the teams who have the farthest to go. We have pre-determined times to give fair allowance to all.

"The closing bugle will sound at 4:30 PM sharp. After that time, there won't be much light to see by anyway. Be back here by five o'clock for the final tally. Anyone not here by that time will be disqualified from all prizes and will not receive a supper chit. I'm sure that everyone who has been in the race before knows how fine a spread we put on at the Turnverein Hall. All you can eat plus leftovers to take home—if you hungry lads leave any.

"In addition to the supper, you will earn for your team to share and share alike three cents for each dead rat..." He shook an admonishing finger, "...and five cents for each one you bring in alive. The two teams, the courier cats and the wharf rats, will also receive a bonus of ten dollars per thousand rats.

"This year, because we have so many rat catchers, we will be giving a dozen oranges to each boy in every crew of twenty that catches at least five hundred rats.

"And, we have another treat that's new this year. We will name one boy as rat king. Yes, the boy who brings in the largest number of rats, dead or alive, will become the Rat King of St. Louis and wear this crown for a year." Amidst hoots of derision, he held up a tin crown with a stuffed rat atop.

"But don't think honor alone is the reward of being Rat King. The Rat King will win a permanent job which lasts a full year. The job will, of course, be rodenticide—as befits the Rat King's area of special expertise. And the pay will be three dollars per day—as much as a skilled workman earns."

Appreciative whistles went up at this. Every boy would start the Rat Race with his eye on the prize. Of course, Jemmy did not; but then, Jemmy was a girl.

The rat master continued his spiel. "At each building, you will find the tallyman's wagon at the main entrance. Take your rats there. The tallymen will also have a good supply of sacks and twine. For any other tools, you're on your own.

"All rewards will be announced and given out at the Turner Hall." The speaker's eyes made a majestic sweep of the crowd. "So, what do you say, boys? Are you ready to declare war on the St. Louis riverfront rats?"

The boys sent up a resounding, "Yes!"

The speaker announced the first group to go—Jemmy's own. She had not even noticed that Nipper had pushed, and wormed, and edged their way into the group slated to go to the most distant warehouse. She wondered how he managed—and why. She watched as Nipper grabbed a sack and the two set out for the warehouse along with the other teams.

Jack the Ripper in St. Louis

As their breath made little puffs of steam while they jogged along in the chilly air, she asked, "Why did we want to go to the place that uses up the most shoe leather?"

Nipper said, "You'll see."

"You were wrong about the rats. They want live rats—not dead ones."

"We'll just have to be careful not to kill them, then, won't we."

Jemmy had too little breath to ask any more questions. When they arrived at the Wunderlich Flour Warehouse, she stopped and gasped for air with her hands on her knees. Nipper yanked her inside the building and downstairs. The place smelled of wheat straw and dust. Only a few narrow aisles allowed passage among the flower-printed sacks piled heavenward in wooden stanchions.

Jemmy and Nipper had beaten all but five or six of the other racers. Nipper staked out a territory on the bottom floor where Wunderlich stored whole grain waiting to be ground.

Nipper unrolled screen wire from his clanking sack to create a barrier in a likely looking corner. He handed Jemmy a shovel and a wooden spoon. He said, "Go to the middle and beat and holler. When I yell 'come,' you get back here on the double to help me clobber 'em."

Jemmy nodded and followed orders—up to a point. When she returned, she saw Nipper bashing and smashing with his shovel inside the screen-wire barricade. She stood mute in fascinated horror as the creatures squealed during their last tortured moments.

Nipper hollered an impatient, "What's the matter with you? You're letting them get away. Do your share before I come after *you* with *this*." He waved the back of his bloody shovel in Jemmy's direction and spattered her with flecks of blood and gray hair matted with gore.

At that Jemmy awoke with a start. She smacked her shovel on the floor and clipped a tail. The shock sent her target rat into a tizzy. It circled behind her, then lost the direction of safety and crawled over her shoe. From that moment on, Jemmy became a rat-killing machine. She kicked off that audacious rat and bashed it mightily when it fell. She slammed after escapees with the fury of demonic possession.

As he scooped their gruesome loot into the gunny sack that Jemmy held, Nipper said, "You're not too quick on the draw, but once you start duelling, you're a shooting fool."

Flushed with kill-fever, Jemmy said, "What now?"

"We have another gunny sack to fill. This time, we'll set up the wire in the center aisle. You go all the way to the far wall and scare them to me."

Their second pass would have netted far fewer rodent corpses had it not been for Jemmy's frenetic rush to kill rats seeking to escape execution. Jemmy was all excitement as they dragged their catch to the tallyman's wagon. "Did you see that fat brownish one? It splattered blood on my trousers 'most up to my knees. And look at your shoes. There is blood all over them."

Nipper stuck two fingers in the red ooze seeping through his gunny sack and pointed his bloody index finger at Jemmy's face. Jemmy ducked back in surprise. Nipper said, "War paint—like the Indians. Bathe in the blood of the enemies you slew."

Jemmy laughed and dipped her own fingers in the gore—then challenged Nipper's finger to a duel. While the tallymen weighed and counted the rats, the pair sparred until Jemmy managed to plant a daub of the red stuff on Nipper's cheek. "Touché ."

Nipper bowed ceremoniously as he said, "I yield to the knight of the rats."

When the tallyman asked what name to attach to each gunny sack, Nipper held his head higher, "Jem and Nipper—share and share alike."

Nipper took twine and four more gunny sacks. Back inside the warehouse he headed not for the basement, but for a side window. The pair slipped out.

Nipper said, "Now you'll see my pied piper secret. Look all around—and keep looking all the way. We don't want anyone to follow us and find out what we're up to."

Jemmy had no notion of what to expect, so she kept a good lookout and followed through the empty Sunday streets along the riverfront.

She followed Nipper south until he turned east and headed for the Mississippi. The hard packed mud was rutted with hoofprints and icy puddles that made for slow going.

After a time, Nipper stopped at the foot of a rocky embankment and began to scrape away sand and caked mud from a spot in the ground. Before long Jemmy could see a wooden manhole cover in a round metal frame. The hatch was secured with an iron crossbar pulled through two pairs of iron handles. The remains of a hinge clung to the bar on one end. The padlock that had once secured the other end from would-be thieves had disappeared.

Nipper pulled the metal bar from the handles with much scraping and flaking of orange-red dust. The cover lifted to reveal a rusty iron ladder straight down.

Jemmy stated the obvious, "That's not a warehouse."

"It was once, sort of, a warehouse for beer—caves to store it and keep it cool. They don't use this one any more on account of floods. Too close to the river."

"You expect me to go into a flooded cave?"

"It's December, and we haven't had a big snow yet—or any rain for a couple of weeks. The cave probably won't be flooded again until the snow melts upriver in the spring."

"Maybe we'd get caught when the tide comes in."

Nipper snorted in derision as he tossed the iron bar into the cave with a clatter and thump. "You dumb dick. This is a *river*—no tide on a river."

Nipper climbed down the stairs calling, "Wait until I light the lamp. Then come down. And pull the trap shut when you come."

Jemmy took a deep breath and descended. Pulling the lid down brought a rain of sand and little clods of dirt on Grandpa's cap. With real alarm she said, "The ceiling is falling down on my head."

Nipper said, "Cave's been here a thousand years, a million maybe. Take an earthquake to bring down the ceiling. Don't be a pansy."

She said no more, but looked at a pile of rubble which seemed to say Nipper didn't know as much about caves as he seemed to think. Her stomach sank lower with every step down. She could think of no easy way to get out of this hole.

At the bottom, she turned to see Nipper holding a coal oil lantern waist high. The dusty rays sent shadows the wrong way round on his face. His chin and nose blazed with light while his lips looked black. His eyes became no more than glints in dark holes. Jemmy fancied that he might be a ghoul when he said, "Watch the water."

She looked down to see that she had one foot in a rivulet which sloped downward toward the far wall. She hadn't even noticed that one foot was wet or that she had backed as far away from Nipper as the cave would let her.

Jemmy picked up the soggy foot and kicked off drops that sprayed the side wall. Nipper held the lantern higher to reveal a cave carved by water from sandstone zigzagged with red-orange veins of iron. The cave was not large—perhaps twenty feet wide. Jemmy could stand up straight, but Nipper had to stoop when he walked.

He put his finger to his lips when Jemmy started to say something. "Shhhh—hear them?"

Jemmy could hear them all right. The scrabbling claws and squeals of rats magnified a thousand times as they echoed off the hard rock.

He turned to lead the way as he said in a hushed voice. "Try to keep your feet out of the stream. The splash might spook them."

Jemmy walked gingerly along the water. She slipped in the gooey clay and wishing she really did have a job as companion to an elderly invalid—a job that would keep her warm, safe and dry on cold Sunday afternoons.

Jemmy carried both shovels and the gunny sacks as Nipper led the way to a crumbling brick wall. He stooped down to a hole he had to squeeze through and held out his hand for a shovel and a wooden beating spoon.

As he backed through the opening, he took the lantern. He said in a low voice, "When I start banging the rats your way, hold a gunny sack over this hole. When one sack is full, gather up the neck and put your foot on it, but get a new sack over the hole first. I want to bring 'em all back alive."

"But you're taking the lantern. How can I see what I'm doing?"

"I've got to take the lantern. I got to go back two more rooms—can't do that in the dark, now can I?"

Jemmy gave a little shudder. "But, won't the rats bite me?"

"I been bit, lots of times. Didn't kill me, did it?"

Jemmy knelt down to the hole and watched it zigzag into a smaller patch of light until it disappeared altogether into the far recesses of the cave. Before long she could no longer hear Nipper's brogans scraping along the rocks dislodging pebbles that clacked together like a game of marbles.

She was in a cold blackness so total and so suffocating that a thousand yards of black executioner's hoods could not so utterly swath her in dread and foreboding. She thought about skedaddling up that iron ladder. Her legs were just about to head in that direction when she heard banging and hollering from the deep recesses of the cave.

She took a deep breath and set her jaw. "After we catch these rats, I have a few questions for the Nipper. He's going to tell me what happened to Grandma, and why."

Even so, she very nearly bolted when she heard the frantic scrabbling and squealing of hundreds of rats aiming themselves in her direction. She gritted her teeth as the first creatures raced into her gunny sack. She was ready for the noise and for the roiling movements in the sack. What took her unawares was the smell.

The rats in the warehouse were grain eaters, but these rats were not half so fastidious. The stink of dung, decay and rotting meat came close to making her retch. When she closed off her nose to the stench, she had to open her mouth to the poisoned air.

She came near to passing out. She might have given way but for the fact that her sack was full and a rat came clawing its way over her hand. She clamped the bag shut without remembering Nipper's admonition to put a new bag over the hole before removing the first. She let out a screech between her clenched teeth as rats poured over her ankles. But she finally got her foot on the mouth of the old bag and opened the new bag across the hole.

The third try went smoother. Still, a goodly number of rats got by her. She felt as if ten baths with lye soap would never make her clean from this putrid job and this filthy cave.

At length, the rats came in lesser numbers then stopped altogether. She tried to keep her jaw and the sacks clamped shut while counting the minutes, the seconds, until Nipper returned to tie the bags.

When he did return, she scarcely noticed. He said, "Only two-and-a-half bags, huh? I thought sure we would have three or four. Oh, well, I bet it's way more live ones than most boys will get."

He began using twine to tie off the necks of the gunny sacks. He started with the two sacks Jemmy clamped shut with her feet. She used her free hand to rub her sore calf muscles. Jemmy had such a death grip on the last one, the half bag, she didn't notice that Nipper had tied it off and that he had looped twine around Jemmy's own wrist.

That is, she didn't notice until he yanked the loop at the same time as he pulled her other hand from massaging her leg. He neatly tied the two hands together behind her back as if she were a steer in a calf-tying contest.

She found herself with the wind knocked out as he shoved her over a boulder and proceeded to truss her feet to her hands. By the time she realized her peril, she was helpless as a gnat stuck in flypaper.

Chapter Nineteen

Nipper placed the lamp on a ledge above Jemmy's face then moved back into the dark. She could barely make out his form as he sat on a rock with his arms around one leg while he smoked a cigarette. He chuckled. The more Jemmy struggled against the layers of twine, the more he chuckled. Jemmy stopped struggling.

Nipper tortured Jemmy with this story. "Big Nose George Parrott was a thief and a rustler in Wyoming. 'Bout twenty years ago he killed two deputies while robbing a train. It took the vigilance committee a couple of years; but the good men of Rawlins, Wyoming finally got their man. Rawlins had a sheriff—but no judge. The circuit rider wouldn't be along for some time. So they saved the county the expense of another mouth to feed. They hanged old George off a telegraph pole.

"Now, none of that seems unusual—not in the days of lawlessness in the old wild west. It's what happened to Big Nose after he died that's worth tellin'. The vigilantes gave his body to Dr. John Osborne. And Dr. Osborne had plans for old Parrott that would bring old Big Nose more fame in death than his life as an outlaw ever did.

"The Doctor sawed off the top of old George's skull and used it for an ashtray. He soaked the old sinner's carcass in salt water, then skinned it like you would a rabbit. He sent the skin to Denver to be tanned and made into leather goods. The chest—with nipples still on if he had his druthers—made into a doctor's bag and the thigh skin into a pair of shoes.

"The upstandin' tanners and leather workers of Denver said not a word about how right or fittin' it might be to make shoes out of a man's skin, but some things are just too much to stomach. They sent him a doctor's bag all right—but without nipples.

"Dr. Osborne was uncommon proud of those shoes. I know because I was in Wyoming in '93 when he ran for governor. I had nothing better to do so I went to hear him stump. He pointed to those shoes—funny looking things—like regular shoes in the back—but pale colored in the front.

"I'll never forget it." He said, 'I wear shoes made of thief-hide.' Then he stamped his foot. 'Every one of you can now bear witness to the fact that John Osborne takes a tough stand on crime.'"

Nipper laughed at his own joke, if laugh you could call it. It sounded like a horse's neigh crossed with an eagle scream. He emerged from the darkness still laughing and poked his face near Jemmy's to deliver his punch line. "If you ask me, Parrott-skin shoes made Dr. John Osborne governor of Wyoming.

"Doctors is funny folk as I have good reason to know. You're funny folk, too. No screamin'. Not even talkin'. I thought by now you'd have asked me a hundred times or more why I tied you up."

Jemmy looked in his direction in what she hoped was a penetrating way. "I can guess—you want all the rat money for yourself. But I would like to know why you told that ridiculous and disgusting Parrott lie."

"God's own truth. I swear."

"I don't believe you."

"Believe what you want, but that's a true story, and Osborne isn't the only doctor that's funny folk as I have good reason to know."

Jemmy heaved a sigh as if from boredom. "It's obvious you want me to ask you why doctors are funny folk. So, Nipper, please. Do tell me why doctors are funny folk."

"Well, my doctor is sure funny folk." He paused.

"Do tell. In me, you have a captive audience."

"Well, I'm not sure I should. You didn't seem to like my last story. I don't imagine you'll take to this one no more'n that."

Jemmy heaved another sigh. "It's a matter of complete indifference to me whether you tell it or not. Suit yourself."

"I think I will tell it. It will give you something to think on while I am gone."

"Do, do tell."

"What would you think if I told you that Doctor Tumblety is not who you think he is?"

"I don't think he is anything."

Nipper adopted a quizzical tone. "Not even a doctor?"

"All right, yes, I think he's a doctor. So I suppose you're going to tell me he isn't."

"He's a quack, a jimcracky of a quack. Started out using walnuts to color his face brown like a Hindu and selling medicine no better'n snake oil. In Montreal he called the stuff Dr. Morse's Indian Root Pills. Nothin' but Turkish tobacco. But when he held up a bottle for folks to see, he promised the stuff would cure anything from a tumor the size of a watermelon to a mother-in-law's bad disposition. He put advertisements in the paper saying he saved patients who were given up by all doctors. Said he could cure Pulmonary Consumption in its last stage. Folks thought so much of him they wanted him to run for office; but he was a salesman, not a public servant.

"Doctor T was born an Irish Canuck, but then his people moved to Rochester. That's in New York State in case you don't know. No medical degree, I can tell you that for certain. He sold French postcards and picked pockets on the Erie Canal boats. Made a handsome living, but wanted something more refined.

"He started out his doctorin' career in Dr. Lispenard's drug store at the back of Reynolds Arcade. I'm sure you know that drug stores sell all manner of pills to rid females of unwanted offspring. Sometimes the pills didn't work, so the Doctor offered more direct means—learned how in the Rochester hospital."

Jemmy said, "Do you have to start when he was an infant?"

"All right, all right." A note of irritation shrilled Nipper's voice. "When he was all grown up, he claimed he knew secrets of healing from India and the Orient. Before the Civil War, he peddled his cures from Nova Scotia to Montreal to Detroit and back. Sold a lot of Pimple Destroyer. Made three hundred dollars a day and was living high. It was about then he started his collection, but I'll tell you more about that later. Folks say he was a charmer and handsome, too. He made quite a bit of money I do believe.

"But there's always someone out there sneakier than a fellow. The Doctor has taught me that sly someone is always going to be a woman. You see, it was a woman tricked him good. Got him to marry her and him thinkin' she was white as a lily petal. Come to find out she was a whore—with a good dose of the French pox at that. He annulled the marriage, but he couldn't do much about that permanent gift she gave him. Since he kicked her out, all anyone has to do is say the word, 'woman' and the Doctor is off in a hissy fit."

Nipper gave a bitter chuckle. "He's tried every syphilis cure you've ever heard of and a whole bunch you haven't. He's tried everything from Salversan to a Pawnee sweat ceremony. Nothing works.

"It was women always got him in trouble. He doesn't even call the gentler sex 'women.' He calls them 'cattle.' I once heard him say he would rather give his best friend poison than see him with a woman.

"Many's the time he had to leave town one step ahead of the law—most times for nothing more than trying to keep some poor soul from living a short and miserable life as a poxy whore's bastard. As I have good reason to know, he was doing the child a kindness—and the world—and even the whore, too.

"Of course, I don't suppose his procedure felt so good. I bet it burned 'til a female wanted to put a bullet through her head. Know what he used?" Nipper chuckled deep in his throat. "Cayenne pepper, aloes, juniper oil and cantharides—better known as Spanish Fly."

Jemmy had never heard anyone praise abortion. She had read of such things, but nice girls wouldn't contemplate such an act any more than they would go outside in the summer without wearing a hat. "What you're talking about is illegal."

"Now, yes, it's illegal most places. But it wasn't then. Drug stores advertised French pills in the newspaper. Doctor wrote a book and spent a lot of time inspiring young girls and lads to read it. In secret, of course. They wouldn't want their families to know they were reading *Dr. Tumblety's Private Medical Treatise.*"

"If it was legal, why was the Doctor arrested? Police don't arrest a man for writing books."

"You're just about too smart for your own good. All right, so the Doctor wasn't arrested for helping women out of the family way. If you want to know, he was arrested mostly for gross indecency and for indecent assault—at least that's what he was arrested for in London—'course, sometimes it was for poisoning people with his Indian Herbal Cure. I don't see how it could have done that, though. He told me it wasn't nothing but molasses and water. I think the police just wanted him out of town."

Nipper warmed to his subject. "Here in St. Louis, police arrested him more than once for wearing military medals he did not earn in battle. Arrested him for impersonating an officer and a hero.

"He has plenty of nerve, as I have good reason to know. When the Civil War broke out, he moved to Washington DC. Claimed to be an army surgeon on General McClellan's staff, a friend of President Lincoln and a bosom buddy of General Grant.

"Now *that* got him in trouble. Well, not directly. What got him in trouble was the name he chose. He was always a great one for disguises and aliases. My favorite was when he tricked himself out like an English sportsman with huge spurs and shiny patent leather boots. How proud he was of his small hands and dainty feet. I was something to see, too. I walked ten paces behind him wearing a turban and golden slippers curled up at the toes like a eunuch in a harem.

"That was the only time I knew him to have bad luck. He picked the wrong name—J. H. Blackburn. He didn't know that lots of folks were looking for Dr. L.P. Blackburn. The military thought Blackburn had tried to infect Union soldiers with yellow fever by giving them diseased blankets from Bermuda. If I'd been around then, I could have told them he wouldn't do nothin' like that. The Doctor admired soldiers. Women, that's the ones he hated—just women—not people.

"Here's the funniest story about the Doctor. He loved publicity. He sued the Canterbury, which was a ten-cent Music Hall in the nation's capitol. Sued them for libel when they put on a burlesque poking fun at him. And who do you think was playing Dr. Tumblety? None other than Doctor T himself." Nipper laughed out loud and slapped his knee.

"I just about forgot the time St. Louis police arrested him for plotting to kill Lincoln. He was mighty out-of-joint over that one. He even wrote a little book, *The Kidnapping of Dr. Tumblety*, to clear his name."

Jemmy's hands were numb because the twine loops cut off her circulation. "I don't suppose you could come to the point before gangrene sets in, could you?"

Nipper felt her hands, then slipped two ends of rope under the twine to ease the pressure on her wrists. Icicles pricked Jemmy's fingers as the feeling started to flow back into her hands. "I take it that means you still have lots to tell."

Nipper took out his pocket watch and said, "Too early. I want to turn in my rats, our rats, just before four-thirty. Then on to the celebration at the Turner Hall. Too bad you'll miss it. But, of course that's why I'm telling you this story. So you'll have plenty to think about.

"One thing I regret is that I couldn't show you his collection when we invited you and Annie up for lunch. I am too polite. Seeing the jars might have put you off your feed. Of course, we have only two here. The rest are in Rochester."

Nipper sounded triumphant. "Now, where did I leave off?"

Jemmy droned in an automatic voice. "The Kidnapping of Dr. Tumblety."

"Yes. The next chapter in the life of Francis J. Tumblety takes place in London.

"Ten years ago, no, nine—nine years ago he rented a room in the East End—22 Batty Street—practically a slum. That's not at all like the Doctor as I have good reason to know. He loves luxury. Stays at the best hotels and eats at the finest restaurants. Never gets up before eleven in the morning. Says anything before he takes his pint of ale is an uncivilized hour.

"He's one for the high life. He stays in hotels even when he has an apartment like he does here over at Annie's place. Loves the theatre, matinees especially. Been all over—England, France, Saratoga, Boston, New Haven, Philadelphia, Dublin, New York, Jersey City, Pittsburgh, San Francisco—now it's mostly Rochester, Baltimore, New Orleans and St. Louis.

"He makes it a point to stay at the Lindell Hotel right here in St. Louis because back in Civil War days, it was the largest hotel in the world, seven stories tall. He was a great one to strut about in fancy duds pretending to be a blueblood.

"So it's not like him to lodge at a seedy little house in a dodgy neighborhood. London police were already watching him. They thought he helped the Fenians blow up Scotland Yard three or four years earlier.

"They also thought he might be in disguise. Thought he might be some doctor from Guyana. Fellow name of Hamilton Williams who brought in the amputating knives used to assassinate the Irish Secretary in Phoenix Park—you know, Balfour, the man keeping Ireland in chains.

"I can't vouch for the truth of that one. The Doctor can fool them or anyone else any time he wants. You've never seen such a hand with disguises. One time I saw him when I didn't know him. He was got up like a black Negro in a long flowing dress that looked like the flags of all the nations put together. And he wore gold earrings and a high fur shako hat with a plume. He had an overcoat covered with decorations. His own mother wouldn't recognize him.

"Well, his snooping landlady there in London gave the police one of the Doctor's shirts that was all soaked with blood. You can imagine what police thought. Doctor T became their number one suspect.

"By now you have probably figured out that the Doctor is an invert."

Jemmy had no earthly idea what an invert might be. She said, "Yes, of course."

Nipper snorted in derision. "Probably saved his life—liking men and hating women. Lots of people, especially the big men in law enforcement, seem to think loving the one is worse than killing the other. London police arrested the Doctor for murder but knew they couldn't prove it so they arrested him for gross indecency. Those dumb dicks couldn't so much as keep him in jail.

"Judges put off the trial and let him out on bail TWICE." Nipper snorted again. "The Doctor didn't hang around after the last one. He skipped across the channel and took the steamer from Boulogne to good old New York City. Called himself Frank Townsend.

"Those dimwits at Scotland Yard had no idea how to catch their number one suspect. If they had seen him in the street, they would have tipped their caps and smiled—never recognizing the Doctor on the run and one step ahead of the law."

Nipper snorted his derision. "They couldn't keep him in jail, couldn't drag him back to England because they had no real proof that he had anything to do with murdering fallen women. So naturally they covered up the fact that he ever was IN London at all.

"I'll give them this much. They cared enough about New Yorkers to tip the city police. The London dimwits turned everything over to the New York dimwits. One high-ranking dimwit named Byrnes followed the Doctor until the dimwit lost him altogether.

"I bet Byrnes is the one what tipped off the press that the Doctor was staying at Mrs. McNamara's. It was all over the papers. I think that's why he only dispatched one in New York—and that not up to his usual standard—dressed like a common seaman—and with a filed-down cooking knife. Shows how far he'd tumbled down.

"Blamed his misery on the press. How he hated news hounds! Know what he did? Wrote another book. *Dr. Francis Tumblety—Gifted Eccentric and World Famed Physician*. Called the reporters 'snakes and slanderers.'

Jack the Ripper in St. Louis

Made up a bunch of quotes supposed to come from important people. That man is a wonder to behold as I have good reason to know.

"Then the Doctor outwitted them all—not, of course, that it is any great feat to outwit dimwits. After just three years the London police closed the case—you think that wasn't to cover their own hind ends? They didn't know anything. The only thing they knew for certain was that the Doctor was trying to add to his collection.

"You see, the Doctor went to a medical museum in London and asked if they had any female 'matrices' for sale. They reported him. I guess they don't have many calls to sell wombs. Yes, that's the Doctor's pride and joy—his collection. I don't even know how many he has, but he started collecting them before the War Between the States. Puts them in jars of formaldehyde, now. Olden days he used vinegar, brine, whatever he could. Some of those didn't keep too well.

"I bet the world famous Scotland Yard now has no record and no recollection of even arresting the Doctor. Mind you, they sent two dozen men to chase Dr. T to Canada and the U.S. Would they do that for anything less than murder? Just proves how slick the Doctor is. I bet they have not even one file anywhere to prove there ever were any murders at all in Whitechapel.

"Want to know where he went when they couldn't find him?" Nipper lowered his voice and said in a conspiratorial tone, "South. Jamaica—Nicaragua. He did better business there than in London—six females slashed in dark alleys in Managua in less than ten days.

"Yes, the Doctor sure has a clever way with words as I have good reason to know. I can't tell you how many times I have heard him say that all the trouble in this world is caused by women." Nipper chuckled. "Then, when he wants to cover up anything he might be doing at night, he says he's been to a monastery to pray for his dear departed wife."

Nipper laughed out loud. When the sounds softened to a nasty giggle, he looked at his pocket watch. As he snapped it shut, he said, "Time for me to leave you."

With the harangue ended at last, Jemmy thought she could devote herself to slipping free of those twine binders. She longed to get herself out of this miserable rat-infested cave. She tried to say something nonchalant. "Since you're going to the banquet without me, maybe you would be so kind as to bring me some dessert. A doomed man deserves a last wish."

Nipper's voice dripped with sarcasm. "Even if the doomed male is a female?"

Electricity surged through Jemmy's veins. Nipper knew that she was not a boy. She struggled to raise her head. With the lantern behind him, she could see nothing but a brown void inside a man's shape of light. The shape began to shake with mirth.

"You didn't think I knew, did you?"

"Know what? Do you have some fool idea that I'm a female?"

"I know you are."

"Some fool you are, then. You KNOW something that isn't so."

Nipper laughed. "You should take lessons from the best, the Doctor, like I have. Your boy act isn't terrible. It might fool your average man—but it doesn't fool me."

Jemmy could see the shape of a shovel attached to the brown void's arm, separate from the body, and raised high over her head. She braced for the blow. It didn't come.

Instead, Nipper bent low to her face and whispered in her ear, her bad ear. But she could hear what he said perfectly well in the dark stillness of the cave. "You know who the Doctor is, don't you?"

When Jemmy said nothing, Nipper leaned even closer and kissed her on the cheek. "Say it. Say who he is."

"I don't know. YOU tell me."

"Yes, you know. You remember their names. He made them famous. Martha Tabram, Mary Ann Nichols, Annie Chapman, Lizzie Stride, Catherine Eddowes, Mary Kelly. Left the middle part of old Katie Eddowes in the hole they were digging to build New Scotland Yard. Right under their own proper noses—a body without arms, legs, or a head."

A dam burst in Jemmy's brain. The terrifying memories of an eight year old girl who overheard hushed grownups telling of unspeakable horrors far away across the ocean flooded into her consciousness. All the clues that she had been shutting out, all the memories of Grandma in the basement at Bromschwig's and the virgin mutilated in the snow gurgled the words up through her teeth.

Nipper bit her ear and hissed, "You know that I am his humble apprentice and you know who he is. Say his name. Say it!"

Tears rolled out with the name as Jemmy's revulsion reached a crescendo. A volcano of acid gushed up from her stomach as she vomited out the words, "Jack the Ripper."

The shovel came down on her head, and Jemmy slipped down into the brown void.

Chapter Twenty

Jemmy awoke with a drum thumping in her head and a bitter taste in her mouth. In the profound inkiness she could see nothing, but she could hear a faint scratching and squealing of rats.

The loops of twine scraped her wrists and ankles. She had no choice but to remember where she was, and why. Was Nipper there? She raised her head to see. No lamp. Nothing but black, not even a trace of brown. She wondered how long he'd been gone. Had the sunset come and gone? Was there any hope of rescue?

No, of course there wasn't. No one knew Nipper had convinced her to join the rat race. Annie had been deep in conversation with the fancy man and the Doctor when Jemmy and Nipper had talked about it. Even if Annie would consider something so outlandish as going to the police over a missing errand boy, she wouldn't go until tomorrow.

Jemmy faced reality. Annie would never go to the police and even if she did, it would be much too late.

Jemmy would be missed at home, but no one there had any idea that she was in an old beer cave—less than a mile from home.

She had to get out of this on her own. With her hands and feet tied together behind her, any movement only made the twine tighten. Maybe she could loosen it. The water. Yes, the water.

She edged over toward the trickle of water. The mud oozed through her opened greatcoat to sap her body heat. Her hands numbed in the clammy mud, but she could feel the twine stretching. She edged in closer to wet a longer stretch of the hemp.

With one hand nearly freed, her hopes collapsed in a frenzy of fear—a fear she dared not show. The cave cover grated open and steps descended the ladder. Even though the outside darkness revealed no feature of the person, she knew Nipper had returned. He said, "I see you've been waiting for me like a good girl."

She pretended grogginess and realized her only chance for survival was to free her hands and surprise him. She had to play for time. "Oh, it's you, and I was having such a nice dream. It was all about dessert—crullers, apple cake, and snickerdoodles. What did you bring me to eat?"

"You might wait until I light the lamp." Nipper set the lamp on a ledge and began peeling an orange. Jemmy smelled its pungent sweetness and wished she really were hungry. She forced herself to chew as Nipper slipped sections into her mouth. She kept up a discreet pulling and twisting behind her back. One of the strands gave a fraction of an inch. A flicker of hope popped up from her despair.

Nipper said, "The banquet was nice. We got a good price for the live rats and a good overall turn-in. I thought they might make me Rat King, but some yokel must have cheated—had seventeen more than I did."

"What happened to 'Nipper and Jem, share and share alike'?"

"Sure, I claimed all the live rats. You'd never even have known about them except for me. I gave you half credit for the Wunderlich rats, one

209

hundred and eighteen. I'll be happy to give you your share. Half of three dollars and fifty-six cents. That's one dollar and seventy-eight cents. Of course, I'm afraid you'll have very little time to spend it—and no place at all. This is Sunday. Even if you were free, no shops are open."

"I'm more interested in the food. What did they have for dessert?"

"Rice pudding and oatmeal cookies. I would give you some of those cookies—for after the orange—but I'm afraid there won't be time. You see, the Doctor expects me."

Jemmy's heart beat so fast she thought Nipper could surely hear it. She stuck out her chin and told it to slow down. She didn't want to give him the satisfaction of knowing how petrified she was. She said, "How did you know I wasn't a boy?"

"I just knew."

"But what did I do wrong?"

"Your hands."

"What's wrong with my hands?"

"Too soft, too clean. Boys chop wood and drive teams of horses. They have callouses and dirty fingernails."

The twine loops were giving, stretching ever so slowly. She ignored the pain as the fibers ground into her wrists. A few more seconds and she might have a hand free. What then? Nipper was bigger and stronger and she would still have her feet tied. She had to have more time—more time.

Her brain raced. She had to think of something, but what? What would hold his interest? What would keep him talking? The idea came in a rush of impatient breath. "Well, get on with it then. At least you won't be telling me any more of your stupid stories."

"So, you like my stories. I suppose I might have time for one or two more." Jemmy felt the fibers give an eighth of an inch. Nipper hadn't noticed. "Here's one of the Doctor's favorites. It's about the great surgeon,

Robert Liston, who could amputate a leg in under three minutes. He once cut off two of his assistant's fingers—the fellow didn't get them out of the way fast enough."

Jemmy gritted her teeth and pulled one hand from one loop, but that only seemed to bind her tighter. She had to stay calm, to think how to unwind the twisted twine.

She forced a yawn. "Most enlightening. Now will you let me go?"

Nipper seemed to be enjoying the moment. "Wait 'til you hear this one. The best Dr. Liston story is about a fellow who had a tumor on his balls so big he had to cart it around in a wheelbarrow. It was so big doctor Liston missed his three minute standard. He had to spend four minutes to cut off the man's balls—all three of them.

"Oh, but I shouldn't tell you such a story. What would a girl know about— Well, I doubt you see the humor."

Jemmy managed a chuckle if for no other reason than to keep from screaming. "Oh, but I do. You finally told a story that makes sense."

"So, you like sensible stories. I'm glad I found one to please you."

"I've just figured out why the Doctor keeps you around. He needs someone to tell his lies to. And you're just stupid enough to believe them, aren't you?" Jemmy nearly dislocated her wrist in twisting it around to scrape off the first loop of twine.

"You can think what you want, but I believe his stories even when I know they're not true. He paints such a fine picture of himself riding a coal black charger across a twenty foot ravine to escape the Rebs in McClellan's Peninsula campaign in the big war. You'd swear you could hear the horse's hoofs." Nipper shoved the last orange section into Jemmy's mouth and stood up.

Jemmy spat out the orange. "Of course, *you* would believe the stories. You'd believe anything he said, but that doesn't make you his apprentice.

You'd never have the nerve to kill anybody. That's why I'm not scared.

"The time to be scared is when HE shows up. That is if anything you say at all is true. Mostly, I think it's just a bunch of cornpone to scare me. Maybe teach me a lesson because I pretended to be a boy so I could pick up a few tips and make a living."

"Oh, I have the nerve all right. You'll find out. The Doctor isn't coming. He doesn't know anything about this."

"Yes, fine. Well, just tell me the rest of your boring stories and let me go. Get on with it."

Annoyance crept into Nipper's voice, "I'll admit I don't have the experience of the Doctor, but I'm not exactly a virgin in this business."

Jemmy bit sarcastic words off with her teeth. "And I'm the famous hoochie coochie dancer Little Egypt. What's the grand tally? How many females have you butchered?"

"If you mean before I kill you, just one. Someone you know."

"Someone I know?"

"The skinny one with freckles—the one at the auction the Doctor swore was a virgin."

"I don't believe you. Do you really think I'm going to fall for your cornpone lies? I know her fancy man did it."

"You know? Well, you know wrong. What makes you think he did it?"

"I was in his room. He had bloodstained money—the money Mrs. Nanny gave her."

"I'm no thief; I have my pride. I suppose he found her and took the money. Why not? It was his."

Jemmy had slipped one hand from its loops and was pawing at the twine on the other. This conversation was no longer going in a direction Jemmy liked. What if Nipper really had killed the professional virgin? If he was crazy enough to believe that Doctor Tumblety was Jack the Ripper, maybe he was crazy enough to follow in the Ripper's footsteps.

She demanded, "If you killed her, prove it."

Nipper pulled out a string from his shirt. From it dangled an object. He stuck it close enough to Jemmy's face for her to identify. A ring. Annie's peacock ring that the virgin had stolen. Jemmy ground her teeth as a bolt of fear shot down her throat.

He said, "I can't show you my real trophy. It's at home. I don't mean the womb. That's the Doctor's collection. I'm collecting fingers. Why shouldn't I take whatever is on them, too?"

Jemmy said, "That only proves you were there after the fancy man killed her, like the ugly vulture you are."

"Keep on talking. You'll see soon enough that I was the one. I do like having someone to tell my secrets to. Sad, though, that you won't be able to tell anyone else."

Jemmy had edged both hands free but couldn't think how to reach her foot bindings without arousing Nipper's attention. She needed more time. In desperation she tried to get him to launch out in a new story. "By now you must have run out of stories to try to scare me. Why don't you just give up this game and let me go?"

"Oh, I can think of more stories—lots more stories. But there's only one I want to tell. I want to tell you every step of what I did to her in the alley."

He spoke in low even tones without a single touch of warmth or compassion—not even excitement. "Once the Doctor was back at the hotel, I sneaked back to Mrs. Nanny's place. I stayed out back behind the shed. I could hear them in there, laughing and carrying on. I knew, sooner or later, one would come out alone and I'd have my chance."

Nipper kept on talking in a voice as bereft of emotion as a cement column in front of the Post Office. Jemmy's mind flashed around the cave seeking a weapon. Her fingers tried to pry a bit of rock from the mud. Then she remembered she was carrying a much better weapon if only she could reach it. The virgin's derringer. She had not thrown it in the Mississippi or a trash barrel. It was still in the inner pocket of Father's greatcoat.

Of course, the gun might not be loaded. It might misfire. Mustn't think like that. It's the best chance. Maybe the only chance.

But she couldn't remember which inside pocket. She moved around to test for bulges. She began pulling up the soggy overcoat from the mud but stopped when the sucking sounds drew Nipper's attention. He asked, "Getting uncomfortable are you? Well, not much longer now."

Jemmy could no longer maintain her calm defiance. In a voice that was near a scream, she shrilled, "Why did you do it?"

Nipper said, "So you believe me now?"

"Why did you do it? What did she ever do to you?"

"Nothing—just being a whore. Like the Doctor, I hate whores."

"Then why pick on me? I'm no whore."

"How do I know you're not a whore? You work for whores."

"I'm not a whore. I'm a virgin—a real virgin. Even if you hate tramps because they gave you the French pox like some tramp gave the Doctor, you can't blame me. You can't tell me that I or any virgin gave you the French pox."

"No, the Doctor gave me the French pox if you must know."

"Then why don't you kill him?"

"Because I'm going to kill you."

"But I'm not a whore and I didn't give you a disease. You don't have a single reason to kill me."

"I hate virgins. Especially a young one the Doctor intends to take my place."

"You're jealous. Is that it? Believe me, no power on earth would make me the Doctor's girl."

Nipper countered, "You don't understand."

"You're doing this for jealousy. Disgusting."

"You just don't understand."

"Pitiful. You're pitiful. Killing a girl in some pathetic hope of pleasing the Doctor." Jemmy realized too late she had said the wrong thing.

Nipper regained his composure. "How dare you pity me. It's almost funny. You're the one who deserves pity."

"Will you answer me one thing about why monsters like you and Jack the Ripper kill in cold blood? Is it nothing but revenge or hate?"

"It's not about jealousy or hate or even revenge. It's about pride."

Jemmy almost had the derringer in her hand. The cold metal of the twin barrels boosted her courage. She screeched, "Pride? How can you take pride in jumping out of the dark in an alley and butchering someone you don't even know? Someone who is half your size—defenseless?"

"No, no you don't see at all. She has nothing to do with it. Nothing at all. It's about impressing someone you want to impress. With the Doctor, it was the police. He wanted to impress the police."

"And you? Who are you trying to impress?"

"The Doctor." Nipper's voice saddened. "After I tell him you were pretending to be a boy, after I show him that you are a fraud—after I give him the gift, then maybe he will take me back."

"So the Doctor booted you out?"

"Last night."

"Why? Did he find out that you killed the virgin?"

"He found out that she could be me."

For the first time Jemmy looked at Nipper's face—too smooth for shaving yet the tiny wrinkles around his eyes said he was no longer young. She formed the words in surprise. "You're a woman."

Nipper stood up so fast that he banged his head on the cave ceiling. "I'd

215

sooner be a squirrel in a tree."

Jemmy had hit a sore spot. "But you're not a squirrel. You are a female."

Nipper said nothing.

"But you've been with the Doctor for a long time. How is it that he didn't know?"

"I'm good at disguises. I learned from the master."

The handle of the little gun firm in her hand, Jemmy said, "It won't work. He won't take you back."

"Yes, he will."

"No. You just told me why. Pride."

"He has to take me back."

"Your deception hurt his pride. Every time he looked at you, he'd remember."

Nipper sobbed quietly and dropped her head. Jemmy rolled into a ball and undid the knots from the twine around her ankles with her right hand while she clung to the derringer with her left.

When she stood, Nipper looked up in alarm. "How did you get loose?"

Jemmy pointed the gun at Nipper. "Just move away from the ladder. I don't want to shoot you. I just want to leave."

Nipper backed up squarely against the ladder. "Kill me. Without the Doctor I don't want to live. You're right. He'll never take me back; he'll find someone else—some young pretty boy like you."

"Step aside. I don't want to shoot you."

"You're going to have to." Nipper walked closer to Jemmy. "Put the gun right here." She placed an index finger over the spot. "Shoot me in the heart." She reached out toward the gun. "Let me steady your hand. I don't trust your aim."

Jemmy was standing no more than four feet away. But the gun was shaking far too much for clear aim. Even worse, every moment her taxed arm muscles cramped more painfully, she knew her aim would worsen. How else could she get Nipper away from the ladder? How would she escape?

Before the rumbling began, the rock beneath her feet quivered. Dirt and pebbles fell from the ceiling. Jemmy knew it was a tremor, but Nipper stood transfixed as the lantern tumbled from its ledge and snuffed out the light.

Jemmy moved to her left in hopes of getting behind Nipper and shoving her away from the ladder. Nipper lunged toward the spot where Jemmy had been. Instead of grabbing Jemmy, she hit the derringer, which clacked against a rock as it fell to the floor. Nipper fell to her knees from her own momentum then fumbled around to find the gun.

Jemmy began to climb the ladder taking care not to make a sound. She held her breath as her heart pounded in her bad ear like a blacksmith's hammer. She climbed up to the point where she had to thrust up the manhole cover—then two rungs more. From a low crouch, she braced her back against the wood and shot it up amidst a shower of dirt clods and sand.

She could see the night stars of freedom overhead. She heard Nipper scrambling to stand up and the clang of a brogan hitting the bottom rung of the ladder. Jemmy erupted from her cave prison and slammed down the hatch. She sat on it as Nipper pushed and heaved to open it from below. Jemmy looked around for the iron bar which would seal off Nipper's escape, but it was gone. Nipper had tossed it down into the cave.

Jemmy pulled her wet greatcoat around her but it only seemed to worsen the chill. She looked around for help. Nothing moved but the wind in the poplar trees across the river. Who would have thought she would miss the comparative warmth of the cave?

If she didn't find a way to fasten the hatch soon, someone would find her frozen on top and Nipper still alive, below. Could she outrun Nipper? She wouldn't have much of a head start if Nipper kept up those bangs and shoves on the hatch. She could wait—and get colder and colder or she could make a run for it.

No, there had to be a better way. She remembered the virgin's knife. She dug around until she found it. She managed to lodge it with blade on one side and hilt on the other of the pair of handles on one rim of the hatch. It was a start, but she also had to have something to keep the other side shut.

She felt around for something to use as a bar. Her hand met a bit of driftwood. Just the thing. She growled in frustration when she tried to wedge it through the handles, but it refused to slide through no matter how hard she pushed. Too thick. It wouldn't fit.

She pulled open the greatcoat and caught her breath as the wind dug ice picks into her chest. She turned her back to it and began searching the pockets. Grandpa's spyglass. Too thick.

She searched again as hope began to desert her. Then she found something she had utterly forgotten—a second knife—Nipper's own knife. She smiled—imprison him with his own knife. Not as permanent as the end Nipper had planned for her, but with a savory smack of irony.

She tried to stick the knife through the hatch handles—too broad. She took the blade out of its sheath and tried again. Still too broad, and the tip alone would not hold.

Jemmy was just about to dissolve in tears when one last hope entered her brain. She picked up the driftwood and whittled down a section. Her fingers were too numb to make much speed. And she had to take care lest Nipper's occasional assaults on the hatch might cause her to maim herself.

After a half hour or more, she managed to fit the whittling into the hatch handles. None too soon either, for Nipper must have found the virgin's gun. Jemmy heard the shot when she was no more than a few yards away. She didn't go back to see if the bullet had pierced the hatch cover. She was free.

Chapter Twenty-One

When she found herself standing in front of the Lafayette Park Police Station, Jemmy's eyebrows shot up in surprise. She had been so grateful and gleeful at her escape that her legs fairly flew over the mile and a half from the river. She arrived breathless without giving a single thought to what she would say.

She burst into the station house and stopped. She must have wavered on her feet because the sergeant came out from behind his desk. He was a balding fellow with a strip of white hair down the center of his head that looked remarkably like a leghorn chicken feather. He led her to a chair. "What's the trouble, Lad?"

She flopped down as her panting slowed and she regained the power of speech. "Woman in a cave—killer."

"A woman killed in a cave you say?"

Jemmy shook her head. "The woman is trapped in the cave. And she's a killer. She killed..." Jemmy stopped amid sentence. She didn't know what to say. She had never known the virgin's name. "...that girl in the alley a week ago. You know, the one that was cut up."

"Been drinking, have you lad?" The sergeant leaned over to sniff Jemmy's breath. He looked surprised when he smelled nothing. "I'm not falling for pranks—not early of a Monday morning. Go on home and tell your pals this is one jape that didn't rope in the sergeant." He chuckled as he stood up. "Ladies cutting up other ladies in such a frightful way? Next you'll think you can make me believe President McKinley is going to be assassinated at the fair."

It had never occurred to Jemmy that anyone would disbelieve her.

Anger and determination set her mind to cool logic. "Sir, if I were playing a prank, would I have tied myself up and rubbed my wrists so raw they bleed?" She held up her red wrists and turned them so he could see.

The wrists turned the sergeant back into a policeman, if not a true believer. He said, "Looks like you've been tied up, all right. I'll get my report form."

"Please, Sir, don't you think the first thing is to get some men and go arrest her?"

"No, the first thing is for me to find out who you are and who tied you up. *The Police Manual* tells us how to proceed, and generally it gets us to the criminal in the end."

Jemmy had to hold her impatience and her tongue.

He asked, "Name?"

"Nipper—Nipper with an N."

The sergeant repeated as he wrote. "Please say so if I write down anything that's not right. Nipper. Last name?"

"Just Nipper, that's all I know."

"You mean that is *her* name." He erased what he had written. "I was asking for *your* name."

"*My* name? Why do you need my name? I'm not a criminal."

Jack the Ripper in St. Louis

"We have to know who you are. We can't put criminals behind bars without the help of the public to bear witness. We have to know who you are so we can find you. So you can tell us what you know so we can solve crimes. Now, Lad, what's your name?"

Jemmy thought about bolting through the door and leaving Nipper in the cave to be rescued or not as the fates decreed. But no, her conscience wouldn't let her. "Jemima McBustle."

The sergeant looked at her with a new curiosity, but he didn't ask why she was dressed in men's clothes. That wasn't a question on his form. He droned on asking for her address and a description of Nipper and a statement of what had happened. When he asked why Jemmy thought Nipper to be the killer, Jemmy thought the fact that Nipper had confessed should be enough. Still, she told about the peacock ring and the finger.

At length he ran out of questions and used a whistle to summon the two night officers who were patrolling their beats. When the men arrived, he said, "Miss Jemima McBustle here says she's got a killer trapped in a cave by the river."

One of the men just looked bored as he warmed his hands over the coal stove. But the other—a lanky fellow Jemmy had often seen twirling his nightstick while sauntering through Lafayette Park peered into her face and said. "It is. It is Miss Jemima McBustle. What's the prettiest girl in the neighborhood doing tricked out the like of this?" He chucked her under the chin as if she were a five year old.

Jemima slapped his hand away and said, "I am an undercover journalist on assignment." She could stand answering questions if she had no choice; but no way would she tolerate being treated like a puppy, even if she had to lie like a dog.

She stood up. "Now, if you gentlemen have no further questions or other delays in mind, shall I show you the cave—and let you catch a murderer?"

221

The sergeant said, "You'll catch your death in that wet coat. He motioned the bored officer toward the empty lockup. "Fetch a blanket from off the cot." To Jemmy he said, "It's not much, but it will be better than the muddy coat."

The sergeant folded the wool blanket into a triangle and wrapped it around Jemmy shawl-like. As she led the three policemen back to the cave, she was grateful for the lightness and the warmth the blanket gave her.

She and the sergeant walked in front. The other two trailed far enough back that Jemmy could hear laughter but no words. She tried to shrug off the belief that they were laughing at her; but it sat on her shoulder like a spider that went into hiding when she tried to brush it off, then popped out the minute she thought it was gone for good.

When they reached the cave, Jemmy warned, "She has weapons. She fired the derringer once, but it has two barrels. She must have a knife, too." A pang of fear followed by relief caught the words in her throat. "She wouldn't be able to k-k-cut off my finger without a knife."

The sergeant looked at Jemmy with a mite more respect when the lantern light revealed her means for locking down the hatch cover. He pulled out the driftwood and said, "I wouldn't hire you to carve a toy for a tyke, but if I had need of a toothpick you'd be the one I'd call."

Seeing the knife hilt and blade securing the hatch cover gave Jemmy a profound sense of relief. Nipper must still be down below. Her knees weakened in the first rush of comfort she'd felt since early that afternoon— before she had become a rat-killer and very nearly a killee of a lady-killer. The sergeant stamped on the wooden cave lid and put on a cheerful voice. "Is someone trapped down there. We're going to let you out. Be just a minute before we free you."

The policemen stood on opposite sides of the hatch cover. The lanky one extricated the knife. Then nodded to the bored one who yanked off the hatch cover. It rolled down the embankment and plopped on the dirt. They stood back from the opening and waited. No sound.

The sergeant hallooed, "Anyone down there. Are you injured? Can you make any sound?" Nothing.

The sergeant knelt down, dipped his lantern into the cave and swung it around. The bored officer kept Jemmy too far back to see in the cave, but the sergeant stood and said. "I see a foot. Somebody down there. Maybe playing possum."

He pulled his sidearm from its case and nodded toward the lanky officer as he motioned for the man to go below. He handed the bored officer the lantern while he held his pistol at the ready.

The lanky officer looked grim as he slipped in smooth rapid motion down the ladder. When he hit bottom, with nightstick raised, he edged toward the body. He prodded a leg with his toe, then poked other places until he was satisfied that the body was not going to move on its own.

He yelled up, "I think this one is done for." The Sergeant replaced his sidearm and climbed down the ladder. He and the lanky officer poked around for what seemed hours.

Jemmy began shivering. She tried to distract her mind by thinking how to write the story. The bored officer unstrapped his rain cape and covered her with it. It helped a little.

The sergeant and the officer came up from the cave. The sergeant assigned the bored officer to keep watch for the rest of the night. He told the lanky officer to take Miss McBustle home. But before they left, he said. "You'll be happy to know I don't suspect you of the murder."

Jemmy's mouth fell open in bewilderment. How could anyone think her capable of murder? "Was Nipper murdered?"

"No. You said Nipper fired the derringer. It must have been enough to cause a big chunk of the roof to cave in. Looks like she got trapped in all the dirt from the slide. Probably suffocated. No, the murder I meant was the murder of the girl in the alley—which you, Miss McBustle, seem to know a surprising quantity of information about."

"You suspect me of—murder?"

"Well, not so much now. We'll check out the ring with the peacock on it; and we found something else in her pocket—a finger—her eleventh, one too many. She already had her proper ten."

"She told me she left her trophy finger at the Doctor's apartment."

"We'll pay a visit to the Doctor as well."

The bored officer at last spoke up. As he pointed to Jemmy, he said, "Maybe this one put the ring on that one—and planted the cut-off finger, too."

The sergeant shook his head. "No. The pocket was all full of dried blood. Week old finger won't bleed. Whoever wears that coat was the one did the deed. Easy enough to find out was the Nipper wearing the coat last Saturday."

On the way to St. Ange Street, Jemmy realized she would face an arduous ordeal at home. How would she be able to write down the story she'd been rehearsing in her mind? Mother would fuss over the rope burns on her wrists and ankles and would see she had a bath and a hot meal. But then, she would berate Jemmy for hours for causing such worry, for doing such dangerous unladylike things, and for being a daughterly disappointment in general.

She said in her most winsome way, "Officer—I don't know your name."

"Officer Spilker."

"Well, Officer Spilker, I am in desperate need of a great favor from you. I have no right to ask it, but your kindness to me and your thrilling bravery embolden me. Have I any hope you may help me, save me?"

"I would be more than pleased to aid you, if I can."

"Go to my home and tell my mother that I am perfectly well but that I am needed to help with the police investigation. That I long to come home but I cannot possibly do so until the case is put to rest."

Officer Spilker sounded mystified. "But why don't you simply go home?"

"May I tell you the truth? Can I trust you with my deepest secrets?"

"Of course. I wouldn't be much of a policeman if I couldn't keep to myself all the things which ought not cause a burden to decent people."

"I must have time to write the story and take it to the newspaper before anyone else does. If I go home, Mother will fuss and scold and keep me from doing what I must do."

"You need the care of your mother and medical attention for those wrists. You can't possibly think a newspaper story is more important than your health. Who could believe a slip of a girl like you could do a man's job anyway?"

"Please, I can't tell you how much this means to me." She stopped and pulled his lapels to face him in a pool of lamplight. "My whole future depends upon your answer. I beg you to help me. Surely I will find an opportunity in the future to thank you properly."

Jemmy had never known tearful plea and batting eyelashes to fail to work on any man—until Officer Spilker. He placed his hands on her shoulders and turned her in the direction of home. He then marched her up St. Ange to her front door. Jemmy didn't even have to tell him the number. He knew.

On the way she half-listened to what she knew would be the first harangue of the night. He started with the voice of calm concern. "I mean to see you home as I have been ordered to do. It's for your own good. Even without orders, I would be remiss to leave you defenseless against the night." He had apparently forgotten that she had sufficient defenses to keep from being knifed by a devotee of Jack the Ripper.

He took a more imperious tone. "Young ladies ought not to be abroad alone after dark. I might add that young ladies ought not to wear men's clothes. The Bible says it's a sin all unto itself." He paused for a reply.

Jemmy knew better than to speak up. He spoke faster and in a more stentorian voice. "Even if the Bible says nothing about females writing stories about evil doings, any right-minded person would know ladies ought to stay far away from all things which would stain their purity and soil their reputations. I warn you to leave off, and I mean to say as much to your mother. Though I hate to add to the poor woman's grief at having so wrong-headed a daughter on her hands. More wicked than a serpent's tooth is an ungrateful child."

No doubt he had more to say, but had to stop his sermonizing when Mother answered his pounding on the front door. She had not changed into nightclothes. Her red eyes attested to her state of worry. She pulled Jemmy in from the cold and inspected her for damage.

Officer Spilker followed Jemmy in and pulled the door shut against the cold December wind. Mother clucked her tongue over Jemmy's raw wrists and made Jemmy wince when she touched the lump on her head. When she determined that Jemmy would very likely live, she ordered her to the kitchen where Gerta had pots of water heating and a galvanized tin wash-tub waiting. Jemmy needed a hot bath to warm her. The kitchen was more convenient than carrying hot water upstairs to the bathroom—which, of course, had only cold water piped in.

When Jemmy started to protest, Mother gave her a look that persuaded her to stay mute and head toward the kitchen. Mother looked to Officer Spilker for an explanation. He said, "Your girl has more spunk than sense. I trust you'll see to it that she stops these fool notions about being a journalist. Not a fit job for females. Not fit for young girls to dress themselves up like men, neither.''

Jemmy could hear the edge in Mother's voice. "Officer, I am most grateful that you have brought my daughter home. What you advise I shall contemplate under careful scrutiny." Jemmy curled up her bottom lip. The officer's high-handedness was rubbing Mother the wrong way.

While Jemmy was peeling off her clammy clothes behind a closed kitchen door, the voices grew louder. Officer Spilker might have been a preacher at a camp meeting. "I only say this for your own good. Keep a tight rein on her or she'll end up dead or worse."

Mother upped her voice a few decibels. "Thank you for your concern. Now, I'd be obliged if you would tell me exactly what happened."

"Best you don't know. Just be warned."

Even though Jemmy couldn't see Mother, she could imagine red indignation creeping up Mother's neck. Her voice cracked like ice on a not-quite-frozen pond. "With all due respect, Officer, are you going to tell me what happened or not?"

"No need to get huffy."

Jemmy could hear the door creaking open as Mother said, "Goodbye, Officer—Officer Spilker, is it? I do appreciate your bringing my daughter home. Good night."

Jemmy couldn't hear whether Officer Spilker protested. Mother shut the door with a definitive bang and slid the lock bar too. With Officer Spilker locked out, Jemmy had first crack at convincing her mother nothing really bad had happened.

It turned out she didn't need to. Officer Spilker had upset Mother so thoroughly and insulted her so fully that she forgot her own objections to Jemmy's desire to be a stunt reporter—not that she had known Jemmy wanted to BE a stunt reporter.

She even forgot the fact that Jemmy had stolen Easton's clothes and very probably ruined them. After Officer Spilker left, she came out into the kitchen and rummaged through the remedies to find bandages and Cloverine Salve. As she applied the petrolatum and beeswax with just a touch of healing oil of turpentine, she looked into Jemmy's eyes and asked, "Are you all right? Are you truly all right?"

In that instant, Jemmy's love for her mother flooded her with the realization that she could never be worthy—never deserve such tenderness. She gulped down the lump in her throat and said. "I am truly all right. I can't tell you how guilty I feel when you are so kind to me and I don't deserve it, not even a little bit. Please, please, scream at me or shake your finger. Preach to me. Do something to make me feel better."

"I mean to lay down the law, but not tonight. Tomorrow will be soon enough. Now you need hot food and bed."

Mother smiled and dished up leftover chicken and dumplings heated in the warming oven.

With a full belly, Jemmy climbed the two floors to the former ballroom she shared with her sisters and Gerta. She went to bed, but not to sleep.

She pulled a pencil stub and a tablet with a red Indian on the cover from her lap desk. She hardly noticed her numb fingers as she began to write. "Would-Be Jack the Ripper Caught in St. Louis."

Chapter Twenty-Two

Jemmy awakened with the lapdesk across her legs and tablet still open. The coal oil in the lamp had burned out. She took the story to the window to read by dawn's early light. Her words made her feel again the damp and the mud and the rat claws on her hand. She nodded in satisfaction.

She dressed and slipped down the front stairs. She could hear Gerta banging pots in the kitchen. Mother's voice said, "I can't abide deception. What am I going to do about the girl? Maybe I should let her Uncle Erwin send her to Lindenwood. Maybe farther away would be better—Bryn Mawr or Wellesley."

Jemmy yearned to eavesdrop on the rest of Mother's musings, but she had to get out of the house before anyone noticed. She intended to get to the *Illuminator* as fast as public transportation would allow. On the way she changed a word here and there in her story to build even more excitement and horror.

Still clutching her tablet, she stopped in front of the *Illuminator* building and looked up to the fifth floor. Well, here it was, the moment she had been yearning for. Her big chance—her only chance—to choose the life Jemima McBustle would lead.

She took a deep breath and marched into the main office. She asked to see Mrs. Willmore. The frizzy-haired blond behind the desk didn't even look up from her filing. "Mrs. Willmore doesn't see anyone until after she's read the papers."

"How long does that take?"

"She comes down to get a cup of something at ten or ten-thirty."

Jemmy looked at the clock. In bold Roman numerals, it displayed the time—quarter to seven.

"I can't possibly wait that long."

Still without looking up from her filing, frizzy-hair said, "Come back later. Do you want to leave your name?"

Jemmy slapped her tablet down on the counter. "I must see Mrs. Willmore and it must be now."

Frizzy-hair jumped at the sound. She looked at Jemmy for the first time. "No need to throw things about." She was edging back toward a door—apparently to get help.

Jemmy saw she was about to be trapped. She ran out the office door and up the stairs. Thank heaven in a handbag she knew where to find Mrs. Willmore's office. Of course it would have to be on the top floor. By the time she arrived on the third floor landing, she could hear heavy boots on the stairs below.

She ran faster, but her stays cut off her wind. Her skirts kept tripping her feet until she pulled them past her knees in most unladylike fashion. She pounded up the last flight and arrived at Mrs. Willmore's door. At that moment she felt arms around her shoulders yanking her back from the doorknob. She landed two kicks forward against the door. Then she shot a heel back against whoever was grabbing her arms. Her heel connected with something solid. A man's voice yelped in pain, but he didn't let go. Instead, he twirled her to face him and raised a hand to slap her. Jemmy wrenched away and fell back against Mrs. Willmore's door.

The man, a burly fellow in a dark canvas apron and fingers blackened by newsprint, grabbed her again. He turned her toward the stair—this time taking care to keep her as far away from his shins as was practical.

With knitted eyebrows Mrs. Willmore opened the door and demanded, "What's this commotion?" She looked to the man who had started pushing Jemmy down the stairs in front of him.

"Sorry for the botheration, Ma'am. This wild girl was told to come back later and not bother you now. She has no respect for your station. Would you have me put her in her place?"

"No, just take her outside." Mrs. Willmore started back in her office.

Stung that Mrs. Willmore didn't recognize her, Jemmy yelled, "Kick me out. Go ahead. I have a story would make any paper in town sell ten thousand copies. I don't need you." She wrenched free from her captor and started stomping down the stairs.

Mrs. Willmore walked to the railing and said, "I remember you. You're that McBustle girl. Do you really have a story?"

"I have the best—the most exciting story of the year—of the decade." Jemmy stopped and turned at the landing to see Mrs. Willmore's reaction.

"Well, what's the story about?"

"Jack the Ripper."

Mrs. Willmore grunted. "That's just what I need—another crackpot Jack the Ripper story."

"I'm no crackpot. Jack the Ripper is right here in St. Louis—right now. If you don't believe me, call the Lafayette Park Police Station."

Mrs. Willmore motioned to the man to leave. To Jemmy she said, "Come on up, then. Show me."

The man said, "Take care, Ma'am. This one's a wildcat. Shall I stay close by?"

Mrs. Willmore grunted again. "No thank you. I'll be safe enough." As she escorted Jemmy into her office and motioned for her to sit, she said, "Now what's this about Jack the Ripper?"

"Not the Ripper himself. Well, there's a man in town who may be the Ripper. I don't know whether he is or whether the girl who said so was simply out of her mind. I do know she was out of her mind. She confessed to murdering a girl—and she tried to murder me. But whether the man she called the Ripper really is Jack the Ripper or whether she just thought he was Jack the Ripper? That I can't prove."

Mrs. Willmore cocked her head. "Just what can you prove?"

Jemmy shoved the red-covered tablet at her. "Read my story."

Ten minutes later Mrs. Willmore was on the phone to the police. As she returned the earpiece to its cradle, she said, "The police are calling upon Doctor Tumblety this morning." She tore the story sheets from the tablet as she led Jemmy down two floors to the office of her news editor, Suetonius Hamm.

She motioned for Jemmy to stay out of sight. She knocked on the door, then walked in without a by-your-leave. She left the door open. Dismissing pleasantries, she shoved the pages at him and ordered, "Read this."

Minutes later he said, "Is this factual?"

"I've verified the body in the cave with the police. Here's the interview information from Lafayette Park officers." She set a paper on his desk blotter. "You can interview the writer now. Without other verification, we'd be on solid ground if we print the first six pages."

Jemmy could hear Hamm's chair scraping against the floor. "Is the writer here? Let me talk to him."

"The writer wants a job. I promised one if you like the story. Is it good?"

"The writing is good—if the story is accurate."

"So, this is a reporter you would hire?"

"Yes, if he can come up with more stories like this."

Without turning around, Mrs. Willmore raised her voice, "You may come in now and meet your new boss."

Still clutching her tablet, Jemmy walked into Hamm's office and bounced over to his desk with a big grin on her face. She stuck out her hand in most unladylike fashion.

Hamm looked at the hand, and at Jemmy, then at Mrs. Willmore. "That little bit of a female wrote this?"

Mrs. Willmore beat Hamm at his own game. Instead of letting him punctuate his sentence with Latin bromides, she quoted Juvenal, "*Fronti nulla fides*. Don't believe appearances."

Hamm chomped his cigar.

Mrs. Willmore turned to Jemmy. "Welcome to the staff of the *Illuminator*." She shook the outstretched hand which Hamm had spurned, then introduced her protegee. "Miss Jemima McBustle, I'd like for you to meet our News Editor, Mr. Suetonius Hamm. Mr. Hamm, Miss McBustle."

Hamm was so flabbergasted his cigar burned his thumb when he caught it as it fell from his mouth. Mrs. Willmore went on. "Trial period, of course. Six months. Get her a desk. She may not use it much, though. She's a stunt reporter—like Nellie Bly." Mrs. Willmore breezed out.

Hamm looked as though someone had filled his sugar bowl with termites. He looked as though he wanted to spit out whatever disgusting substance he had on his tongue, but couldn't find his hankie.

He said, "Miss McBustle. I will follow up on the rest of this story with great diligence, and as the owner of the *Illuminator* said, we will print the first six pages today. I give you fair warning—if you have misrepresented anything at all, you will have less time as an employee of this newspaper than a stewing hen has to primp for Sunday dinner."

He dinged a bell on his desk. Hamm handed the copy boy Jemmy's wide-lined papers and said, "Copy editor. Tell him to put it on page one—lead story. Move the item on the Dingley Protective Tariffs. Tell him I know 91% is much too high a tariff on woolen goods, and that's a much more important story to the lives of everyday people. But our first job is to sell papers. This Ripper story will make the locals sit up and shiver—and tell everyone they know to read today's *Illuminator*."

He turned to Jemmy and started asking questions until she began to feel the weight of her ordeal, compounded by sleeplessness and lack of food, she was on the verge of collapse when he said, "Just like a female. You're about to pass out on me, aren't you?"

Jemmy straightened her back. "No, Mr. Hamm. It's just that I haven't had breakfast."

He gave her fifteen cents from his own pocket. "Turn right. Two streets down is a place serves food." He shooed her out of the office. "I'll call the front desk. After you eat, fill out the personnel forms. Then go home and get some sleep. Be here at eight in the morning and try not to bring a headache with my name on it."

Hamm muttered to no one in particular. "*Super visum corporis*. First I must see the body. Then we'll see whether this Ripper story holds up."

Under his breath, though not entirely out of Jemmy's hearing, he muttered. "How will I keep that one from getting underfoot for the next six months. Carries a grammar school tablet, yet."

Jemmy followed orders, well some of them. After becoming a genuine employee of the *Illuminator* complete with an identification card that said so, she took the streetcar to Annie's place. When she arrived, two police wagons were standing outside. The bell tinkled as she entered. Annie was pinning pheasant feathers to a mustard-colored hat. When she saw Jemmy, she took the pins from her mouth. She adopted a big smile in her best pro-prietress-of-a-hat-shop fashion. Then stopped.

Jemmy knew Annie recognized her. She said, "I came to explain in person why I can't be your errand boy."

Annie replied, "That's clear enough. You aren't a boy." Her voice warmed as she said, "Now I know why I told my secrets to you. I think I always knew you were too much like me to be male."

Relieved at how easy telling Annie had been, Jemmy felt as if she had gained a true friend, a grownup friend, the first she could claim. In spite of herself, Jemmy teared. "I can't tell you how relieved I am. How kind you are not to hate me after I deceived you."

Annie teared up—but not on Jemmy's account. "You didn't deceive me. Looks as though I have deceived myself. I haven't had a single buyer all morning."

Jemmy pointed out the obvious. "With two police vans outside, who could blame them?"

Annie refused to be cheered. "As soon as they're gone, customers will come flooding in to find out what the scandal was all about."

"Would it be so terrible if they did? They would look at your lovely hats and buy them in spite of themselves."

Annie dabbed at her eyes. "You make me feel better."

Jemmy moved closer to Annie. "The police will be gone soon. Do you know what's going on up there?"

"No, but if you want to sneak up the front stairs, I won't stop you." She ducked through the portieres and returned with a glass. "Putting this to your ear might help."

When she produced another glass from behind her back, both giggled. Annie locked the front door and turned the "open" sign to the "closed" side.

The pair slipped through the side door and up the stairs to stand outside the Doctor's apartment. Jemmy put the glass to her good ear.

The Doctor's voice articulated calmly, "Officer, I swear to you that I thought Nipper was a boy. Why would I doubt him? You surely are not accusing me of unnatural or indecent acts with that young man. The law courts of this nation will prove me innocent of such slander."

A nasal voice said, "Now, now, Dr. Tumblety. I'm not accusing you of anything. I'm informing you of the facts. A young woman dressed in men's clothes is dead of apparent suffocation caused by the partial collapse of a cave. This person was reputed to have confessed to a most gruesome murder committed Saturday a week. That is my only subject of investigation. Did this Nipper have a real name as well as the nickname Nipper?"

"Not so far as I know."

"No aliases?"

"None that I know about."

"How long have you known the deceased?"

A jangling crash, perhaps from glass breaking, brought a rush of talk from the Doctor. "I resent your men tossing about my property. Where is it written in the law that they have the right to throw things on the floor?"

"I have shown you our search warrant, properly executed."

"The warrant doesn't give authority to ruin my home."

"You know what we're looking for. Perhaps I can persuade them to be a bit less thorough if you give us what we want."

"Very well." Steps of two men walking blurred the next words.

The Doctor spoke again. "I want you to understand that Nipper brought me these two matrices. I thought he—she bought them for me from an undertaker. That's what he-she told me."

"And which undertaker would that be?"

"Brom—Brom-something."

"Bromschwig and Husmann?"

"Yes, I think so."

"And I'd be wondering why the deceased would make you presents of such an unusual nature. Why would you want female body parts, Dr. Tumblety?"

"I make no secret of it. It is quite well-known that I have a collection of uteruses, diseased organs for study. I keep them at my sister's house in Rochester in New York state, my summer residence. It's all perfectly circumspect and aboveboard."

"Not if your Nipper has been killing off females to provide you with your objects of study."

"You wrong me, Officer. I am guilty of nothing—except, perhaps being overly trusting."

"Can you verify that this coat belongs to the person you call Nipper?"

"Yes."

"And was the person known as Nipper wearing this coat on Saturday, the eleventh of December, and also the following day, Sunday the twelfth?"

"Yes."

"And are you aware that the deceased person accused you of perpetrating the Whitechapel murders in London in 1888?"

"No. She must have been quite mad to say such a thing. And you would have to be equally mad to believe it."

"Have you anything to add?"

"Just that I am impressed with the efficiency of the St. Louis Police. You seem to have solved a murder in a week and a day. The London Police haven't been able to solve half a dozen murders in nearly a decade."

As the policeman shuffled off, Jemmy and Annie slipped back downstairs. Annie reopened the store. Both were sitting demurely when the officer, whose voice Jemmy recognized as the interrogator, stuck his head in the door and touched the brim of his hat. "We're leaving now, Ma'am. I hope our wagons didn't chase off your customers."

"Thanks for taking the time to say so, Officer."

He held up Nipper's coat. "Ma'am, might I ask you whether you recognize this coat?"

"Yes, Officer. Doctor Tumblety's boy wore that coat."

"Did the Doctor ever wear it?"

"Not that I know of. I'd judge it to be much too small across the shoulders."

"Would you know whether the boy was wearing this coat on Saturday a week ago?"

"I don't know. The Doctor and the boy moved in here just two days ago. But I will say that I never saw the boy wear any other coat. And, of course, it's winter."

The officer touched the brim of his cap as he said, "Thank you, Ma'am, for the help. I'll see you get that ring back, the one with the ruby eye, just as soon as we finish up our paperwork. I wish you much success with your new shop." And he was gone with a jingling of the door bell.

Jemmy turned to Annie and took her hand. "You already forgave me, but I want to tell you everything. I want to be your friend. That's why I want to—need to—explain and apologize."

Jemmy looked into Annie's eyes. "I am a stunt reporter. I wasn't a journalist then, but I am now. I was trying to get a story."

"Well, you got a story. A humdinger of a story, by the sound of it."

"That was just by chance."

Annie sounded wary. "What story were you trying to get?"

"A story that I now know I could never write—about fallen women—about—" Jemmy had to steel her nerve to say it. "I was going to write about you—but I was wrong. There is a story in you—a story of courage. But I can't tell it. I won't tell it. I would never ruin your story's happy ending."

Jack the Ripper in St. Louis

The look passing between them said more clearly than words, "I trust you."

Annie smiled and patted Jemmy's hand. "Your hands are cold. Let's warm them up with some hot cocoa."

Jemmy warmed herself by the stove while Annie prepared hot chocolate and toast. As they ate, Jemmy said. "I hate to bring this up, but because I count you as my friend, I must. What will you do about the Doctor upstairs? Nipper said he was Jack the Ripper. What if he is? You're in terrible danger—and the girls on the third floor, too."

"Annie is armed and knows how to be careful. I'll see to it that Hannah and Fifi are careful, too. After his lease is up, Dr. T will be going home to New York. When he returns—if he returns—I'll have the top floor rented to someone else. I'll be fine."

Jemmy wasn't entirely reassured, but she could do no more. Well, she could do one thing more. "I'd like you to make me a hat. As a professional journalist, I need a suitable hat—a hat Nellie Bly would be proud of."

Annie hopped up and said, "It would be a great pleasure for me to design my very first custom creation for you—my friend—" Annie stopped in surprise. "But I don't know your name. All I know is Jem."

"That is my name. Jem—Jemmy—Jemima McBustle."

Annie raised her cocoa cup in a toast. "Well, then, to Jemmy—friend—boyfriend, girlfriend and Annie's first sale."

The pair spent a happy quarter hour making millinery decisions of great moment. At last they settled on a black felt with removable notions. A few alterations would change it from hat for society maven to hat for serious woman of commerce or to any hat disguise in between. The perfect hat for an undercover journalist.

As Jemmy left Annie's shop, a mother with a hatless little girl came in. Jemmy could hear her say, "I cannot keep anything on the child's head. I know she's going to catch her death of cold. Please, can you help me?"

Jemmy beamed as she pulled the door shut with its jolly twinkle. It looked as though Annie's business would be a smashing success.

Chapter Twenty-Three

Jemmy went home triumphant in her new job and braced to face Mother's ire, but Mother had gone off to Soulard Market. Jemmy had spun a plausible story and was a bit miffed she couldn't try it out while she had her courage up.

"Mother Dear, you know how I need money for Christmas presents. Well, Nipper told me about the rat race. Naturally, no girls are allowed, so I dressed up in Father's old clothes. I know now how wrong and foolish I was—even though my heart was in the right place. I realize how lucky I am to have escaped. I would never dream of allowing myself to get into such a fine fix ever again."

She practiced looking sincere in the mirror and conveniently forgot that she was supposed to be earning money at her respectable job as lady's companion. Impatience to test the story caused her to sulk a good ten minutes.

She looked at the hall clock to find the hour only a little past ten in the morning. All of a sudden, her valor turned to pallor. An attack of nerves persuaded her to postpone her interview with Mother. She beat a hasty exit to run a convenient errand.

She set off to Lafayette Park Police Station to return the loaned lock-up blanket and the officer's rain cape. The day sergeant traded her for Father's greatcoat. It was stiff with mud, but she was glad to have it back. After all, it had saved her life.

The day sergeant looked regretful as he said, "We have something else that you should have. He set an object wrapped in black wool jersey on the counter. He removed the cloth to reveal a glass jar. Inside a pear-shaped object the size of a fist floated in liquid.

He pointed to the label. Jemmy gasped when she read it.

Matrix of McBustle, H.
Died, October 1897, Age 75
St. Louis, Missouri
(Water solution with Formalin 14%, Glycerin 5%, Sodium Borate 3%, Boric Acid 1%. Collection and preservation delayed 4 days.)

"Miss McBustle, I am sorry for what I am about to ask of you. I am hoping to spare your mother the need for seeing this. And from your statement, I know that you were already aware that this—this—" The sergeant couldn't bring himself to say it, "—had been taken from your grandmother.

"I'd like to do what I can to ease your family's burden. I know it's little enough, but I can send a man with you to the cemetery to help you have this—this—properly seen to. Of course a member of the family must be present or I would not trouble you at all."

Jemmy choked back the tears but said nothing. Her bad ear buzzed, "You and me and Dr. T."

Jemmy's struggle to keep from crying flustered the sergeant. He threw up his hands in a gesture of helplessness. "I apologize. I should have taken this to Mr. Erwin McBustle and not have upset you. It's just that if my mother were the lady—if that fiend took this—this from my mother, I'd rather not know. But you, you already know and have been keeping the secret—"

His searching look bucked up Jemmy's courage. "You've done just the right thing, Sergeant." She mustered every ounce of her self-control as she covered the jar and took it in her arms. Through quivering lips, she said, "I am ready whenever you have an officer you can spare."

The sergeant blew a pattern on his whistle and escorted her to the front door. An officer arrived with a lock-up wagon.

As he handed her up on the front seat with the driver, the day sergeant said, "I wish we had another conveyance, but it's this or horseback. You may ride in the back where we transport the prisoners if you would find that more comfortable."

Jemmy shook her head. "You've been more than kind. I appreciate your discretion and your help." He handed up the mud-caked greatcoat with the words, "I think most of the mud will come out with a good brushing. The crescent knife is in the inside pocket and the other knife, too, and a spyglass as well."

Jemmy thought about the knives. How ironic the pair. She felt a pang of guilt over the wavy bladed knife which might have been used to save a life—if only Jemmy had persuaded Mrs. Nanny to give it back to its owner. The other was a gift to her, albeit a gift given begrudgingly, from the person who had meant to use it to end life. Perhaps Jack the Ripper himself had forced Nipper to give her the knife—by the hilt—the opposite of his usual practice when supplying women with cutlery.

The two knives together had saved her life—albeit in an odd way. Jemmy felt compelled to keep them both—at least until she could understand what they meant. How doubly ironic. She was starting a sin-stained collection of knives as macabre as Dr. Tumblety's glass jars of matrices. Of course, hers was not quite so gruesome.

Jemmy asked the officer, "Have you arrested Dr. Tumblety?"

"No grounds, Miss. The murder evidence is all against the woman in the cave. Nothing to show he knew a thing about it."

"She accused him of being Jack the Ripper. Are you investigating that?"

"Not as I know, Miss. St. Louis Police don't have time to waste on the words of hysterical females."

"What about the women she said he killed in South America? Can't you at least find out about that?"

"Don't see how we could. I heard they don't even talk English down there."

"Surely there are translators and the telegraph so you could at least ver-ify—"

"Don't get yourself worked up, Miss. I'm sure that if the sergeant thinks it proper, he'll inform the captain who will do what's best."

She nodded to the jar cradled in her arms. "And what about this? The Doctor took this from my Grandmother. Can't you at least arrest him for that?"

"Not as I think, Miss. We have laws to protect medical men who study persons deceased as a part of their profession."

"And what if she wasn't deceased? What if he killed her?"

"Well, that's something else entirely. If you have proof of murder, we'll investigate—though I'd think you'd have given your proof when she died—two months ago was it?"

Jemmy had no defense to that. She had no proof. She had no more than a suspicion. Perhaps it was no coincidence that Grandma had died hours after the Doctor left and that he returned to try to take charge of the body without even being summoned. But that was not proof. Even if Grandmother had been killed, it could just as well have been by Nipper—

a confessed murderer.

The officer was still waiting for Jemmy's answer. "Well, Miss, do you have any proof that the doctor harmed your grandmother?"

Jemmy hung her head. "No real proof, Officer."

The officer patted her hand, "Leave it to the men, Miss."

Jemmy tried to keep her exasperation in check. "Would you suggest to the men that they keep a careful watch on the doctor—just in case he is the Ripper. I'm sure you would feel terrible if he takes to murdering the ladies of St. Louis."

The officer reassured her. "Don't trouble your head, Miss. I believe he plans to go to New Orleans. He said something about having Christmas dinner at Antoine's Restaurant in the Vieux Carré ."

Jemmy had to bite her tongue to keep from uttering the sarcasm which perched there. She longed to point out how callous he sounded. Did he really think it proper and Christian to leave the ladies of New Orleans at the tender mercies of Jack the Ripper so long as he left the ladies of St. Louis alone?

Jemmy fumed but knew better than to push the officer any farther. She tried to think of something else.

She began picking clods of dried mud off Father's dirt-encrusted great-coat. It reminded her of the fouled kilts of the fighting pipers at Grandma's burial. Who would have thought that from the muck would rise such strange events—both bad and good. A young woman lost her life and Jemmy nearly followed suit. Yet, somehow Jemmy had managed to cheat death and flimflam a job from Suetonius Hamm.

She had what she wanted. Her only problem was deciding whether she really wanted it. Did she did long for a career as a journalist, or did she just want to prove that she could get one? Would this success lead her to become the new Nellie Bly or was it no more than scratching a childish itch? Maybe so close an encounter with disembowelment should convince her to take her expected place in St. Louis Society.

She had learned much, but the answers to the big questions eluded her. She took stock. Annie taught her that the world can force people into a life of pain and debasement, but that it can't keep them there. Doctor Tumblety taught her that some people pretend to befriend but in reality butcher the people they are supposed to aid.

From Mrs. Willmore she learned that women have power to help women. From Nipper she learned that women have power to prey upon women.

From Officer Spilker she learned that a girl dressed like a boy is a flop at flirting. She even learned two things from Grandma—don't shoot the grandchildren and be sure you open the right door before you hoist your nightgown and turn around.

When they reached Bellefontaine Cemetery, the officer fetched the gravedigger who looked none too happy to be asked to redig a grave. "Can't dig 'er up for less than five dollars."

The officer started to haggle. "Let's be reasonable, now. The ground is soft because the grave is new. You shouldn't expect the same as for digging in hard earth."

"Four-fifty, then. No less."

The officer said, "I'm sure Miss McBustle doesn't carry so much."

Jemmy said, "I do have that much. How long will it take?"

"With my helpers, it will take an hour or thereabouts."

Jemmy dug into her reticule and handed the man a five dollar bill.

He said, "Got no change. I'll go back to get your fifty cents."

"No need. I want you to have the rest. I know we're imposing on you."

"I have to go back for the men and the shovels, but if you still want me to keep the money, I'm much obliged." He tipped his cap and left.

The officer said, "That was generous, Miss McBustle. I see you have a warm heart."

Not until then did Jemmy realize the man was young and good looking in a blond, Teutonic sort of way.

Something clicked in the back of her mind. She said, "You're a young man to have such responsibility. No doubt you have had many interesting adventures since you joined the force. It would cheer me greatly to hear some while we are waiting. It would get my mind off..." She motioned toward the mound of Granny's grave.

The officer said, "Well, most of what we policemen do is too ordinary to be worth mentioning. We walk our rounds and haul in sots who are disturbing the peace. Stop young fellows who have the urge to scrap with one another. The rest of what we do is not fitting for a young girl to hear."

When Jemmy looked downcast, he said, "Well, there is one story I might tell. It's about the time a big dog helped us catch a pickpocket." He smiled down at Jemmy. "You know the dog—belongs to your neighbor. Huge white animal with long ears and brown spots. What kind do they call it?"

"Saint Bernard."

"Yes, Saint Bernard. Well, I was on duty at the big Oracle parade. And hot? Well, you know August in St. Louis. A pickpocket was doing a dandy business because lots of fellows were watching the parade and not paying attention to their valuables. Then the dip picked on the wrong fellow. Your neighbor, Mister—Mister—"

"Bappel."

"Yes, Mr. Bappel. Well, when the dip was stealing Mr. Bappel's pocket watch, Mr. Bappel caught him by the collar. To keep Mr. Bappel from chasing him, the man grabbed Mr. Bappel's crutch and made his getaway. Then Mr. Bappel's dog—what's the dog's name?"

"St. Augustine."

"St. Augustine. Well, St. Augustine must have known his master had to have that crutch so he took out after the pickpocket. That's when I heard the fracas. What a sight. A man waving a crutch and running on two good legs just as fast as those legs would carry him. When I blew my whistle, he turned to see how far off I was. At just that instant, St. Augustine barreled him right over backwards and knocked him out cold."

By now the officer was laughing at the memory. "I could hardly believe it. Once the man was down, I swear the dog tried to rescue him. Licked him all over the face until the man came to."

"I swear the other officers and I couldn't so much as return the poor man's crutch for laughing. We were that doubled over. Mr. Bappel had to one-leg it leaning on the shoulder of that lazy son of his."

This wasn't the shocking story Jemmy had hoped for; but in spite of the let-down, a headline formed in her mind: "St. Aug the Wonder Dog." Mark Twain started out as a newspaper humorist, didn't he? What Mark Twain could do, Jemima McBustle could do.

Postword

"There are liars, damned liars, and people who write books bout Jack the Ripper."
—Jack Hammond, retired antiquarian crime book dealer

Jack the Ripper

Is our enduring fascination with the slippery shadow of the first media-star serial killer a true mystery, or nothing more than a sloppy cover up for slipshod police work?

One thing is clear, the British police simply lost track of their prime suspect, Francis J. Tumblety (1833-1903). Perhaps to save face, Scotland Yard downplayed Tumblety's existence. They closed the Ripper case as unsolved in 1892, only three years after the most sensational murders of the nineteenth century. One might speculate that they closed the case because they knew the identity of the Ripper, but didn't believe he would ever again pose a threat in England.

Some years later all information and arrest warrants on Francis Tumblety disappeared. Today, New Scotland Yard has no files on the murders, no details of the inquiries. But at the time, the American press, along with British and American police, followed the prime suspect across the Atlantic.

December 1, 1888, The London Branch of *The New York World* newspaper, reported:

> The last seen of Dr. Tumblety was at Havre, and it is taken for granted that he has sailed for New York. It will be remembered that the doctor, who is known in this country for his eccentricities, was arrested some time ago in London on suspicion of being concerned in the perpetration of the Whitechapel murders. The police, being unable to procure the necessary evidence against him in connection therewith, decided to hold him for trial for another offense.

Fedora Amis

Was Francis J. Tumblety Jack the Ripper?

Suspects in the 1888 Whitechapel murders are as numerous as they are far-fetched—Oscar Wilde, Lewis Carroll, Lord Randolph Churchill, the "Elephant Man" John Merrick—even in the royal household itself—Prince Albert Victor Christian Edward. Many Ripperologists suspect Canadian-born quack doctor Francis J. Tumblety because the murders stopped when he fled England on November 24th. Tumblety, almost certainly, was the infamous "Batty Street Lodger"—as handsome and charming as Ivor Novello of silent movie fame who portrayed "The Lodger."

The tale begins before the Civil War at a Rochester New York abortion hospital where Tumblety worked as a cleaner. On the side he peddled porn on Erie Canal boats. Too late he discovered his young wife to be a prostitute and annulled the marriage.

In 1850, still in his teens, he moved to Detroit where he painted his face brown, concocted patent medicines, and called himself an herb doctor from India. In Montreal in 1857 he was arrested (but not tried) for trying to abort the pregnancy of a local prostitute. He fled to Boston from Nova Scotia to elude a Coroner's Inquest verdict of manslaughter in 1860.

With the outbreak of the Civil War, he moved to Washington D.C. While claiming to be an army surgeon on General McClellan's staff, he proudly displayed his extensive collection of preserved female body parts to dinner guests—all male, of course. When a guest asked why he did not invite any single women, Tumblety replied that women were nothing more than "cattle" and that he would rather give a friend poison than see him with a woman. Francis Tumblety preferred the company of men. The mere mention of a woman could send him into violent rage.

In 1863 St. Louis police arrested him for impersonating a military officer. Later they picked him up for questioning in two crimes which facts later proved he had not committed. One was a plot to infect Northern soldiers by sending them blankets infected with yellow fever; the other was a plot to assassinate President Lincoln.

In June of 1888 he took lodgings at 22 Batty Street in London's seedy East End—not the most elegant hostelry in town as was his customary choice. Scotland Yard took an interest in his comings and goings because they suspected him of having a part in the blowing up of Scotland Yard which they attributed to the Fenians in 1884.

Tumblety gained even more notoriety when he visited a pathological museum and

Jack the Ripper in St. Louis

inquired whether any uteruses might be for sale.

When his landlady found a blood-soaked shirt in his room and gave it to the police, Tumblety became the Yard's number one Ripper suspect.

They arrested him on November 7th on charges of gross indecency—a genteel way of calling him a homosexual—and let him out on bail. He pleaded not guilty on November 20th at the Old Bailey and was given bail again with the trial set for December 10th. He skipped on November 24th to Boulogne, France, then to New York City under the alias Frank Townsend.

New York City's Chief Inspector Byrnes kept Tumblety under surveillance at Mrs. McNamara's boarding house on East Tenth Street. They couldn't arrest him because the crime for which he had skipped bail was not extraditable. New York City knew Tumblety was in town and trembled that he might commence ripping. On the 5th of December, Tumblety—always a master of disguises—disappeared.

On the 24th of April, 1891, drunken prostitute "Old Shakespeare" Brown was strangled and mutilated—perhaps by a copycat—or perhaps by the Ripper himself. The murder of son-net-reciting Carrie Brown took place in Manhattan, New York.

Tumblety doesn't resurface again until 1893, a year after the Yard closed the Ripper case. He and his jars of uteruses resided with his sister in Rochester. Tumblety roamed about living in hotels in Baltimore, New Orleans and St. Louis. He suffered a long and painful illness, perhaps syphilis, which might have caused his hatred of women—especially prostitutes.

In April 1903 he checked himself into St. John's Hospital and Dispensary at 23rd and Locust in St. Louis, a hospital for indigents, though he was far from broke. He left an estate of more than $135,000 to his niece, Mary Fitzsimmons of Rochester.

Francis Tumblety died May 28th, 1903. His personal belongings included a collection of preserved uteruses in glass jars and some extremely expensive jewelry. He also had two cheap brass rings—perhaps savage souvenirs of Ripper victim Annie Chapman who had been found with throat savagely cut, organs torn from her body, and both her rings missing.

Even death did not end the oddities in the Tumblety case. Baltimore attorney Joseph Kemp challenged Tumblety's will of May 16, 1903. Kemp claimed Tumblety had written a will in October of 1901 that left $1,000 to the Baltimore Home for Fallen Women—a halfway house for prostitutes. The claim was thrown out of court. I imagine Tumblety would have approved.

September 23, 1913, twenty-five years after the Ripper murders, Inspector John Littlechild, head of the Special Branch in England, wrote to journalist George Sims:

> I never heard of a Dr. D. in connection with the Whitechapel murders, but amongst the suspects, and to my mind a very likely one, was a Dr. T. He was an American quack named Tumblety and at one time was a frequent visitor to London and on these occasions constantly brought under the notice of police, there being a large dossier concerning him at Scotland Yard. Although a 'Sycopathis Sexualis' subject, he was not known as a sadist, but his feelings toward women were remarkable and bitter in the extreme.

The entire theory of whether Tumblety was Jack the Ripper hinges on the date that he was released from jail in London. On November 7, Tumblety was arrested for "unnatural offenses." Some records say he was released on bail November 16. Others cite his release on November 8.

On November 9, the Ripper claimed his last victim, Mary Kelly. Tumblety was arrested on suspicion of her murder on November 12. He was released without being charged and then vanished from Whitechapel. A quick look at the dates of release would seem to dispel doubts. He was released on bail on *both* November 8 and November 16—otherwise how did police pick him up on November 12th to question him about the murder of Mary Kelly?

A Ripper Chronology

Ripperologists debate the actual number of Ripper murders—which might be as many as eleven. Even among the six which occurred during the Ripper panic of August and November 1888, many doubt whether all were the work of a single man.

Many exclude Elizabeth Stride, because Stride and Eddoes were found just 12 minutes apart, and unlike all other victims Elizabeth screamed three times, and because none of her parts were missing, many suspect Aaron Kosminski as using the Ripper's crimes to provide an opportunity for him to dispatch Ms. Stride.

Another question mark is Mary Kelly. It is altogether possible that Tumblety, under police observation as a suspect, may not have killed and mutilated Mary Kelly. If so, authorities might well have dismissed him from consideration as the Ripper.

Jack the Ripper in St. Louis

Date in 1888	Name	Place
Tuesday 7 August	Martha Tabram	George Yard, Whitechapel
Friday 31 August	Mary Ann Nichols	Buck's Row, Whitechapel
Saturday 8 September	Annie Chapman	29 Hanbury St, Spitalfields
Sunday 30 September	Elizabeth Stride	40 Berner St, Whitechapel
Sunday 30 September	Catherine Eddowes	Aldgate, London
Friday 9 November	Mary Jane Kelly	Millers Court, Whitechapel

More and more people have come to believe that Tumblety was the Ripper. In their 1996 book, *Jack the Ripper: First American Serial Killer*, Evans and Gainey outline fifteen reasons why they believe Tumblety should be considered a top suspect in the Whitechapel murders.

On-line, Ripperology central "Casebook: Jack the Ripper" devotes a page to the most popular Ripper suspects. Tumblety stands second—and "the lodger" stands eighth in the poll. Add them together and I'd say Francis J. Tumblety is the odds-on choice.

Splendid mystery writer Patricia Cornwell brought her considerable talent and resources to bear on the Ripper question. Her DNA saliva test results convinced me that artist Walter Sickert wrote the Ripper letters, but even in 1888 there was scant belief that the man who wrote the letters was the man who did the deeds.

Her conclusion when she "closed the case" was primarily psychological—based on Sickert's dark art, pained body and twisted brain. If Sickert wrote the letters, he clearly had a fascination with the Ripper—which explains the art. In my humble opinion if one compares the pair in grisly pain and gruesome twist, Sickert may have been a sick puppy; but Tumblety was a big dog ripping in the tall weeds.

Bibliography

Abrahamsen, David. *Murder & Madness: The Secret Life of Jack the Ripper*. New York: Donald I. Fine, c1992.

Casebook: Jack the Ripper. "Who are the most popular Ripper suspects?" Poll October 20, 2007, http://www.casebook.org/suspects/suspect_av.html

Cornwell, Patricia. *Portrait of a Killer: Jack the Ripper, Case Closed*. New York: G.P. Putnams' Sons, c2002

Evans, Stewart P. and Paul Gainey. *Jack the Ripper: First American Serial Killer*. New York: Kodansha International, c1996

Graysmith, Robert. *The Bell Tower: The Case of Jack the Ripper Finally Solved in San Francisco*. Washington D.C.: Regnery Publishing, c 1999.

Hannaford, Scott. "A Theory on Francis Tumblety." *Casebook : Jack the Ripper*. 1996. Thomas Schachner. 23 March 2012. http://www.casebook.org/dissertations/tumb-art.html

Ryder, Stephen P. (Ed.). *"Francis Tumblety (1833-1903) a.k.a. J. H. Blackburn, Frank Townsend." Casebook: Jack the Ripper. 1996.* Thomas Schachner. 23 March 2012. http://www.casebook.org/suspects/tumblety.html

Taylor, Troy. "The Whitechapel Murders: Could Jack the Ripper Have Been an American?" *Dead Men Do Tell Tales*. C2004. Whitechapel Productions. 23 March 2012. www.prairieghosts.com/ripper.html

"The Enduring Mystery of Jack the Ripper." *Metropolitan Police*. 2012. Metropolitan Police Service, 23 March 2012.

"The Enduring Obscurity of Jack the Ripper." *The Goldonian*. 2001. Goldonian Web. March 2012. http://www.goldonian.org/sub_pages/jacktheripper.htm

Wagner, Gillian. *Barnardo*. London: Weidenfield and Nicholson, 1979

"Who are the most popular Ripper suspects?" *Casebook: Jack the Ripper*. 1996. Thomas Schachner. 23 March 2012. http://www.casebook.org/suspects/suspect_av.html

I am also greatly indebted to the librarians and collections at the St. Louis Public Library, St. Louis County Library and the Library of the Missouri Historical Society.